Ludwig Bruck

Guide to the Health Resorts

in Australia, Tasmania, and New Zealand

Ludwig Bruck

Guide to the Health Resorts
in Australia, Tasmania, and New Zealand

ISBN/EAN: 9783337272357

Printed in Europe, USA, Canada, Australia, Japan

Cover: Foto ©Andreas Hilbeck / pixelio.de

More available books at **www.hansebooks.com**

GUIDE

TO THE

HEALTH RESORTS

IN

AUSTRALIA, TASMANIA,

AND

NEW ZEALAND.

EDITED AND COMPILED BY

LUDWIG BRUCK,

Author of " The Australasian Medical Directory and Hand-Book."

CENTENNIAL EDITION.

PUBLISHED AT THE "AUSTRALASIAN MEDICAL GAZETTE" OFFICE,
35 CASTLEREAGH STREET, SYDNEY.

LONDON : BAILLIERE, TINDALL & COX, 20 KING WILLIAM STREET, STRAND.

1888.

NOTIFICATION

Of any omissions or errors for correction in future issues of this Guide, will be gratefully received by

L. BRUCK, Medical Publisher,

35 Castlereagh Street, Sydney.

INTRODUCTION.

WHILST Europe may boast of a number of works on climatology and balneology, these branches of study, though of great importance, are as yet, in these colonies, still in their embryonic state. Little is known of the Health Resorts in Australasia, even by those residing on the spot, and, excepting the New Zealand thermal springs, hardly anything has been written on the subject. Considering the great variety in temperature, owing to the wide range of latitude under which these colonies lie, the numerous mineral and thermal springs, and sea-bathing places to be found in all parts of Australia, Tasmania, and New Zealand, the author may be permitted to hope that this guide will prove of some value to invalids, as well as to members of the medical profession when called upon to select a suitable climate or mineral spring for their patients. In it will be found a concise, but complete and accurate description of upwards of 200 Health Resorts, with the analyses, temperature, and special indications of nearly 100 mineral waters throughout Australasia. In the fourth division, which may be termed the key to this guide, all the Health Resorts named have been arranged in twenty-eight different classes and sub-classes, each class being accompanied with prefatory remarks as to its characteristic nature; at the same time the diseases are named which are benefitted by it, the whole forming an excellent means for ready reference.

The climatology has been compiled from official documents, and contains a complete outline of the climates of Australia, Tasmania, and New Zealand.

The description of the New Zealand thermal springs districts, written by the Hon. Sir W. Fox, K.C.M.G., has been re-printed, by kind permission of the Honorable the Colonial Secretary of New Zealand, from a pamphlet published by the New Zealand Government a few years ago.

For the convenience of non-professional readers a division has been added, giving a definition of all the technical terms, medical and chemical, which occur in the book.

The editor trusts that any errors and short-comings, which no doubt will be observed, and which unavoidably occur in a book of this description, especially when it is the first edition as in this case, will be pardoned, the more readily when it is borne in mind that the information contained in it relates to an expanse of territory nearly as large as the whole of Europe.

In conclusion he begs to tender his most cordial thanks to those gentlemen who have afforded him information and assistance. Amongst them he may mention the Hon. J. M. Creed, M.L.C., Sydney ; Dr. J. T. Chapman, Drysdale ; R. L. J. Ellery Esq., F.R.S., Government Astronomer, Melbourne ; Dr. A. Ginders, Medical Superintendent, Sanatorium Rotorua ; R. B. Gore Esq., Meteorological Observer, Wellington, N.Z. ; Chr. Gunsser Esq., of the Ballan Mineral Springs ; Sir James Hector, K.C.M.G., F.R.S., M.D., Director of the Colonial Museum, Wellington, N.Z. ; Dr. T. Hope Lewis, Auckland, formerly Medical Superintendent at Rotorua Sanatorium ; J. K. McDonald Esq., Chairman of the Whaingaroa Hot Springs Domain Board ; Dr. J. A. Reid, Sale ; J. Shortt Esq., Meteorological Observer in Hobart ; Dr. W. I. Spencer, Napier ; Karl Theodor Staiger Esq., F.C.S., Brisbane ; J. Stewart Esq., Superintendent of the Hanmer Springs ; Dr. Guido Thon, Rockhampton ; Dr. W. H. Tibbits, Manly ; C. Todd Esq., C.M.G., F.R.A.S., Meteorological Observer, P.M.G. & S.T., in Adelaide ; Dr. F. W. Towle, Drysdale ; Dr. J. H. Townsend, Christchurch; Dr. D. Turner, Melbourne ; Dr. Alfred Wright, Te Aroha ; also to a large number of medical practitioners, proprietors of hotels and boarding-houses, various postmasters, and other gentlemen in all the colonies.

LUDWIG BRUCK.

35 Castlereagh-street,

    Sydney, January 26, 1888.

CONTENTS.

———◆———

CLIMATOLOGY

OF THE

AUSTRALASIAN COLONIES.

THE CLIMATE OF NEW SOUTH WALES.

THE climate of New South Wales is very similar to that of Southern Europe, but, as the colony extends from latitude south, 28° to 37°, much variation is experienced, from the cold at Kiandra, where the mean minimum temperature is 21° F., to the heat in the inland plains, where the thermometer sometimes reaches 140° F. in the shade, and is generally from 100° to 116° F. for the greater part of the summer. The summer temperature of the coast regions of New South Wales is much the same as that of Lisbon and of the Mediterranean coast, *i.e.*, like Naples, Algiers, and Gibraltar, whilst the winter temperature is like that of Sicily or the south of Africa. The summer heat on the coast is less than in the interior, but to many persons it is more trying, because it is a moist, tropical heat, whereas in the interior, to the west of the Great Dividing Range, it is extremely dry, and though hot, it is not enervating ; on the contrary, it produces great elasticity of frame, and an increased power of endurance. This region, and especially the Riverina district, consisting of vast inland plains, bounded on the south by the River Murray, and lying between its chief affluents, the Darling, Lachlan, and Murrumbidgee Rivers, can, in dry seasons, be strongly recommended to the consumptive, as possessing one of the most suitable climates in the world for the effectual climatic treatment of phthisis, even if attended with hæmoptysis, provided out-door occupation, especially station life, is resorted to.

In most parts of the colony the winter mornings and evenings are very cool, and a fire is found agreeable. The temperature of the coast districts is beneficially affected by a warm equatorial current setting south along the coast, furnishing moisture in summer and mitigating the cold of winter. Snow lies for months on the mountains, *i.e.*, at Kiandra (4,600 feet above sea level), where eight feet of snow have fallen in a single month, whilst it is almost unknown in the coast districts. The average annual rainfall to the east of the Dividing Range is over 40 inches, and the number of rainy days 102; but in the interior, on the western side of the mountains, it is only about 14 inches, with 70 rainy days, and sometimes two or three years have passed by without rain in some parts, or at least not sufficient to wet the ground. Moreover, the evaporation is enormous, sometimes reaching 12 inches a month for several consecutive months ; at these times the rivers cease running and the whole country gets burnt up with the heat. Such seasons of drought occur at regular intervals, and, of course, produce the greatest distress. The heavy rains come with winds from eastward and are often intercepted by the mountains, therefore it sometimes happens that floods on the coast districts are simultaneous with droughts inland. Southerly "bursters" frequently set in between the months of November and February, and are always attended with clouds of dust, penetrating everywhere.

June, July, and August are the coldest months, December, January, February, and March are the hottest, and with the exception of these last four months the climate is delightful and highly salubrious.

The diseases most prevalent in Sydney and suburbs during the summer months are dysentery, diarrhœa, and enteric fever, and in winter the greatest number of deaths are due to phthisis.

The mean annual temperature in the shade at Sydney (lat. 33° 52') is 62·4° F.; at Casino (lat. 28° 50'; height, 139 feet; distance from the coast, 30 miles), 67·1° F.; at Grafton (lat. 29° 40'; height, 40 feet; distance from the coast, 22 miles), 70·6° F.; at Armidale (lat. 30° 34'; height, 3,278 feet; distance from the coast, 80 miles), 56·2° F.; at Newcastle (lat. 32° 55'), 64° F.; at Bathurst (lat. 33° 24'; height, 2,333 feet; distance from the coast, 98 miles), 56·8°F.; at Goulburn (lat. 34° 45'; height, 2,129 feet; distance from the coast, 58 miles), 55° F.; at Kiandra (lat. 35° 52'; height, 4,640 feet; distance from the coast, 90 miles), 45·3° F.; at Cooma (lat. 36° 13'; height, 2,637 feet; distance from the coast, 53 miles), 51·8° F.; and at Deniliquin (lat. 35° 32'; height, 410 feet; distance from the coast, 280 miles), 58° F. The hottest month, generally, is January, and June is the coldest month.

The mean daily range of temperature in the shade at Sydney, is 14·7° F.; at Casino 28·6° F.; at Grafton 21·1° F.; at Armidale 30·8° F.; at Newcastle .17·9° F.; at Bathurst 29·9° F.; at Goulburn 25·4° F.; at Kiandra 24·7° F.; at Cooma 25·6°, and at Deniliquin 31·8° F.

As regards the average annual amount of rain and the average number of rainy days in the year, Sydney shows 141 rainy days, with 48·697 inches of rain; Casino 111 days, with 42·996 inches; Grafton 123 days, with 44·990 inches; Armidale 102 days, with 39·560 inches; Newcastle 102 days, with 44·662 inches; Bathurst 74 days, with 23·222 inches; Goulburn 96 days, with 24·188 inches; Kiandra 105 days, with 60·590 inches; Cooma 112 days, with 19·165 inches, and Deniliquin 62 rainy days in the year, with an average annual rainfall of 13·285 inches.

THE CLIMATE OF NEW ZEALAND.

NEW ZEALAND, extending as it does from latitude south 34°
to 47°, has of course a very varied climate ; it is not unlike
that of Great Britain, but it is more equable, the extremes
of daily temperature only varying throughout the year by an
average of 20° F., whilst London is 7° F. colder than the
North, and 4° F. colder than the South Island of New Zealand.
The mean annual temperature of the North Island is 57° F.,
and of the South Island 52° F., whilst that of London is
51° F. The mean annual temperature of the different seasons
for the whole colony is—in spring 55° F., in summer 63° F.,
in autumn 57° F., and in winter 48° F. The climate on the
west coast of both islands is more equable and agreeable than
on the east, the difference between the average summer and
winter temperature being nearly 4° F. greater on the south-
east portion of the North Island, and 7° F. on that of the
South Island than on the north-west. Especially the climate
of Canterbury, on the east side of the South Island, is
extremely variable ; it has been said to be a mixture of the
climates of the south of France and the Shetland Islands,
the winter being most severe, and for two or three months
the Canterbury Plains are covered with snow, whilst the
summer is very hot ; moreover the annual fluctuation of
temperature at Christchurch (Canterbury), on the east coast,
is greater by fully 18° F. than at Hokitika, on the opposite
west coast of the South Island, which has a mild winter
and cool summer ; whilst Invercargill, 11° further south
than Auckland, has hotter days in summer than Auckland. In the North Island the probability of rainfall in
winter is twice as large as in summer. In the South
Island, however, the rainfall, though irregular, is distributed
more equally over the year, with the difference that on
the west coast spring rains prevail and summer rains on

the east coast. The contrast between the rainfalls on the east and west coasts is most striking ; thus, in the North Island, Napier on the east has only half the amount of rain that falls in Taranaki on the west ; and in the South Island, at Christchurch, on the east coast, the average annual rainfall is 26 inches, and at Hokitika, on the west, 112 inches. The winter snow line on the Southern Alps is 3,000 feet on the east side, and 3,700 feet on the west side. The south-western coasts of New Zealand and the straits between the islands are exposed to stormy weather ; thus at Wellington on Cook Straits, and at Invercargill on Foveaux Straits, the winds are generally very boisterous throughout the year, but no part of the islands suffers from hot winds. On the whole, the climate, being free from extremes of heat or cold, is mild and bracing, and in almost all parts highly salubrious, the death-rate being lower than in the healthiest rural districts of England. The diseases most prevalent during the summer months are diarrhœa and dysentery, and throughout the year a number of deaths occur from phthisis.

The mean annual temperature in the shade at Auckland (S. lat. 36° 50') is 59·54° F. ; at Napier (lat. 39° 29') 57·56° F. ; at Wanganui (lat. 39° 56') 55·90° F. ; at Wellington (lat. 41° 16') 55·58° F. ; at Nelson (lat. 41° 16') 54·86° F. ; at Hokitika (lat. 42° 42') 52·34° F. ; at Christchurch (lat. 42° 33') 52·88° F.; at Dunedin (45° 52') 50·72° F., and at Invercargill (lat. 46° 17') 50·36° F.

The mean daily range of temperature at Auckland is 17·82° F. ; at Napier 17·46° F. ; at Wellington 12·06° F.; at Nelson 20·16° F. ; at Hokitika 13·14° F. ; at Christchurch 17·10° F. ; at Dunedin 13·68° F., and at Invercargill 20·16° F.

The mean annual rainfall at Auckland is 47·008 inches ; at Napier 36·004 inches ; at Wellington 51·542 inches ; at Nelson 61·599 inches ; at Hokitika 111·653 inches ; at Christchurch 25·536 inches ; at Dunedin 31·682 inches, and at Invercargill 49·732 inches.

THE CLIMATE OF QUEENSLAND.

In a country like Queensland, containing 669,520 square miles within 17 or 18 degrees of latitude, a variety of climate must be experienced and no accurate conception of its . wide diversities can be given in any general account. In the interior, to the west, comprising the districts of Maranoa, Warrego, Mitchell, North and South Gregory, the atmosphere is pure, extremely dry and hot, yet exhilarating, and it has one of the most suitable climates in the world for phthisical patients. The summer heat in the daytime is very great, but by no means oppressive, for a fresh and singularly invigorating breeze plays incessantly over the downs and plains. When the sun sets the temperature falls rapidly, and there is hardly any dew at night. In winter the cold is quite severe, and 4° or 5° of frost during the night or early morning are not uncommon. The rainfall is scanty and irregular, and varies from 20 to 10 inches, and even less, according to the distance from the coast; the greater the distance the less is the rainfall, and becomes altogether uncertain, whilst the evaporation increases.

Another portion of the interior, the Darling Downs, the so-called " Garden of Queensland," on the western slopes of the Main Dividing Range, comprising the important towns of Toowoomba, Warwick, and Dalby, enjoys many of the advantages of the coast districts. The climate is temperate and bracing, the atmosphere is fairly charged with moisture and the rainfall more regular.

Following the coast districts from south to north, the first division at the southern extremity of the colony is that of East and West Moreton, lying between the Main Dividing Range and the sea, the principal towns of which are Brisbane, the capital, and Ipswich, twenty-three miles to the south-west of it. The mean temperature at Brisbane is 70° F., or about the same as at Funchal, on the Island of Madeira, and the changes of the thermometer are far less extreme than at Sydney or Melbourne, while cool southerly breezes prevail throughout the year, so that the heat which is, of course, greater than in the more southern colonies, is rarely felt to be oppressive ; besides, the nights are longer and cooler, producing a revival after the heat of the day, and moreover, the hot winds from which the other colonies suffer are here not experienced. The winter season, say from May to November, throughout Southern Queensland is most delightful ; the mornings and evenings are cool, the days bright and warm, the sky cloudless, the atmosphere dry and exhilarating ; frosts are experienced but they are not severe. The rainfall is more evenly distributed throughout the year, though the largest amount generally falls between December and April. The air is fairly charged with moisture and a nightly fall of dew is the rule not the exception. The mean annual rainfall at Brisbane is 50 inches, with 128 rainy days. The next districts are those of Wide Bay and Burnett, including the towns of Gympie, Maryborough, and Bundaberg. The climate here is very similar to that of the Moreton district, though perhaps a little warmer—but even frosts are not unknown here. At Gympie, thirty miles from the coast, the annual amount of rainfall is 44 inches. Further north are the districts of Port Curtis and Leichhardt, with the important seaport of Rockhampton, just within the tropic of Capricorn. In climate these districts occupy an intermediate position between the temperate and tropical portions of the coast country, and the temperature is decidedly high. The rainfall is unevenly distributed throughout the year, but the total amount is satisfactory, about 50 inches during the twelve months. The next districts going northward are those of North and South Kennedy, with the towns of Mackay, Bowen, Townsville, and Cardwell on the coast, and the mining centres of Charters Towers and Ravenswood in the interior. The climate in these districts is distinctly tropical and free from frost ; the summer though hot is not unhealthy, and there is a pleasant exhilarating cool season— the climate in the neighbourhood of Bowen especially, is noted for being so temperate and equable, that the place is used as a sanitarium by the residents of the far north, and even at Townsville the temperature is as a rule most enjoyable during the winter months. The summer months, from December to March, are of course very hot, and as a marvellous amount of rain falls at this time, tropical heat and moisture are combined. All along the coast the rainfall is great, being about 90 inches at Cardwell. In the interior of these districts the air is pure and dry, and the climate generally is not unhealthy for Europeans. The temperature, as a matter of course, is more prostrating in the northern-most districts of Cook and Burke, and the heat of the tropical sun, with moisture combined, is too fierce to be endured with comfort by Europeans. The north-west coasts are visited with periodical rains of great regularity, and are quite free from the seasons of drought that occur in the more southern parts.

Queensland is almost entirely free from endemic diseases ; epidemics are rare, and the climate throughout the colony is on the whole very favourable to the European constitution.

THE CLIMATE OF SOUTH AUSTRALIA.

THE climate of South Australia is very hot and dry, but owing to its dryness, the heat, except on hot wind days, is seldom oppressive. The hottest months are December, January, and February, when the temperature on the plains frequently exceeds 100° F. in the shade, but then the wet bulb thermometer will show only about 65° F., and it is this extreme dryness of the air which enables the residents to bear the heat of the summer without much inconvenience, as perspiration generally affords instantaneous relief. November and March are also hot, but the heat is seldom of long duration, and moreover the nights are much cooler, producing a revival after the heat of the day. The mean temperature in October is 62° F., in November 66° F., in December 71° F., in January and February 73° F., and in March 70° F. in the shade. After March the temperature falls rapidly, very rarely reaching 90° F. in the shade in April, the mean temperature for that month being 64° F., whilst for May it is only 58° F. The coldest months are June, July, and August, the mean temperature of which are 54° F, 51° F., and 53° F. respectively. The weather from April to October is delightful and most enjoyable ; the heat is less excessive, the atmosphere wonderfully transparent, and the rains which generally fall during the winter months produce a delightful freshness in the air. The mean quantity of rain registered in these seven months is 16·721 inches, whilst for the whole year it is 21·091 inches, with 114 wet days. The average number of wet days in May is 13 days, in June 14 days, in July 16 days, and 16 days in August ; the average rainfall being respectively 2·814, 2·915, 2·801, and 2·621 inches for May, June, July, and August. These quantities refer to the plains only, as on the hills and in the south-eastern portion of the colony the rainfall is much heavier, and the temperature of course is also much lower than on the plains above referred to.

Occasionally during the summer the colony suffers from the hot winds which blow from the interior of the continent and generally last for three days ; the temperature of the air is raised to 100° F. and 120° F. in the shade, and the heat of the wind can only be compared to the blast from a furnace.

Clouds of fine dust are a most painful concomitant, in short these hot winds are very much like the sirocco of North Africa. Infants and old persons severely feel these hot winds, in delicate persons they produce determination of blood to the head, inflammation of the throat and eyes, &c., yet they are not unhealthy, as they purify the atmosphere, drying up and rendering innocuous all decomposing animal and vegetable matter and, moreover, as settlement proceeds, the hot winds become less frequent and less severe.

On the whole the climate of South Australia is highly salubrious, although a large number of deaths are recorded every year as due to diarrhœal diseases, phthisis, pneumonia, bronchitis, whooping cough, and enteric fever, principally due, as in all the other colonies, to the toleration of nuisances and bad drainage in townships, bad water, unsuitable dwellings, and a general disregard of many other indispensable observances conducive to health.

THE CLIMATE OF TASMANIA.

TASMANIA, the sanitarium of the south, has a climate equal, if not superior, to that of the healthiest part of Europe ; the winter is not more severe than that of the South of France, and the summer is not hotter than that of London. The temperature is not marked by extremes of heat or cold, and as in summer the nights are always cool and refreshing, the heat of the day is never felt relaxing. The mean temperature at Hobart, in the south of the island, is 54° F. ; the mean maximum temperature is 61° F., and the mean minimum temperature 45° F. ; the mean daily range is 16° F. The hottest months are November, December, January, February, and March, when the extreme temperatures are 92° F., 91° F., 100° F., 86° F. and 96° F., respectively. The coldest months are May, June, July and August; the mean monthly temperatures of which are 49° F., 46° F., 45° F. and 48° F., respectively. At Launceston, in the north of the island, the mean annual temperature is 55° F., the mean maximum temperature 64° F., the mean minimum temperature 43° F., and the daily range 20° F. The monthly mean temperature is highest in December and January, viz., 74° F. and 77° F. respectively, and lowest in May, June, July and August, viz., 38° F., 34° F., 35° and 38° F. respectively.

Rain varies in quantity in different parts of the island, Hobart having little more than 21 inches, with 189 wet days; Launceston nearly 31 inches, with 119 wet days, while Mount Bischoff, twenty-eight miles from the north coast, has 78 inches, with 264 wet days; and Corinna in the north-west, nine miles from the coast, has nearly 69 inches of rain. The climate of the island is certainly much cooler and more equable, and therefore more pleasant and healthy than in Australia, and it is especially favorable to enfeebled constitutions from warmer climates.

THE CLIMATE OF VICTORIA.

THE climate of Victoria is very similar to that of the more favoured portions of Southern Europe, such as Madrid in Spain, Marseilles, Bordeaux, and Nice in France, and Bologna and Verona in Italy; however, the difference between the coldest and warmest months is much less in Melbourne than in any of these places. The annual mean temperature in the shade is 58° F., the highest temperature in the shade has been 111° F., and the lowest temperature 27° F. The spring season generally sets in about the beginning of September, during which month the weather is usually mild and often quite warm, the average temperature being

53° F. The weather in October is genial and pleasant, with a mean temperature of 57° F.; November is characterised by fine, warm, and sometimes even hot weather, the mean temperature in this month being 61° F. The hottest months are December, January and February, with a mean monthly temperature of 64° F., 67° F. and 66° F., respectively. The greatest heat and dryness of the atmosphere occurs towards the end of January or the beginning of February. With March the autumn season sets in, which although subject to stormy weather, gales of wind, and a large rainfall, is the most genial and beautiful portion of the year; the mean temperature in March is 64° F., in April 59° F., and in May 53° F. June inaugurates the Victorian winter; July is the coldest month, the mean temperature being 48° F.; at this season cold northerly winds are experienced. In the higher altitudes it often freezes at night, although the days may be of a summer temperature, but in the lowlands the temperature only occasionally falls below freezing point. The suddenness of the atmospheric changes is felt by some to be trying, but as a rule the climate in autumn, winter and spring, is exceedingly agreeable; the atmosphere is transparent, dry and exhilarating. The sky is brightly blue, and soft breezes breathe a delicious freshness and temper the rays of the sun. Even the summer is not oppressively warm, and the dry heat being cooled by southerly and south-westerly winds, is rather stimulating, and not so exhausting as the moist heat of the coast regions of New South Wales and Queensland. The hot winds and dust storms which occasionally occur are certainly not pleasant, but they generally terminate the second day and never last longer than three days; besides they also act as a kind of scavenger, as explained in the description of the climate of South Australia; it is during these hot winds that the highest temperatures occur. The rainfall is very variable in the different parts of the colony. The average yearly rainfall at Melbourne is 26 inches, with 137 wet days, but the rainfall has been as low as 16 inches and as high as 44 inches. In the highlands, especially towards the east, the rainfall is greater, while the Wimmera district, in the north-west of the colony, is extremely dry, having rarely above 14 inches ; and moreover, the evaporation, which in most parts of Victoria is greatly in excess of the rainfall, is especially large in the Wimmera district, but in sheltered localities, as in the valleys and gulleys at the foot of the mountain ranges, the evaporation. is almost reduced to a minimum. On the whole, Victoria has probably one of the finest climates in the world, though of course not without its drawbacks.

The principal diseases prevalent in Victoria are enteric fever, diarrhœal diseases, pneumonia, phthisis, and heart diseases.

THE CLIMATE OF WESTERN AUSTRALIA.

THE climate of Western Australia is said to be the healthiest of any of the Australian colonies. It is very hot but accompanied by a remarkable dryness of the atmosphere, and therefore the heat is rarely oppressive. The annual mean temperature is 65° F. ; the highest temperature recorded at Perth has been 109° F., and the lowest 34° F. The hottest months are December, January, February and March, with a mean monthly temperature of 72° F., 75° F., 79° F. and 76° F., respectively. The coldest months are July and August, both having a mean monthly temperature of 53° F. The average annual rainfall is nearly 33 inches, with 111 wet days ; the wet or winter season is from May to September, and the largest quantity of rain generally falls in July and August. In winter frosts are experienced, but only in the morning, and the greater part of the winter is temperate and fine.   The rest of the year is extremely dry, but with occasional showers and thunderstorms ; and from October to April the climate is generally most delightful. Hot winds do occur, but they are neither so frequent nor so severe as in South Australia and Victoria.   There is little luxuriant vegetation, and there are no swamps or marshes to produce fevers and ague, and the general sterility of the country may be said to contribute to the healthiness of the climate, which is very suitable for invalids and consumptive persons.

The diseases most prevalent in the colony are heart disease and dysentery ; and with the exception of an epidemic of whooping cough, which made its appearance in the latter part of 1885, epidemics are unknown.

II

AUSTRALASIAN HEALTH RESORTS:

*Being an Alphabetical List of all known Health Resorts in
Australia, Tasmania and New Zealand, giving a general
description of the Climatic Health Resorts, Spas and
Watering-places, with their environs, special indications,
analyses of mineral waters, the names of resident medical
men, and the addresses of the principal hotels and boarding-houses, the quickest and cheapest routes, and other
useful information.*

AKAROA (CANTERBURY), NEW ZEALAND, 56 miles S.E.
of Christchurch, on Banks' Peninsula, very picturesquely
situated at the foot of green hills covered with ferns, on the
shores of one of the finest harbours of New Zealand, in a
dairy farming district. The surrounding scenery is magnificent, and the summer heat being cooled to a delicious
temperature by frequent sea breezes, the town has become a
favourite summer retreat. Sea-bathing ; fishing ; boating.
Post and Telegraph Office ; Cottage Hospital ; Literary
Institute, with Library ; Musical Society.

EXCURSION : Pigeon Bay.

DOCTOR : Dr. A. E. Woodforde.

HOTELS : "Grange's," "Wagstaff's," "Bruce's,"' the
"Criterion."

ROUTE : From Christchurch by steamer or coach ; or by
rail to Little River, thence coach.

ALBURY, NEW SOUTH WALES, 531 feet above sea-
level, 386 miles (by rail) S. from Sydney, 190 miles (by rail)
N.E. from Melbourne, and 170 miles from the coast, a
flourishing town, picturesquely situated on the Murray river.
The principal industry is that of the vine ; grapes are extensively grown at Ettamogah (5 miles from Albury), and in the

Murray Valley surrounding the town. The botanical reserve being a pleasant place of recreation. The surrounding scenery is very pretty, and the climate salubrious and pleasant. The mean maximum temperature, in the shade, during the hottest month is 93·5° F., and the mean minimum temperature during the coldest month 34·3° F., the mean annual temperature is 60·2° F., and the mean daily range 28·1° F. ; the average annual amount of rainfall is 27 in., with 85 rainy days in the year. Hospital ; Post and Telegraph Office ; Mechanics' Institute.

DOCTORS : Drs. A. Andrews, M. Herdegen, P. Kennedy, and W. C. Woods.

HOTELS : The " Globe," the " Rose," the " Albury Club," the " Exchange."

ALDGATE, SOUTH AUSTRALIA, 1,392 feet above sea-level, 12 miles E. of Adelaide, a favourite summer resort, in a fruit growing district. Post and Telegraph Office.

EXCURSION : Echunga goldfields (6m.)

HOTEL : The " Aldgate Pump."

ROUTE : By coach ; or by rail (22m.)

ALEXANDRA, VICTORIA, about 1,000 feet above sea-level, 90 miles N.E. of Melbourne, and 75 miles from the coast, on the Goulburn River, in an agricultural and gold-mining district. The country is mountainous, the scenery magnificent, and the climate bracing and moderately dry. The average annual rainfall is 26 inches. The water of the numerous mountain streams is very fine and clear. Fishing ; shooting. Hospital ; Post and Telegraph Office; Mechanics' Institute ; Free Library ; Shire Hall, with stage ; Race-course.

EXCURSIONS : Mt. Prospect, (3m.) ; Mt. Torbreck, (16m.) ; Cathedral Mountain (11m.)

SPECIAL INDICATIONS : Phthisis ; Renal complaints ; Asthma ; Dyspepsia ; Nervous Affections.

SEASON : From October to March.

DOCTOR : Dr. C. F. Lethbridge (who makes diseases of women a specialty) can accommodate a few lady patients at his delightfully situated residence.

HOTELS : Keene's "Corner," the "Exchange," the "Shamrock," the "Mount Pleasant."

ROUTE : By rail to Yea, thence by coach (20m.)

AMBERLEY (CANTERBURY), NEW ZEALAND, 34 miles by rail N. from Christchurch, on the North Kowai river, in an agricultural and pastoral district. Post and Telegraph Office ; Public Library. Here is situated a cold chalybeate spring which, however, is unfit for use on account of the large amount of organic matter present.

ANALYSIS (in grains per gallon) : Total dissolved solids, 37·6grs. ; Volatile, 8·8grs. ; Fixed 28·8grs. ; Carbonate of lime, 3·6grs. ; Carbonate of magnesia, 2·2grs. ; Chlorine, 10·5grs. ; Iron protoxide, 2·3grs. ; Free ammonia, 0·069grs. ; Albuminoid ammonia, 0·034gr. ; or a total of 11·7grs. of mineral matters in one pint ; Sediment, per gallon, 165·2grs.

DOCTOR : Dr. M. Morris.

HOTELS : The "Crown," the "Railway."

ANGASTON, SOUTH AUSTRALIA, 52 miles N.E. of Adelaide, and 35 miles from the coast, on the Angaston Creek, in an agricultural district. It is noted for its numerous vineyards which produce splendid crops of the finest grapes. The surrounding country is hilly. The total rainfall in 1882 was nearly 18 inches. Post and Telegraph Office ; Literary Institute, with Library.

EXCURSION : Tanunda, (6½m.)

DOCTOR : Dr. H. Ayliffe.

HOTELS : The "Angaston," the "Commercial."

ROUTE : By rail to Freeling, thence coach.

APOLLO BAY, VICTORIA, 144 miles S.W. of Melbourne, a rising watering-place on the N.W. coast of Bass' Straits, near Cape Otway, in a fine timber-growing district, abounding in gigantic blue gum trees and magnificent ferns. The climate is mild and very salubrious. The mean annual temperature is 55·1° F. The mean temperature in January is 60° F., in April 57° F., in July 49° F., in October 53° F., and in December 58° F. The average annual rainfall is 35

B

inches.   The scenery is very pretty.   Fishing;   shooting;
boating ; sea-bathing ; fine beach ; jetty.

SEASON : From November to April.

HOTELS : " Gosney's ;" " Caywood's Boarding House."

ROUTE : By steamer direct ; or by rail to Colac or Birregurra, thence coach.

ARMIDALE, NEW SOUTH WALES, 3,313 feet above
sea-level, 335 miles N. of Sydney, and 80 miles from the
coast, the chief town of New England,. a district of extreme
beauty and fertility.   The scenery is very picturesque, and
the climate is bracing, and cool.   The mean annual temperature
in the shade is 56·2° F., the mean maximum temperature in
the shade during the hottest month 87·3° F., and the mean
minimum temperature during the coldest month 26·6° F., the
mean daily range 30·8° F., and the nights are always cool.
The average annual amount of rainfall is 39·560in., with 102
rainy days in the year.   Hospital; Post and Telegraph Office ;
Free Library.

SPECIAL   INDICATIONS :   Consumption   in   its   early
stages.

SEASON : From October to April.

DOCTORS : Drs. L. G. Mallam, W. Murray.

HOTELS :   " Tattersall's,"   " New   England,"   " Commercial," the " Court House," the " St. Kilda ; " also Mrs.
Gill's Boarding House.

ROUTE : By steamer to Newcastle, thence rail (260m.) ;
or by rail direct.

AUCKLAND, NEW ZEALAND, 260 feet above sea-
level, the largest city in New Zealand, most picturesquely
situated on the shores of Waitemata harbour, on the North
side of the volcanic isthmus where the Waitemata harbour on
the east and the Manukau on the west almost meet ; it is
famed for the beauty of its many sea-views, and sometimes
called the " Corinth of the South Pacific."   The climate is
warm and somewhat moist ; the mean temperature in the
shade in Winter is 52·34° F., in Spring 57·56° F., in Summer 66·92° F., in Autumn 61·16° F. ; the mean temperature
is 59·54° F. ; the mean daily range 17·82° F. ; the mean

maximum temperature during the hottest month is 88·52° F.,
and the mean minimum temperature during the coldest
month 33·26° F. ; the mean annual amount of rainfall is
47·008 inches. Fishing ; sea-bathing ; boating ; yachting.
Post and Telegraph Office ; Hospital ; Free Public Library ;
Museum ; Government House ; Lorne-street Hall ; Temperance Hall ; Theatre Royal ; Opera House ; Choral Hall ;
Albert Park ; the Domain, the principal recreation ground of
the city, with Botanical Gardens.

EXCURSIONS : Mount Eden, 644 feet high (at one time a
Maori pah), with crater and magnificent views (3m.) ;
Remuera, a beautiful suburb at the foot of Mount Eden ; the
Three Kings, a group of volcanic hills, with interesting volcanic caves (5m.) ; North Shore, (by ferry boat), with Mt.
Victoria, once a volcano, now a signal station, affording fine
views (2½m.) ; Lake and Mt. Takapuna ; Ponsonby, a pretty
suburb (2m.) ; Parnell, adjoining Ponsonby ; Waiwera hot
springs, on Hauraki Gulf (24m.)

DOCTORS : Dr. T. H. Lewis, formerly for 3 years resident medical superintendent of the Rotorua Sanatorium, should
be consulted by all invalids passing through Auckland *en
route* for the Thermal Springs district ; Drs. J. C. Mac-
Mullen, C. H. Haines, G. T. Girdler, H. C. Wine, C. N.
Cobbett, H. Walker.

HOTELS : The " Albert," the " Star," the " Royal Mail,"
the " Clarendon," the " Nevada," the " Governor Browne,"
the " Waitemata," the " Thames," the " Auckland," the
" Imperial," the " Masonic," the " Thistle," "Oram's."

PRIVATE BOARDING HOUSES : " Claremont House,"
" Harbour View House."

BAIRNSDALE, VICTORIA, 185 miles E. of Mel-
bourne, and 10 miles from the coast, pleasantly situated on
the banks of the Mitchell River, in a hop-growing district,
near the Gippsland lakes. Surrounding country partly low,
partly mountainous. The average annual rainfall is 26
inches. Fishing ; shooting ; boating. Post and Telegraph
Office ; Mechanics' Institute ; Race-course ; Cricket and
Rowing Clubs.

EXCURSIONS : Eagle Point (the beauty spot of the lakes) (5m.) ; Rosherville ; Cunningham.

DOCTORS : Drs. F. A. Bennet, J. Duncan.

HOTELS : The " Victoria," " Commercial," " Imperial," " Club," " Bridge," and " Court."

ROUTE : By rail to Sale (127m.), thence steamer (46m.) ; or by steamer direct.

BALLAARAT, VICTORIA, 1,437 feet above sea-level, 100 miles (by rail) W. from Melbourne, and 60 miles from the coast, the second city in Victoria, enjoys a temperate climate, and its noted salubrity makes it a place of resort by invalids requiring a bracing yet not too cold an air.   The mean annual temperature is 54·3° F. ; the mean temperature in January is 63° F. ; in April, 54° F. ; in July, 42° F. ; in October, 52° F. ; and in December, 60° F.   The average annual rainfall is 26 inches.   Turkish and Swimming Baths ; Hydropathic establishment ; Post and Telegraph Office ; Hospital and Benevolent Asylum ; Mechanics' Institute ; Public Library ; Academy of Music, with Fine Art Gallery ; Alfred Hall ; Masonic Hall ; Liedertafel ; Musical Union ; Ballarat and Commercial Clubs.

OBJECTS OF INTEREST : Lake Wendouree, a beautiful sheet of water of 600 acres in extent (fishing, boating, yachting) ; Botanical Gardens, with its fernery and statues ; City Hall, with the Alfred Memorial Bells ; Bourke and Wills Memorial Stone ; Eureka Monument ; Burns' Statue ; School of Mines ; the Gold-mines.

EXCURSIONS : Mount Warrenheip 2463 feet, and Mt. Buninyong 2,448 feet, affording splendid views ; Mounts Pisgah, Blowhard, and Hollowback, the three bald hills of Dowling Forest ; the water reserves in the forest, especially near Kirk's reservoir ; Lal Lal Falls, a favourite spot for picnics (14m.) ; Moorabool Falls.

HOTELS : " Lester's," replete with every comfort and convenience ; " Craig's Royal," one of the finest hotels out of Melbourne ; the " Unicorn," the " George," " Brophy's Club," Sayle's " Edinburgh Castle," the " North Grant," the " Earl of Zetland," the " Buck's Head," the " Royal Standard," " Saunders."

DOCTORS : Drs. R. D. Pinnock, W. P. Whitcombe, T. F. Jordan, R. J. Owen.

BALLAN, VICTORIA, 1,650 feet above sea-level, 45 miles (by rail) N.W. from Melbourne, on the Werribee River. The climate is healthy, cool, and agreeable. The average annual rainfall is 33 inches. Fishing ; shooting. Post and Telegraph Office ; Mechanics' Institute ; Race-course ; Recreation Reserve.

Mineral Springs of a highly medicinal character known as the " Ballan Mineral," or the " Victorian Seltzer," are situated on the border of the Ballarook Forest, about 7 miles from the Ballan railway-station, and over 2,000 feet above sea-level. The water is clear, sparkling, inodorant, mildly pungent, and of an alkaline character ; it has been in use for the last twenty years.

ANALYSIS (in grains per gallon) : Carbonate of soda (with traces of potash), 68·8grs. ; Carbonate of lime, 19·2grs. ; Carbonate of Magnesia, 22·4 grs. ; Carbonate of iron, 1·6gr. ; Chloride of Sodium, 5·4grs. ; total, 117grs. of solid matter in one gallon. Also traces of Bromine and Sulphuric Acid, but Phosphoric Acid, Iodine, and Fluorine, though carefully sought for by the Analyst, Mr. J. Cosmo Newbery, were not detected. The water is bottled at the Ballan Mineral Springs by Mr. Chr. Gunsser, but as the water, as it comes out of the rock, does not contain sufficient carbonic acid to keep the different minerals in solution when the water is bottled, a gas-holder has been erected at the springs, to collect the free carbonic acid which the springs give off continually, and with this natural carbonic acid gas, the water, as it comes from the springs, is impregnated, producing a very palatable and refreshing beverage.

SPECIAL INDICATIONS : Indigestion, Affections of kidneys and bladder, Costiveness, Heartburn, and Rheumatism ; in large doses useful in reducing corpulence, and in small doses in diarrhœa and dysentery. Also suitable for infants, if mixed with equal parts of milk.

HOTELS : The " Ballan," the " Commercial," the " Shannon," the " Freemason's," the " Orwell," the " Railway," the " Hanrahan."

BATHURST, New South Wales, 2,153 feet above sea level, 145 miles (by rail) W. from Sydney, and 98 miles from the coast, the emporium of the western interior, on the Macquarie River. The climate is extremely healthy and invigorating, though frequently very cold in the winter months. The mean maximum temperature in the shade during the hottest month is 86·8° F., and the mean minimum temperature during the coldest month 28·1° F., the mean annual temperature is 56·8° F., the mean daily range, 29·9° F., and the average annual amount of rainfall 23·222in., with 74 rainy days in the year. Hospital ; Post and Telegraph Office ; School of Arts.

Doctors : Drs. W. F. Bassett, D. T. Edmunds, W. Finlay, T. A. Macbattie, W. W. Spencer.

Hotels : The " Royal," " Metropolitan," " Duke's," " Tattersall's," " Newmarket," " Oxford."

BEECHWORTH, Victoria, 1,795 feet above sea-level, 171 miles (by rail) N.E. from Melbourne, and 126 miles from the coast, the capital town of the Ovens district, picturesquely situated and surrounded by lofty mountains. The scenery is magnificent, and the climate is extremely salubrious ; the air is pure, mild and dry, though cold in Winter. The mean annual temperature is 55·7° F. ; the mean temperature in January is 70° F. ; in April, 58°F. ; in July, 40° F. ; in October, 58° F. ; and in December, 67° F. The average annual rainfall is 30 inches. Good shooting in the neighbouring ranges and gullies. Post and Telegraph Office ; Hospital ; Public Library and Burke Museum ; Athenæum ; Star Hotel Theatre ; Masonic, St. George's and Oddfellow's Halls ; Recreation Reserve, beautifully kept ; Race-course ; Cricket ground.

Excursions : Lake Kerford (4m.) ; the Dingle Ranges ; the Red and One-Tree Hills ; Stanley (6m.), and Mt. Stanley, 3,444ft., commanding splendid views (12m.) ; Buffalo Mountain ; numerous Gold Mines.

Special Indications : General Debility, Chest Affections.

Doctors : Drs. W. A. Dobbyn, D. Skinner, H. T. Fox.

HOTELS : The " Commercial," a fine roomy hotel ; the " Star," the " Victoria," the " Alliance," the " Corner," the " Post Office," the " London Tavern," the " Oriental," the " Albion," the " Imperial."

BEENLEIGH, QUEENSLAND, 24 miles (by rail) S. from Brisbane, and 10 miles from the coast, near the Albert and Logan rivers, in a farming, sugar, and arrowroot growing district. Climate very fine. The total rainfall in 1884 was 54 inches, with 88 rainy days. Post and Telegraph Office.

HOTELS : The " Beenleigh," the " Railway," the " Royal."

BELFAST, VICTORIA, 190 miles (by steamer) S.W. from Melbourne, an important seaport town and sea-side health resort at the mouth of the river Moyne, on Port Fairy Bay, in a fine agricultural and pastoral district. The surrounding country is undulating and the scenery picturesque. The climate is salubrious and bracing. The average annual rainfall is 29 inches. Good sea and river bathing ; excellent fishing (trumpeter and crayfish) ; splendid shooting (kangaroo and plover) ; boating. Hospital ; Post and Telegraph Office ; Botanical Gardens ; Mechanics' Institute ; Oddfellows Hall ; Temperance Hall ; Cricket and Bowling Clubs.

EXCURSIONS : Tower Hill, a remarkable volcanic mountain, with a perfect extinct crater, standing in the Tower Lake (9m.) ; the " Crags," a favourite place for picnics (5m.) ; Lady Julia Percy Island, much frequented by seals ; Koroit (12m.)

DOCTOR : Dr. T. Stanton.

HOTELS : The " Star of the West," the " Bank," the "Commercial," the " Albion," the " Caledonian," the " Victoria," the " Market," the " White Hart," the " Union."

BELMONT, NEW SOUTH WALES. *See* LAKE MACQUARIE.

BLACKHEATH, NEW SOUTH WALES, 3,494 feet above sea-level, 73 miles (by rail) W. from Sydney. There are numerous mountain springs in the district, the water of which is very fine and of the purest quality. Post and Telegraph Office.

EXCURSIONS : Govett's Leap, an unbroken descent of about 500 feet; the Trinity Cascade ; the Gorge of the Grose ; Mermaid's Glen ; Mt. King George, (3,620ft.) ; Mt. Toomah, (3,240ft.) *See* also KATOOMBA and MT. VICTORIA.

HOTEL : The " Victoria House," with superior accommodation.

BOOROOLONG, NEW SOUTH WALES, 4,328 feet above sea-level, 375 miles N. of Sydney, and 87 miles from the coast, situated in the centre of the New England Tableland ; the scenery is picturesque, and the climate very mild and bracing. The average annual rainfall is 34·58 inches with 105 wet days ; the mean temperature in 1885 was 43° F. Post Office.

EXCURSION : MacLeay Water Falls.

ROUTE : By steamer to Newcastle, thence rail (281m.) ; or by rail direct.

BOWENFELS, NEW SOUTH WALES, 2,972 feet above sea-level, 97· miles (by rail) W. from Sydney, and 78 miles from the coast, situated on the Blue Mountains. The surrounding country is mountainous and well wooded, with splendid scenery. The climate in summer is very mild, dry, and equable, and all through the year it is most invigorating and salubrious. Good walks. Post and Telegraph Offices.

EXCURSIONS : Lithgow ; Hartley ; Eskbank.

SPECIAL INDICATIONS : For Convalescents ; (not suitable for advanced phthisis.)

DOCTOR : Dr. M. Asher, from Lithgow.

HOTEL : The " Royal " ; also Cook's Boarding-house.

BOWRAL, NEW SOUTH WALES, 2,171 feet above sea-level, 80 miles (by rail) S. from Sydney, and 30 miles from the coast. A pretty little town at the foot of the " Gib," surrounded by open meadows, grassy slopes and gentle undulations. Noted for its extreme healthiness, which is attracting numbers of well-to-do residents of Sydney during the heat of summer. The atmosphere is dry and exhilarating. The average annual rainfall is 28·41 inches, with 97 wet days. Post and Telegraph Office ; School of Arts.

EXCURSIONS : The " Gib," a high cliff deriving its name from a fancied resemblance to the rock at Gibraltar, from the top of which an extensive view is obtained ; Berrima.—*See* also MOSS VALE and MITTAGONG.

DOCTOR : Dr. B. J. Newmarch.

HOTELS : The " Royal," the " Commercial," " Neich's."

BOARDING-HOUSES : " Groves'," " Shelly's," " Horton's," " Mackenzie's," " Carter's," " Monk's," " Hodgson's," " Chapel's."

BRIGHTON, SOUTH AUSTRALIA, 9 miles S.W. from Adelaide, a favourite sea-side resort, prettily situated on the shores of the Gulf of St. Vincent. Jetty, affording a pleasant promenade. Sea-bathing ; fishing ; boating. Post and Telegraph Office ; Literary Institute.

EXCURSION : Glenelg (2½m.)

HOTELS : The " Brighton," the " Thatched House," the " Sea-side."

ROUTE : By rail to Glenelg, thence tram.

BRIGHTON, VICTORIA, 8 miles (by rail) S.E. from Melbourne, on the eastern shore of Port Phillip Bay, a favourite watering-place and one of the healthiest and prettiest suburbs of Melbourne. The atmosphere is invigorating, pure and salubrious. The average annual rainfall is 27 inches. Long sandy beach ; two fine piers ; Sea-baths ; fishing ; boating ; yachting ; shooting. Post and Telegraph Office.

HOTELS : The " Retreat," " Duke of Edinburgh," " Royal Terminus," " Grimbley's," " Marine," " Red Bluff." Also the " Wellington and Cambrian House," a high-class boarding-house containing 40 rooms.

BUNDABERG, QUEENSLAND, 272 miles (by steamer) N.W. from Brisbane, the port of a rich agricultural and sugar-growing district, on the Burnett River, in close proximity to the sea, noted for the salubrity of its climate ; average rainfall 30 inches, with 80 wet days.   Summer heat seldom exceeds 90° F. in the shade.   Hospital ; Post and Telegraph Office ; School of Arts ; Racing Club.

DOCTORS : Drs. T. H. May, W. D. Thomas, D'A. Sugden.

HOTELS : The " Grand," the " Custom House," the " Imperial," the " West End," the " Royal," the " Criterion," the " Terminus," the " Mulgrave," the " Sydney."

BUNINYONG, VICTORIA, 1,600 feet above sea-level, 106 miles W. of Melbourne.   The surrounding country is elevated, the air very bracing, and fresh water springs are numerous.   The average annual rainfall is 29 inches.   Post and Telegraph Office ; Public Library.

EXCURSIONS : Mount Buninyong (1½m); Mount Warren-heip.

HOTELS : The " Buninyong," the " Crown," the " Court House," the " Royal Exchange."

ROUTE : By rail to Ballarat, thence car (7m.) ; or by rail to Yendon, thence car (5m.)

BURRADOO, NEW SOUTH WALES, 2,168 feet above sea-level, 82 miles (by rail) S. from Sydney, and 24 miles from the coast.   A charming summer retreat.

Every attention is shown to visitors by Mrs. Livingston at her comfortable private boarding-house, close to the plat-form ; terms moderate.

EXCURSIONS : *See* BOWRAL and MOSS VALE.

BUSSELTON, WESTERN AUSTRALIA, 142 miles (by steamer or coach) S. from Perth, a sea-side health resort on the shores of Geographe Bay.   Frequented by residents of Perth and invalids from India.   It is the shipping-port of a jarrah timber-growing district.   Grapes, as well as other fruits are plentiful.   The surrounding scenery is very pleas-ing ; the climate is salubrious and pleasant.   Sea-bathing can be indulged in almost throughout the year.   Splendid sea-fishing ; jetty 2,800 feet long, forming a pleasant promenade ; sandy beach, extending 25 miles.   There are numerous walks and drives in the neighbourhood.   Post and Telegraph Office ; Mechanics' Institute.

SPECIAL INDICATIONS : General Debility ; Convalescence.

DOCTOR : Dr. R. J. Lepper.

HOTEL : The " Vasse."

CAMBOOYA, QUEENSLAND, 1,524 feet above sea-level, 124 miles (by rail) S.W. from Brisbane, on Hodgson's creek Climate bracing. Post and Telegraph Office.

CAMDEN, NEW SOUTH WALES, 42 miles S.W. of Sydney, and 24 miles from the coast, pleasantly situated on the river Nepean, in a vine-growing district ; dry, salubrious climate. The average annual rainfall is 21·18 inches, with 31 wet days. Post and Telegraph Office.

DOCTORS : Drs. R. E. Beattie, C. G. Leacock.

HOTELS : The " Camden," " Crown," " Commercial," " Plough and Harrow."

ROUTE : By rail to Campbelltown (34m.), thence by tramway (8m.)

CAMPBELLTOWN, NEW SOUTH WALES, 210 feet above sea-level, 34 miles (by rail) S. from Sydney, and 18 miles from the coast. Eminently healthy and picturesque. Soil much impregnated with salt and mineral substances. The average annual rainfall is 22·77 inches, with 74 wet days. Post and Telegraph Office.

EXCURSIONS : Broughton's Pass ; Jordan's Pass ; Pheasant's Nest ; Friendly Falls ; Bulli Pass.

HOTELS : The " Royal," " Jolly Miller," " Railway," " Sportsman's Arms," " Forbes Hotel."

CAMPBELL TOWN, TASMANIA, 660 feet above sea-level, 42 miles (by rail) S.E. from Launceston, and 91 miles (by rail) N. of Hobart, an important though quiet township, pleasantly situated on the Elizabeth River, 38 miles from the coast. The air is dry, cool and bracing ; the annual rainfall in 1886 amounted to 20 inches, with 95 wet days. Good shooting. Hospital ; Post and Telegraph Office ; Institute with Library.

EXCURSIONS : Waterworks Lake, covering an area of 1,200 acres (good shooting—wild duck and swan) ; Mount Campbell, 2,356 feet high.

DOCTOR : Dr. H. G. H. Naylor.

HOTELS : The " Caledonian," the " Criterion," " Kean's."

CHARLTON, VICTORIA, 173 miles (by rail) N.W. from Melbourne, and 148 miles from the coast, situated on the Avoca river, in an extensive agricultural district. The country is flat, and lightly timbered. The climate is remarkably warm, dry and equable ; no sudden changes of temperature ; the Winter is mild and short ; the average annual rainfall is 16·7 inches. A mineral spring, of supposed medicinal value, at Yawong (4m.) Post and Telegraph Office ; Mechanics' Institute.

SPECIAL INDICATIONS : All Chest Diseases, especially Phthisis, and Hydatids of Lung.

DOCTOR : Dr. T. G. Beckett, who makes diseases of the chest his special study. ·

HOTELS : The " East Charlton," the " Golden Fleece," the " Globe," the " Cricket Club," the " Vale of Avoca."

CHOWDER BAY, NEW SOUTH WALES, a favourite watering-place, prettily situated on the northern shore of Port Jackson, 6 miles (by steamer) from Sydney. Beach ; sea-bathing ; fishing. Pavilion, accommodating 2,000 persons.

HOTEL : The " Marine," overlooking the beautiful harbour of Port Jackson, is most elaborately furnished, and replete with every convenience.

CLARENDON, SOUTH AUSTRALIA, 18 miles S.E. of Adelaide, on the Onkaparinga River, in a fine vine-growing district. Adjoining this township is the celebrated Clarendon vineyard, situated at an elevation of nearly 800 feet above sea-level, and thickly planted with choice vines. The surrounding country is mountainous, with fine valleys and undulating flats ; scenery varied and beautiful. The mean annual rainfall is 40 inches. Post and Telegraph Office ; Literary Institute ; Oddfellows' Hall.

HOTELS : The " Royal Oak," the " Clarendon."

ROUTE : By rail to Blackwood (11m.), thence coach.

CLEVELAND, QUEENSLAND, 20 miles E. of Brisbane, a favourite watering-place on the shores of Moreton Bay. The total rainfall in 1884 was 48 inches, with 79 wet days. Oranges and bananas are extensively grown. Jetties ; sea-baths. Post and Telegraph Office ; School of Arts.

HOTELS : The " Cleveland," the " Pier," the " Brighton."

ROUTE : By coach or steamer.

CLIFTON SPRINGS, VICTORIA. See DRYSDALE.

CLYDE OR DUNSTAN (OTAGO), NEW ZEALAND, 156 miles W. of Dunedin, on the Clutha River, in a gold-mining and fruit-growing district. The climate is extremely salubrious ; the surrounding scenery is wild and weird. Shooting (rabbits). Hospital ; Post and Telegraph Office ; Athenæum ; Public Library.

EXCURSIONS : Cromwell (10m.) ; Alexandra.

DOCTOR : Dr. G. A. Lewis.

HOTELS : The " Dunstan," " Port Phillip," the " Junction."

ROUTE : By rail from Dunedin to Lawrence (60m.), thence coach via Roxburgh.

COIMADAI, VICTORIA, 33 miles N.W. of Melbourne. In the neighbourhood are mineral water springs, whence is obtained the well known " Coimadai Water."

HOTEL : The " Coimadai."

ROUTE : By rail to Diggers' Rest (20m.), thence coach (13 miles).

COOGEE BAY, NEW SOUTH WALES, a favourite watering-place, 5 miles (by tram) S. from Sydney, beautifully situated on the Pacific Ocean. Fine sandy beach ; sea-bathing ; fishing. An Aquarium, with hot and cold salt-water baths, is to be erected shortly.

HOTELS : The " Baden Baden," the " Coogee Bay."

COWES, VICTORIA, 55 miles S.E. of Melbourne, a seaside health resort on the northern coast of Phillip Island, fronting Western Port Bay. The country is elevated and undulating, the eastern portion is lightly timbered, and the western open country. Fine climate. Sandy beach; seabathing; shooting (wallaby, hares, pheasants, partridges, quails, &c.); fishing. Post and Telegraph Office; Free Public Library.

EXCURSIONS: Swan and Green Lakes (8m. S.W.), abounding in fish and waterfowl (wild ducks).

HOTELS: The "Isle of Wight," at which visitors are well cared for by Host Bauer; "Wood's Family."

ROUTE: By rail to Frankston (27m.), thence coach to Hastings (15m.), thence small steamer.

CROOKWELL, NEW SOUTH WALES, 2,995 feet above sea-level, 160 miles S. of Sydney, and 76 miles from the coast, pleasantly situated on the Crookwell river, well sheltered from cold westerly winds. The climate is healthy and bracing, the temperature dry and equable. The average annual rainfall is 28·73 inches, with 94 wet days. The scenery is varied and pleasing. Fishing; excellent shooting. Post and Telegraph Office.

OBJECTS OF INTEREST: The famous Womberan Caves.

SPECIAL INDICATIONS: Lung Diseases; General Debility.

SEASON: From November to March.

DOCTOR: Dr. A. E. FitzPatrick, who makes diseases of women and children his special study.

HOTELS: The "Commercial," "Tattersall's," the "Crookwell"; also an excellent Temperance Boarding-house.

ROUTE: By rail to Goulburn (134m.), thence coach (26m.).

DALBY, QUEENSLAND, 1,123 feet above sea-level, 152 miles (by rail) W. of Brisbane, and 112 miles from the coast, in the pastoral district of Northern Downs. The climate is dry and bracing. The total rainfall in 1884 was 18 inches, with 62 wet days. Hospital; Post and Telegraph Office; School of Arts; Race-course.

HOTELS : The " Royal," the " Post Office," the " Queen's Arms," the " Golden Fleece," the " Criterion," the " Sovereign," the " Railway."

DALVEEN, QUEENSLAND, 2,906 feet above sea-level, 194 miles (by rail) S.W. from Brisbane. The surrounding country is mountainous, the scenery beautiful, and the climate very bracing. Post and Telegraph Office. At present there is no accommodation for visitors at Dalveen.

DANDENONG, VICTORIA, 69 feet above sea-level, 18 miles (by rail) S.E. from Melbourne, and 16 miles from the coast, a pretty and pleasant township, lying on a flat under the Dandenong Ranges. The average annual rainfall is 30·4 inches. Scenery in the ranges extremely wild and picturesque. The State Forest, close by, is full of red gum and blackwood trees of an enormous size. Good shooting ; fishing. Post and Telegraph Office ; Mechanics' Institute.

EXCURSIONS : The Fern-tree Gullies, celebrated for their picturesque scenery (12m.)

HOTELS : The " Royal," the " Bridge," with first-class accommodation ; the " Shamrock," the " Albion."

DAYLESFORD, VICTORIA, 2,039 feet above sea-level, a rising health resort, picturesquely situated on Wombat creek, near the Loddon river, 78 miles (by rail) N.W. from Melbourne, and 70 miles from the coast. The surrounding district is elevated and mountainous, and the scenery is exceedingly beautiful ; the climate is bracing ; the nights are always cool. The average annual rainfall is 36·8 inches ; the mean annual temperature is 53° F.; the mean temperature in January, is 58° F. ; in April, 52° F. ; in July, 42° F.; in October, 52° F., and in December, 60° F. English fruits are grown to perfection. Fishing ; shooting. In the neighbourhood are some highly carbonated chalybeate springs, (see HEPBURN). Hospital ; Post and Telegraph Office ; Mechanics' Institute ; Albert Hall Theatre ; Botanic Gardens, 2,300 feet above sea-level, commanding a grand and extensive view ; Public Park ; Race-course.

EXCURSIONS : Hepburn Mineral Springs (3m.); Sailor's Creek and Waterfall (4m.) ; Stony Creek, with Waterfall ; Kangaroo Creek Falls ; Loddon Falls ; Coomoora (2½m.) ;

Deep Creek, (6m.) ; Glenlyon (6½m.) ; the Coliban Falls, a romantic spot 2½ miles from Trentham (14m.) ; Mt. Blow-hard.

SPECIAL INDICATIONS : General Debility, Pulmonary and Nervous Affections.

SEASON : From October to April.

DOCTORS : Drs. E. H. C. Massy, T. R. H. Willis.

HOTELS : The "Commercial," the "Victoria," the "Royal," the "Albert," the "Terminus," the "Liverpool Arms," the "Raglan," the "Manchester." Mrs. Brown's Coffee Palace (charges moderate), with excellent accommodation.

DELORAINE, TASMANIA, 800 feet above sea-level, 45 miles (by rail) S.W. from Launceston, and 23 miles from the coast, pleasantly situated on the river Meander, the centre of one of the finest agricultural districts in the colony. The total rainfall in 1886 amounted to 37 inches, with 146 wet days. Post and Telegraph Office ; Public Library.

EXCURSIONS : The famous Chudleigh Caves (15m.) ; the magnificent falls of the Meander ; Quamby Bluff, an isolated, lofty montain ; Mount Rolland.

DOCTOR : Dr. J. M. MacNeece.

HOTELS : The "Deloraine," the "Commercial," the "Shamrock," the "Plough," the "Bush."

DEVONPORT or NORTH SHORE, NEW ZEALAND, a marine suburb, 2½ miles N.E. of Auckland. Fine strand ; sea-bathing ; fishing ; boating ; yachting. Post and Telegraph Office. Good hotels.

EXCURSIONS : *See* AUCKLAND.

DROMANA, VICTORIA, 35 miles (by steamer) S. from Melbourne, a favourite watering-place on the shores of Hobson's Bay ; surrounding country mountainous. The average annual rainfall is 29·2 inches. Sea-bathing ; sea-fishing ; shooting (rabbits). Jetty, 1,400 feet long, forming a pleasant promenade. Post and Telegraph Office ; Mechanics' Institute ; Race-course (3m.)

EXCURSIONS : Arthur's Seat mountain ($\frac{1}{2}$m.), and light-house, (1$\frac{1}{2}$m.) ; Mount Martha (3m.)

HOTELS : The " Dromana," with superior accommodation; the " Arthur's Seat."

DRYSDALE, VICTORIA, 212 feet above sea-level, 57 miles (by rail) via Geelong, and 34 miles (by steamer) S.W. from Melbourne, pleasantly situated on the Corty Ule Creek, near the shores of Port Phillip Bay. The surrounding country is undulated and elevated, and the scenery beautiful. The district is considered a very healthy one, and invalids are frequently sent there for the benefit of the air. The average annual rainfall is 19·7 inches. Sea-bathing ; fishing ; shooting ; boating. Post and Telegraph Office ; Free Library.

The celebrated Chalybeate and Sulphurous Springs at Clifton, close to the sea-shore, are 1$\frac{1}{2}$ miles distant from Drysdale ; the water is bright, sparkling, and very brisk, of pleasant taste and highly refreshing, possessing chalybeate, anti-acid, and tonic properties. There are a number of different springs at Clifton, all highly charged with carbonic acid gas ; these natural aerated waters are bottled and sold by the Clifton Springs Company, Drysdale. Hot mineral baths can also be had at Clifton.

1. MAGNESIA SPRING—

ANALYSIS (in grains per pint) : Silica, 0·500gr. ; Carbonate of Iron, 0·700gr. ; Carbonate of Lime, 3·464grs. ; Carbonate of Magnesia, 13·625grs. ; Sulphate of Sodium, 3·244grs. ; Chloride of Sodium, 51·400grs. ; Carbonate of Sodium, 14·667grs. ; total amount of mineral matters per pint, 87·600grs.

Temperature : 68° F.

Specific Gravity (at 60° F.) : 1006·5.

2. SELTZER SPRING—

ANALYSIS (in grains per pint) : Silica, 1·150gr. ; Carbonate of Iron, 0·910grs. ; Carbonate of Lime, 8·064grs. ; Carbonate of Magnesia, 11·130grs. ; Sulphate of Sodium, 3·171grs. ; Chloride of Sodium, 34·411grs. ; Carbonate of

c

Sodium, 35·564grs. ; total 94·400grs. of mineral matters per pint.

Temperature : 60° F.   *Specific Gravity :* 1008.

3. SODA SPRING—

ANALYSIS (in grains per pint) : Silica, 0·840gr. ; Carbonate of Iron, 0·279gr. ; Carbonate of Lime, 5·904grs. ; Carbonate of Magnesia, 10·038grs. ; Sulphate of Soda, 3·028grs. ; Chloride of Sodium, 37·069grs. ; Carbonate of Soda, 28·069grs. ; total 85·227grs. of mineral matters per pint.

Temperature : 64° F.

Specific Gravity (at 60° F.) : 1005·5.

4. IRON SPRING—

The most valuable one, from a medical point of view, very similar in composition to the Rakoczy Spring at Kissingen, Bavaria, but much stronger in Carbonate of Iron.

ANALYSIS (in grains per pint) : Silica, 0·730gr. ; Carbonate of Iron, 1·156gr. ; Carbonate of Lime, 1·536gr. ; Carbonate of Magnesia, 9·768grs. ; Sulphate of Sodium, 9·060grs. ; Chloride of Sodium, 57·250grs. ; Carbonate of Soda, 4·200grs.; total 84·200grs. of mineral matters per pint.

Temperature : 68° F.

Specific Gravity (at 60° F.) : 1005.

SPECIAL INDICATIONS : Chlorosis, Anæmia, Disorders of Digestion, Liver Complaints ; also Rheumatism, Rheumatic Gout, Gout, Sciatica, and Affections of the Joints, if taken in conjunction with the hot mineral baths at Clifton.

EXCURSIONS : Queenscliff (10m.) ; Geelong, (12m.)

HOTELS : At DRYSDALE : The "Bucks Head ;" two large first-class hotels, each to contain about 50 rooms, were in course of erection in 1887. At CLIFTON : The "Clifton," five minutes walk from the springs, where first-class accommodation can be had.   :

DOCTORS : Drs. J. T. Chapman, and F. W. Towle.

DUBBO, NEW SOUTH WALES, 865 feet above sea-level, 2˜8 miles (by rail) N.W. from Sydney, and 182 miles from the coast, a flourishing town situated on the Macquarie river, and the centre of one of the richest mineral and pastoral districts of the colony. The climate is warm and dry, and very efficacious in chest diseases. The average annual rainfall is 22·26 inches, with 75 wet days. The mean maximum temperature in the shade in 1885 was 80° F.; the mean minimum temperature, 48·6° F.; and the mean temperature, 64·3° F. Hospital; Post and Telegraph Office; School of Arts; Masonic Hall.

A cold effervescent mineral spring is situated on Talbrigar Creek, about 22 miles from Dubbo; the water is of an alkaline character, it is clear, free from odour, and highly charged with carbonic acid gas. It contains a small amount of sediment consisting of silica and some organic matter.

ANALYSIS (in grains per gallon): Bicarbonate of Sodium, 183·10grs.; Bicarbonate of Potassium, 12·83grs.; Bicarbonate of Lithium, 0·05gr.; Bicarbonate of Calcium, 11·38grs.; Bicarbonate of Magnesium, 9·36grs.; Iron, 0·70gr.; Chloride of Sodium, 6·92grs.; Aluminum traces; Silica, 0·28gr.; total 224·62grs. of mineral matters in one gallon. Also traces of Phosphates, and Free Ammonia, 00·052 parts in 100·000.

Temperature : 65° F.

SPECIAL INDICATIONS : Acid Dyspepsia ; Disorders of Kidneys and Bladder.

DOCTORS : Drs. H. G. S. Warren, H. M. Gay.

HOTELS : The "Royal," the "Macquarie View," the "Great Western," the "Post Office," the "Imperial," the "Court House," the "Telegraph," "Tattersall's."

DUNSTAN OR CLYDE (OTAGO), NEW ZEALAND. *See* CLYDE.

ECHUCA, VICTORIA (with its border town, MOAMA, NEW SOUTH WALES), 314 feet above sea-level, 156 miles (by rail) N. from Melbourne, and 146 miles from the coast, on the Murray and Campaspe rivers, surrounded by forests of gum trees, which protect these towns from winds and impregnate the pure atmosphere with the balsamic odour of the essential oil of Eucalyptus. The climate is warm, equable, and very dry. The mean annual temperature is 58·9° F.; the average annual rainfall is only 16 inches, with 67 rainy days in the year; there is very little variation of temperature, and hardly any sudden atmospheric changes. The country around

Echuca is rather flat, and the town is liable to severe inundations from the flooding of the river ; the river scenery is very fine.   There are some vineyards in the district.   Fishing (Murray cod, black-fish) ; shooting (hares, turkeys, &c.) ; floating river-baths ; boating.   Hospital ; Post and Telegraph Office ;   Mechanics' Institute ; Free Library ; three Public Parks.

OBJECTS OF INTEREST : Granite obelisk in memory of Henry Hopwood, the founder of Echuca ; the bridge over the Murray, 1,900 feet long.

EXCURSIONS : The Moira lakes ;   the vineyards on the banks of the Goulburn river (6m.)

SPECIAL INDICATIONS : Pulmonary diseases, especially Phthisis, Asthma, Bronchitis.

SEASON : April to November.

DOCTORS : Dr. G. R. Eakins, who makes a specialty of diseases of the chest, also of diseases peculiar to women, is the proprietor of a private hospital, where patients will be received ; also Drs. Graham and Osborne.

HOTELS : Spearing's "Palace Hotel," with superior accommodation; the "Echuca," the "Commercial," the "Pastoral," the "Union Club," the "Steam-packet," the "Rodney," the "Victoria Terminus," the "Caledonian," "Berryman's Temperance;" and at MOAMA : the "Bridge," the "Border Inn," the "Plough and Harrow," the "Vine," the "Railway Terminus."

ECHUNGA, SOUTH AUSTRALIA, 21 miles S.E. of Adelaide, a favourite summer-resort, in an agricultural and gold-mining district.   The climate is very salubrious, and the surrounding country is considerably elevated and of a hilly character.   The total rainfall in 1882 was 27 inches.   Post and Telegraph Office ; Literary Institute.

EXCURSIONS : Mt. Barker (6m.) ;   Hahndorf, (5¾m.) ; Meadows, (6m.) ; Macclesfield, (6m.).

HOTELS : The "Bridge," the "Hagen Arms."

ROUTE : By rail to Aldgate (12m.), thence coach.

EDEN, NEW SOUTH WALES, 107 feet above sea-level, 283 miles (by steamer) S. from Sydney, a sea-side health resort on the north shore of Twofold Bay, in a pastoral, agricultural and dairy-farming district. The town is built on the slopes of, and in the valley formed by two hills, and is well sheltered from all winds. The district is mountainous and the climate mild and very salubrious. The mean maximum temperature during the hottest month is 76° F., the mean minimum temperature during the coldest month 43° F., and the mean annual temperature 60° F. The mean annual rainfall is 36 inches, with 116 wet days. Sea-bathing; fishing; boating; pier. Post and Telegraph Office.

SPECIAL INDICATION : Consumption.

SEASON : Throughout the year.

HOTELS : The " Commercial," the " Pier," the " Great Southern ; " also Silk's and Woollett's boarding-houses.

EDITHBURGH, SOUTH AUSTRALIA, 50 miles (by steamer) S.W. from Adelaide, a fashionable watering-place, pleasantly situated on the eastern shore of Yorke's Peninsula. The mean annual rainfall is nearly 18 inches. Sea-bathing; fishing; boating; pier; sea-beach. Post and Telegraph Office ; Literary Institute.

EXCURSION : Troubridge Island, with lighthouse (4m.)

HOTELS : The " Edithburgh," the " Troubridge," " Temperance Hotel " with 50 rooms.

ELPHINSTONE. VICTORIA, 1,365 feet above sea-level, 70 miles (by rail) N.W. from Melbourne, pleasantly situated on the slope of a hill, commanding extensive and picturesque views of Mount Alexander, and the surrounding country, which is elevated and undulating ; climate very salubrious. Good fishing. Post and Telegraph Office.

EXCURSION : Coliban Water Falls, a romantic spot.

HOTEL : " Lonsdale's."

EMU PARK, QUEENSLAND. *See* HEWITTVILLE.

EVANDALE, TASMANIA, about 1,000 feet above sea-level, 13 miles (by rail) S.E. from Launceston, and 38 miles from the coast, pleasantly situated on the South Esk river, amidst beautiful scenery ; from the absence of hills, much exposed to winds. The climate is dry and very bracing.

Shooting ; fishing ; boating. Post and Telegraph Office ; Public Library.

EXCURSIONS : " Corra Linn," (6m.) ; the White Hills or Breadalbane (5m.) ; the Nile river (7m.) ; Hunter's mills.

SPECIAL INDICATIONS : For Convalescents.

DOCTOR : Dr. C. H. Elliott, who is the proprietor of " Blenheim House " sanitarium, affording accommodation for ten persons, invalids or otherwise.

HOTELS : The " Prince of Wales," the " Clarendon," the " Royal Oak."

FERNSHAWE, VICTORIA, 45 miles N.E. of Melbourne, on Watts river, famed for the extreme beauty of its scenery ; the surrounding country abounds in fern-tree gullies, waterfalls, and lofty mountains ; the timber is of immense height, some as high as 420 feet. The average annual rainfall is 35 6 inches. Shooting ; fishing. Post Office.

EXCURSIONS : Mount Juliet (2m.) ; Mount Monda (2m) ; Black Spur.

HOTEL : " Jefferson's."

ROUTE : By rail to Lilydale (24m.), thence coach (21m.)

FERN-TREE GULLY, VICTORIA, 21 miles S.E. of Melbourne, in the Dandenong Ranges, abounding in mosses, heath, and gigantic ferns, famed for the beauty of its scenery, which is extremely rugged and picturesque. The average annual rainfall is 42·3 inches. Good shooting (kangaroo, wallaby, &c.) Post and Telegraph Office

HOTELS : The " Fern-Tree Gully," the " Hunting Tower."

ROUTE : By rail to Oakleigh or Dandenong, thence coach ; or by conveyance from Melbourne.

FORMBY (WITH TORQUAY), TASMANIA, 82 miles (by rail) N.W. from Launceston, two rising sea-side resorts, connected by a ferry, at the mouth of the river Mersey, on the northern coast of the island, in an agricultural and timber growing district. Splendid climate, but not suitable for pulmonary affections. Sea-bathing ; excellent fishing ; fair shooting ; boating. Post and Telegraph Offices ; Literary

Institute at Torquay. There are two hotels and a coffee-palace at Formby.

HOTEL : At TORQUAY—The "Torquay."

FRANKLIN, TASMANIA, 30 feet above sea-level, 28 miles (by coach) and 60 miles (by steamer) S.W. from Hobart, beautifully situated on the Huon river, 15 miles from the coast, in a fine fruit-growing district. The summer climate is mild, balmy and salubrious, and the surrounding scenery is really beautiful. The total rainfall in 1886 amounted to 31 inches, with 166 wet days. Shooting ; fishing. Post and Telegraph Office ; Mechanics' Institute.

EXCURSIONS : Egg Island, densely wooded (opposite Franklin) ; Victoria (5m.) ; Geevestown (9m.) ; Lakes and Waterfalls near the river Arve.

HOTELS : The "Lady Franklin," the "Kent," the "Temperance."

FRANKSTON, VICTORIA, 27 miles S. of Melbourne, a marine retreat, beautifully situated at the foot of Mount Eliza, on the S.E. shores of Port Phillip. Climate. mild and very salubrious ; the average annual rainfall is 35 inches. Splendid scenery ; fine pier, $\frac{1}{4}$ mile long, affording a convenient promenade ; sea-baths ; fishing ; shooting ; coursing. Post and Telegraph Office ; Public Library.

SPECIAL INDICATIONS : General Debility ; Convalescence.

EXCURSIONS : Schnapper Point, Dromana, Hastings, Phillip Island.

HOTELS : The "Prince of Wales," Davey's "Bay View," the "Pier."

ROUTE : By rail or steamer.

GEORGE'S BAY, TASMANIA.—See ST. HELEN'S.

GEORGETOWN, TASMANIA, 35 miles (by steamer) N.W. from Launceston, a watering-place picturesquely situated at the mouth of the river Tamar ; the summer resort of northern Tasmanians. Sea-bathing ; fishing. Post and Telegraph Office ; Public Library.

EXCURSIONS : Beaconsfield goldfield (10m.) ; Low Head —sub-marine cable to Victoria—(4m.) ; York Town (6m.) ; Garden Island ; the Lighthouse, 140 feet high.

HOTEL : The " New Chum."

GIBBSTON, (OTAGO), NEW ZEALAND, 186 miles W. of Dunedin, in Lake county.   Post Office.

Gibbston's spring is a cold water of an alkaline character, containing 2·3grs. of mineral matters in one pint.   It is stated to be a specific in diarrhœa ; it contains a large amount of organic matter of some astringent quality, to which its medicinal qualities are probably due.

HOTEL : The " Victoria Bridge."

ROUTE : From Dunedin by rail to Lawrence (60m.), thence coach ; or from Invercargill by rail to Kingston, thence by steamer and conveyance.

GLANVILLE, SOUTH AUSTRALIA.   *See* SEMAPHORE.

GLENCOE, NEW SOUTH WALES, 3,794 feet above sea-level, 385 miles N. of Sydney ; surrounded by lofty hills. Splendid climate and pretty scenery.   The total rainfall in 1886 was 18·23 inches with 38 wet days.   Post Office.

EXCURSION : Ben Lomond, the highest mountain in the northern district.

ROUTE : By steamer to Newcastle, thence rail (310m.) ; or by rail direct.

GLENELG, SOUTH AUSTRALIA, 6½miles (by rail) S.W. from Adelaide, the most frequented watering-place of the colony, situated on the shores of Holdfast Bay.   Climate very salubrious.   Sea-baths ; iron jetty, extending about ¼ mile into the sea, forming a very fashionable promenade during the summer months ; fishing ; boating.   Post and Telegraph Office ; Literary Institute.

DOCTOR : Dr. J. H. S. Finniss.

HOTELS : The " Pier," the " St. Leonard's," the " Jetty," the " Terminus," the " Berkshire."

GLEN INNES, NEW SOUTH WALES, 3,518 feet above sea-level, 399 miles N. of Sydney, and 90 miles from the coast, prettily situated at the foot of a hill in Central New England. The climate is cool, and salubrious ; the air pure and bracing. The mean maximum temperature in the shade in 1885 was 74·2° F., the mean minimum temperature 45·6° F., and the mean temperature 60° F. The average annual rainfall is 33·79 inches, with 97 wet days. Shooting ; fishing. Hospital ; Post and Telegraph Office ; School of Arts ; Race-course ; Music Hall.

SPECIAL INDICATIONS : All debilitating diseases.

SEASON : During the summer months.

DOCTORS : Drs. E. S. Tressider, F. H. Wrigley.

HOTELS : The " Great Central," replete with modern improvements; "Tattersall's," affording the comforts of an English hostelry of the first-class ; the "Commercial," the " Royal," the "Telegraph," the " New England," the "Railway," the "Mount Pleasant ; " also Mr. Maund's and Mr. Hawke's private boarding-houses.

ROUTE : By steamer to Newcastle, thence rail (324m.); or by rail direct.

GOODWOOD, (OTAGO), NEW ZEALAND, 32 miles by rail N. from Dunedin, a favourite sea-side resort. Sea-baths.

GOSFORD, NEW SOUTH WALES, 50 miles N. of Sydney, situated on the shore of Brisbane Water, on the north side of Broken Bay, the estuary of the picturesque Hawkesbury river. The country is very broken, the surrounding scenery is beautiful, and the climate is genial. Fruit is extensively grown. Sea-bathing ; excellent fishing ; shooting ; boating. Post and Telegraph Office.

DOCTOR : Dr. R. Calder.

HOTELS : The " Royal," the " Pier," the "Court House," the " Union."

ROUTE : By steamer or rail direct ; or by steamer to Manly, thence coach to Pittwater, thence steamer.

GOULBURN, NEW SOUTH WALES, 2,071 feet above sea-level, 134 miles (by rail) S. from Sydney, and 54 miles from the coast, the commercial emporium of the southern inland trade. The scenery is pretty, and the climate temperate and bracing at all seasons. The mean maximum temperature in the shade during the hottest month is 84·3° F., and the mean minimum temperature during the coldest month 32·2° F., the annual mean temperature is 55° F., and the mean daily range 25·4° F. ; the average annual amount of rainfall is 24·188 inches, with 96 rainy days in the year. Hospital ; Post and Telegraph Office ; Mechanics' Institute.

EXCURSIONS : Lake Bathurst.

DOCTORS : Drs. J. F. Codrington, R. McKillop, S. M. Morton, H. Ray.

HOTELS : The " Royal," the " Commercial," the " Beehive," the " White Horse," " Mandelson's," " Thomas'."

GOWRIE JUNCTION, QUEENSLAND, 1,577 feet above sea level, 108 miles (by rail) W. from Brisbane. Post and Telegraph Office.

GREENMOUNT, QUEENSLAND, 1,651 feet above sea-level, 132 miles (by rail) S.W. from Brisbane. Post and Telegraph Office.

GUYRA, NEW SOUTH WALES, 4,328 feet above sea-level, 362 miles N. of Sydney, on the " Mother of Ducks " Lagoon, which is 13 miles in circumference and is covered with all sorts of waterfowl, affording excellent sport. The climate is splendid, the maximum heat recorded has been 73° F. in the shade, usually between 60° F. and 70° F. ; the winter, however, is extremely cold. The total rainfall in 1886 was 37·76 inches, with 93 wet days. Post and Telegraph Office.

EXCURSION : " Ben Lomond," the highest mountain in the New England district (16m)

ROUTE : By steamer to Newcastle, thence rail (287 miles); or by rail direct.

HALLETT, SOUTH AUSTRALIA, 1,970 feet above sea-level, 120 miles (by rail) N. from Adelaide, and 56 miles from the coast, in a wheat-growing district. Climate bracing and very dry. The total rainfall in 1882 was a little over 10 inches. Post and Telegraph Office ; Literary Institute.

HOTELS : The " Unicorn," the " Hallett."

HANMER PLAINS, (Prov. Nelson), New Zealand,
92 miles N. of Christchurch (Canterbury). The climate is
dry, bracing and salubrious, the mean temperature in the
shade is 70° F. The surrounding country is mountainous,
some of the mountains being over 4,000 feet high ; the
scenery is alpine in character and very picturesque. Shooting (ducks, hares, rabbits, dottrell, pukaki) ; fishing (trout).
Post Office. ·

The Hanmer Plains are 10 miles long by 4 miles broad,
and about the centre (2½m. from the Post Office) there are
situated, at an altitude of over 1,300 feet above sea-level, a
number of hot springs, nine in all, of an alkaline and saline
character, with a strong escape of sulphuretted hydrogen, and
possessing curative properties similar to those at Rotorua.
The Government have constructed bath-houses, plantation
gardens, &c., and have intimated their intention to increase
the bathing accommodation. Mr. J. Stewart is the Resident
Government Superintendent of the springs. The principal
springs are three, known as Nos. 1, 7, and 8.

Spring No. 1.—*Analysis* (in grains per gallon):
Ammonia, Free, 0·156gr. ; Ammonia, Albuminoid, 0·44gr. ;
Potash, 1·63gr. ; Soda, 34·83grs.; Lithium, traces ; Lime,
1·72gr. ; Magnesia, 0·07gr. ; Iron, 2·52grs. ; Alumina,
0·08gr. ; Carbonic Acid, 5·39grs. ; Sulphuric Acid, 4·69grs. ;
Nitric Acid, 0·139gr. ; Phosphoric Acid, traces ; Chlorine,
35·78grs. ; Sulphuretted Hydrogen, 3·29grs. ; Bromides and
Iodides, nil ; Sediment, 3·15grs. ; total 90·339grs. of solid
matter in one gallon.

Specific Gravity (at 60° F.) : 1064.

Temperature : At sides, 97° F. ; in centre, at a depth of
8 feet, 104° F.

Spring No. 7.—*Analysis* (in grains per gallon) :
Ammonia, Free, 0·193gr. ; Ammonia, Albuminoid, 0·016gr. ;
Potash, 1·47gr. ; Soda, 31·61grs. ; Lime, 0·70gr. ; Magnesia, 1gr. ; Iron, 0·25gr. ; Alumina, 0 07gr. ; Carbonic
Acid, 3·69grs. ; Sulphuric Acid, 10·42grs. ; Phosphoric Acid,
traces ; Chlorine, 33·60grs. ; Sulphuretted Hydrogen, Bromides and Iodides, nil ; total, 83 019grs. of solid matter in one
gallon.

Spring No. 8.—*Analysis* (in grains per gallon) : Ammonia, 0·112gr. ; Ammonia Albuminoid, 0·058gr. ; Potash, 0·06gr. ; Soda, 32·38grs. ; Lithium, traces ; Lime, 4·11grs. ; Magnesia, 0·17gr. ; Iron, 0·26gr. ; Alumina, 0·03gr. ; Carbonic Acid, 5·23grs. ; Sulphuric Acid, 7grs. ; Nitric Acid, 0·215gr. ; Phosphoric Acid, traces ; Chlorine, 34·29grs. ; Sulphuretted Hydrogen, 3·43grs.; Bromides and Iodides, nil ; Sediment, 1·4gr. ; total, 88·345grs. of solid matter in one gallon.

Specific Gravity (at 60° F.) : 1103.

SPRING No. 2.—*Analysis* (in grains per gallon) : Chlorine, 35·77grs. ; total solids, 87·40grs.

SPRING No. 3.—*Analysis* (in grains per gallon) : Chlorine, 34·79grs. ; total solids, 83grs.

SPRING No. 4.—*Analysis* (in grains per gallon) : Chlorine, 34·79grs.; total solids, 83·44grs.

SPRING No. 5.—*Analysis* (in grains per gallon) : Chlorine, 27·83grs. ; total solids, 75·80grs.

SPRING No. 6.—*Analysis* (in grains per gallon) : Chlorine, 24·85grs. ; total solids, 89grs.

SPRING No. 9.—*Analysis* (in grains per gallon) : Chlorine, 33·79grs. ; total solids, 134grs.

N.B.—The Ammonia and Albuminoid Ammonia are present in large quantities in these springs, but the water is nevertheless not injurious to drink, but quite the contrary, and in many cases has been found to be very beneficial.

Temperature : From 86° F. to 118° F., and sometimes 120° F.

SPECIAL INDICATIONS : Rheumatism, Sciatica, Gout, Cutaneous Diseases, Nervous Affections, Insomnia, Chest Complaints ; also for Asthma (from October to June only) ; Psoriasis (from September to April only).

SEASON : Throughout the year.

HOTELS : The "Jollies' Pass" (2½ miles from the Springs) ; "Lahmert's" boarding-house at "Jack's Pass" (1 mile from the Springs).

NOTE : A company was formed in August, 1887, for the purpose of building, at the Springs, a first-class hotel, to accommodate 40 visitors, which is to be opened early in 1888.

ROUTE : From Christchurch (Canterbury) by rail to Culverden (Prov. Nelson), thence by coach through the picturesque valley of the Waiau. (*Note.*—There is no communication via Nelson.)

HARLAXTON, QUEENSLAND, 2,003 feet above sea-level, 98 miles (by rail) W. from Brisbane, 3 miles from Toowoomba, and 78 miles from the coast, on the western slope of the main range of the Darling Downs, surrounded by open forests and well-supplied with water from numerous springs. The climate is equable and bracing ; the mean maximum temperature in summer is about 82° F., while in winter the temperature seldom falls below 32° F. The average annual rainfall is 32 inches. Oranges and English fruits thrive well, while a great variety of flowers continue in bloom all the year round. At present there is no hotel at Harlaxton, though as a sanatorium it cannot be surpassed as regards the salubrity and uniformity of the climate.

SPECIAL INDICATIONS : Pulmonary Affections, especially Phthisis ; also Convalescence, General Debility.

HEALESVILLE, VICTORIA, 400 feet above sea-level, 38 miles E. of Melbourne, pleasantly situated at the junction of the Graceburn and Watts rivers, surrounded by lofty mountains ; scenery extremely picturesque. The average annual rainfall is 35·6 inches. Shooting ; fishing. Post Office.

EXCURSIONS : Coranderak Aboriginal Station (2m.) ; Mount Riddell (2m.) ; Mount Juliet (5m.) ; Black Spur, celebrated for its ferns and gigantic trees (7m.) ; Mounts Monda and Disappointment, with fine waterfall (5m.) ; Mount St. Leonards (4m.) ; Fernshawe (7m.)

DOCTOR : Dr. B. Stevenson.

HOTELS : The "Royal Mail," the "Healesville."

ROUTE : By rail to Lilydale (24m.), thence coach (14m.).

HENDON, QUEENSLAND, 1,500 feet above sea-level, 154 miles (by rail) S.W. from Brisbane. Post and Telegraph Office.

HENLEY BEACH, SOUTH AUSTRALIA, 6 miles W. of Adelaide, a favourite sea-side resort, on the shores of St.

Vincent's Gulf.   Sandy beach ; jetty ; sea-bathing ; fishing ; boating.

HOTEL : The " Henley Beach."

ROUTE : By tram or bus.

HEPBURN, VICTORIA, over 2,000 feet above sea-level, 81 miles N.W. of Melbourne ; the country is elevated, mountainous and picturesque, and the climate extremely healthy.   The average annual rainfall is 36·8 inches. Noted for the best mineral spring in Victoria, the water of which is cool, clear, sparkling and inodorous ; it acts as a tonic and alterative, and has proved to be very beneficial to invalids, containing as it does, a large quantity of iron in solution.   In its composition it resembles the waters of Cheltenham, Spa, and Schwalbach.   There is a plant and apparatus at the spring for storing this mineral water and transmitting it in cylinders, charged with its own natural carbonic acid gas, to all the colonies (depot 1 Queen Street, Melbourne.)

Analysis (in grains per gallon) : Carbonate of Lime, 34·40grs. ; Carbonate of Magnesia, 15·12grs. ; Carbonate of Soda, 36·50grs. ; Carbonate of Iron, 2·90grs. ; Alumina, 4·40grs. ; Chloride of Magnesia, 1·20gr. ; Chlorine (otherwise combined), 2·20grs. ; Sulphuric Acid (otherwise combined), 2grs. ; Silica, 3·80grs. ; total, 102.52grs. in one gallon.   Also Carbonic Acid (free), 97·9grs. ; and in combination as bi-carbonates, 77·8grs.

SPECIAL INDICATIONS : Affections of the Liver ; Acute Rheumatism ;   Rheumatic   Gout ;   Flatulence ;   Acidic Dyspepsia ; Chlorosis ; Leucorrhœa ; Menorrhagia.

HOTELS : The " Spring Creek," the " Mineral Spring," the " American," the " Old· Race-course."

NOTE.—A company was formed in October, 1887, for the purpose of building a first-class hotel and sanatorium at the Spring.

ROUTE : By rail to. Daylesford (78m.), thence conveyance (3m.)

HERBERTON, QUEENSLAND, over 2,000 feet above sea-level, 900 miles N.W. of Brisbane, and 50 miles from the coast, the centre of the Northern Tin-fields, situated on the Wild river, is destined to become a health resort. The scenery is very fine, and the climate dry, cool and very salubrious. About 25 miles from Herberton is a thermal spring, the water of which was analysed by Mr. K. T. Staiger, F.C.S., of Brisbane, who reports that the sample analysed by him contained 61·126grs. of solid matter in one gallon, viz. :— Chloride of Sodium, 25·245grs. ; Alumina and Iron, 2 057grs. ; Carbonate of Lime, 2·304grs. ; Sulphate of Lime, 5·230grs. ; Silica, 6·110grs. ; Insolubles, 16·040grs. ; and Organic Matter, 4·140grs. The water deposits a whitish powder, consisting principally of lime and siliceous sinter, and there was also lithium present ; the temperature has not yet been taken, but it is stated that one could boil eggs in it. Post and Telegraph Office ; School of Arts, with large hall ; Hospital ; School of Mines.

DOCTOR : Dr. W. D. Bowkett.

HOTELS : The " Post Office," the " Cosmopolitan," the " Royal," the " Mining Exchange," the " Herberton," the " Australian," the " Criterion," the " Commercial ; " also " Garbutt's," at the Spring.

ROUTE : By steamer to Cairns, thence rail to Redlynch (8m.), thence coach (47m.); or by steamer to Port Douglas, thence coach (85m.)

(NOTE.—A railway from Cairns is in course of construction.)

HEWITTVILLE, OR EMU PARK, QUEENSLAND, 28 miles (by coach) N.E. from Rockhampton, and 20 miles N. of the entrance to the Fitzroy river, a fashionable watering place on the Pacific coast, prettily situated on a plateau, over 50 feet above sea-level, enclosed on the land side, in horse-shoe form, by a chain of bald hills rising to a height of 500 feet. The view, towards the east, of the sea and the numerous islands, is very beautiful. The temperature, though generally refreshingly cool, is liable to sudden changes, especially at night. Sea-bathing, at all times ; splendid fishing. Post and Telegraph Office. A railway from Rockhampton is in course of construction.

EXCURSIONS : Yeppoon (12m.); New Zealand Gully, with

its pillar-shaped mountains ; the Cawarall mines ; the Torangaba gold mines.

SPECIAL INDICATIONS : General and Nervous Debility ; Convalescence from Malaria and Typhoid Fevers, and Barcoo Rot (land scurvy) ; Incipient Lung Disease.

HOTELS : The "Emu Park," highly recommended for comfortable accommodation and reasonable charges ; the "Blue Bell ; " also a private boarding-house, as well as furnished houses to let.

HOBART, TASMANIA, the metropolis of the colony, beautifully situated at the foot of Mount Wellington, on the river Derwent, 12 miles above its junction with the sea. Well sheltered from all winds ; climate very invigorating. The mean annual temperature is 54° F., and the mean daily range 16° F. ; the annual rainfall is 22 inches, with 189 wet days (in 1886) ; surrounding scenery grand and picturesque. Fishing ; shooting ; boating. Hospital ; Post and Telegraph Office ; Museum ; Public Library ; Tasmanian Club·; Hobart Club ; Salt and Fresh Water Baths ; Turkish Baths ; Orchestral Union ; Philharmonic Society ; Racing, Rowing, Rifle, Cricket, and Fishing Clubs ; Theatre Royal ; Royal Society's Gardens.

EXCURSIONS : Mount Nelson, 1,191 feet, a signal station, at the foot of which is Sandy Bay, a beautiful beach ; Battery Point ; Mount Wellington, 4,166 feet, with splendid views ; the "Bower," 1,521 feet ; the Murray Hills, or "Gentle Annie" Falls ; St. Crispin's Well, 2,000 feet ; Kangaroo Point (3m.), with fine beach and bathing places ; Lindisferne ; Bedlam Walls ; Grass Tree Hill ; Mount Direction ; Gunner's Quoin ; Mount Rumney, Seven-Mile Beach ; McRobie's Gully ; Fern-Tree Valley ; Brown's River Beach (10m.) ; Glenorchy Landslip, of June 4, 1872, (5m.)

DOCTORS : Drs. E. O. Giblin, T. C. Smart, C. J. Parkinson, G. H. Butler, R. S. Bright, Crowther, J. W. Agnew, H. A. Perkins.

HOTELS : The "Orient," the "Ship," the "Derwent," the "Rock," the "Criterion," the "Carlton Club," the "Telegraph," the "George and Dragon," "Lloyd's."

BOARDING-HOUSES : "Pressland Lodge," "Alma Lodge," "Bertram's," "Ingle Hall," "Harrington House."

HUTT, (PROV. WELLINGTON), NEW ZEALAND, 8 miles (by rail) N.E. from Wellington, a favourite summer retreat, pleasantly situated on the Hutt river, where it enters the bay. The climate is very equable, the winter mild, and the summer cool ; the mean temperature in winter is 48·74° F., in spring 54·50° F., in summer 62·24° F., and in autumn 56·66° F.; the mean annual temperature is 55·58° F., and the daily range 12·06° F.; the mean annual amount of rainfall is 51·542 inches. Post and Telegraph Office ; Race-course.

OBJECTS OF INTEREST : McNab's gardens ; Old log stockade.

DOCTOR : Dr. J. G. F. Wilford.

HOTELS : The "Railway," "Fraser's," "Cadby's," the "Family."

· IPSWICH, QUEENSLAND, 65 feet above sea-level, 23 miles (by rail) S.W. from Brisbane, and 28 miles from the coast, pleasantly situated on the Bremer river ; climate very salubrious. The total rainfall in 1884 was 33 inches, with 104 wet days. Hospital ; Lunatic Asylum ; Post and Telegraph Office ; Mechanics' Institute ; Albert Hall ; Musical Union Society.

DOCTORS : Drs. H. M. Lightoller, W. H. v. Lossberg, E. R. Webb, P. Thornton, C. Neill.

HOTELS : The "Palais Royal," the "North Australian," the "Victoria," the "Commercial," the "Volunteer Arms," the "Union," the "Criterion," the "Bull's Head."

JAMESTOWN, SOUTH AUSTRALIA, 1,493 feet above sea-level, 175 miles (by rail) N. from Adelaide, and 32 miles from the coast, in a wheat-growing district. Dry climate. The rainfall in 1882 was a little over 13 inches, Hospital; Post and Telegraph Office ; Literary Institute.

DOCTOR : Dr. W. J. Patton.

HOTELS : The "Commercial," the "Jamestown," the "Globe," the "Belalie."

D

KATOOMBA, New South Wales, 3,349 feet above sea-level, 66 miles (by rail) W. from Sydney, and 58 miles from the coast, in the midst of the Blue Mountains, commanding magnificent views of the surrounding beautiful scenery. The climate is equable and invigorating; the total rainfall in 1886 was 42·22 inches, with 107 wet days; the summer temperature seldom exceeds 75° F. Post and Telegraph Office.

EXCURSIONS : Katoomba Falls; Govett's Leap; Wentworth Falls; Nelly's Glen; the Gap; Leura and Lurline Falls; the "Meeting of the Waters;" the Megalong Zigzag; the Katoomba Coal-mine; the Jenolan Caves (26m.)

SPECIAL INDICATIONS : General Debility, Nervous Affections, Liver Complaints.

SEASON : From October to April.

DOCTOR : Dr. G. C. Jackson, who can accommodate a few invalids at his residence.

HOTELS : The "Carrington," (F. C. Goyder, proprietor), situated on a beautiful eminence, surrounded by extensive garden and grounds; "Biles'," opposite the station; the "Katoomba," about ¼ mile on the Bathurst road; "Fryer's;" also "Edwards'" at Katoomba Falls, and the "Mount Allen" at Wentworth Falls.

BOARDING-HOUSES : "Balmoral House," "Montrose House," "Glenample House," the "Clarendon."

KIAMA, New South Wales, an important sea-port town, 92 miles S. of Sydney, pleasantly situated in a rich dairy-farming district. The surrounding country is mountainous and the scenery extremely beautiful. Splendid climate; the total rainfall in 1886 was 41·59 inches, with 122 wet days. Fine sandy beaches; sea-bathing; sea-fishing. Hospital; Post and Telegraph Office; Free Library.

OBJECT OF INTEREST : The "Blow Hole," a subterranean passage near the water's edge, terminating in a perpendicular shaft, into which the sea enters and then is thrown up like a water-spout, often to a height of 200 feet, through the shaft, an aperture in the rocks close to the lighthouse.

EXCURSIONS : Jamberoo (5m.) ; Gerringong (6½m.) ; the " Whispering Gallery," near Jamberoo; Broughton Creek ; Gerringong Waterfall (12m.) ; Saddle-back (5m.)

SPECIAL INDICATIONS : For Convalescents, Nervous Affections, Liver Complaints, General Debility.

DOCTORS : Dr. J. S. Wilson, who could accommodate one good-class patient at his residence; Dr. C. Terrey, who can also accommodate several invalids at his house ; Dr. W. C. Ashe.

HOTELS : The " Royal," the " Steam Packet," the " Kiama ; " also Jackson's boarding-house.

ROUTE : By steamer or rail.

KILLARNEY, QUEENSLAND, 1,691 feet above sea-level, 194 miles (by rail via Warwick) S.W. from Brisbane, and 73 miles from the coast, in a district known as the sana-torium of Queensland, at present in an undeveloped state. Very pretty scenery, and dry, bracing climate. Shooting (marsupials, brush-turkeys, wongas, &c.) ; fishing (bream, cod, &c.) Post and Telegraph Office. Three public-houses.

SPECIAL INDICATION : All Lung Diseases.

SEASON : Throughout the year.

KINGSTON, TASMANIA, 11 miles S. of Hobart, a much frequented watering place, charmingly situated on Brown's river, surrounded by lofty hills ; grand climate and scenery. Good fishing in the river and the sea. Splendid sandy beach. Post and Telegraph Office. Good hotels.

EXCURSIONS : The " Blow Hole " ; the Shot Tower, of stone, 176 feet high, with a gallery round the top from which an extensive view is obtained (4m.)

ROUTE : By coach or conveyance.

KOORINGA, SOUTH AUSTRALIA, 1,151 feet above sea-level, 101 miles (by rail) N. from Adelaide, and 57 miles from the coast, on the Burra creek, surrounded by a chain of undulating hills, in a copper-mining and pastoral district. The mean annual amount of rainfall is 18 inches. Post and Telegraph Office ; Mechanics' Institute.

DOCTORS : Drs. J. R. Sangster, R. Brummitt, W. B. Baker.

HOTELS : The " Burra," the " Commercial," the " White Hart," " Opie's," the "Court-house," the " Pig and Whistle."

KURRAJONG HEIGHTS, NEW SOUTH WALES, 1,870 feet above the level of the sea, 48 miles W. of Sydney, and 35 miles from the coast, a picturesque district, with an equable, extremely salubrious and invigorating climate ; the average annual rainfall is 49·64 inches, with 112 wet days. The mean maximum temperature in the shade in 1885 was 60·3° F., the mean minimum temperature 46·6° F., and the mean temperature 53·5° F. The scenery, consisting of water-falls, gorges, dells, and forests, is extremely beautiful ; there are magnificent views of the surrounding country. The district abounds in extensive orangeries. Shooting ; fishing. Post and Telegraph Office.

SPECIAL INDICATIONS : Alcoholism (nearest hotel, 8 miles), Nervous Disorders, Diseases of the Chest, and for Convalescents.

DOCTORS : Drs. P. L. Guyenot, and L. C. Jockel, both residing at Richmond ; also Dr. J. Callaghan from Windsor.

ROUTE : By rail to Richmond, thence conveyance (10m.)

BOARDING-HOUSES : " Peck's," " Powell's," " Madden's," " Mayo's."

KYNETON, VICTORIA, 1,687 feet above sea-level, 57 miles (by rail) N.W. from Melbourne, lies almost in a basin, surrounded by hills of no great height. Climate exception-ally healthy. The average annual rainfall is 31·1 inches. Splendid shooting (hares, turkeys, rabbits, &c.) ; fishing (trout). Post and Telegraph Office ; Hospital ; Mechanics' Institute ; Oddfellows Hall ; Temperance Hall ; Race-course.

EXCURSIONS : The " Hanging Rock," (9m.) ; the Falls of the Coliban river, at Trentham (20m.)

SPECIAL INDICATIONS : Consumption, Nervous Affec-tions.

SEASON : Summer and spring.

DOCTORS : Drs. S. Smith, R. B. Duncan, W. Langford.

HOTELS : The " Junction," the Newmarket," the " Kyneton," the " Town Hall," " Alexander's," " Wedgwood's."

LADY ROBINSON'S BEACH (NEW BRIGHTON),

NEW SOUTH WALES, 8½ miles from Sydney, a favourite place of resort, celebrated for the beauty of its surroundings, and the purity of the water. Sea-baths; sandy beach, 6 miles long, affording ample scope for equestrian or pedestrian exercise ; fishing ; boating. Assembly Hall.

DOCTORS : Drs. C. Dowd, J. Lamrock, G. Read, from Kogarah (3½m.)

HOTEL : The " New Brighton," containing 40 rooms, and furnished with every requisite for visitors' comfort.

ROUTE : By rail to Rockdale (6m.), thence Saywell's private tramway (2½m.)

LAKE BATHURST, NEW SOUTH WALES, 2,217 feet above sea-level, 153 miles (by rail via Goulburn) S. from Sydney, and 48 miles from the coast, a picturesque sheet of water with an area of 8 square miles, surrounded by well-grassed sloping hills. Splendid climate. The average annual rainfall is 24·18 inches, with 68 wet days. Large flocks of wild fowl frequent the place. Post Office.

LAKE GEORGE, NEW SOUTH WALES, 2,129 feet above sea-level, 177 miles (by rail to Bungendore) S. of Sydney, and 56 miles from the coast, a very extensive sheet of water, 25 miles long by 8 miles wide, situated in a depression between two ranges of hills, some of which, on the western side, rise to 1,500 feet above the lake. The mean maximum temperature in the shade during the hottest month is 72·2° F., and the mean minimum temperature during the coldest month 49·1° F., the mean annual temperature is 56·8° F., and the mean daily range 27·1° F.; the average annual amount of rainfall is 27·190 inches, with 129 rainy days in the year. Fishing ; shooting (waterfowl). Post and Telegraph Office at Bungendore.

HOTELS : At Bungendore—"Lake George," the " Royal," the " Commercial."

LAKE MACQUARIE, NEW SOUTH WALES, 65 miles N. of Sydney, a picturesque inlet of the sea, nearly 20 miles in length, and from 3 to 6 miles in breadth, one of the most beautiful and healthy localities in the colony, 12 miles S. of Newcastle. The scenery is very pretty, and the climate is mild, yet bracing, with a warm, dry, and equable temperature. Sea-bathing ; grand fishing (schnapper, garfish, bream, whiting, mullet, flathead, &c.) ; shooting (kangaroo, wallaby, black swan, duck, &c.) ; boating. Post and Telegraph Office at Belmont, a village on the eastern shore of the lake near its north head.

EXCURSIONS: Coorunbong, Mt. Vincent, Newcastle, Lake Macquarie Heads.

SPECIAL INDICATIONS : Pulmonary Affections, especially Phthisis ; also for Convalescents.

SEASON : From September to April.

HOTELS : The " Toronto " (Albert Jarrett, manager), on the western shore of the lake, opposite Belmont, built on one of the prettiest sites of the lake, with excellent accommodation for families, etc.; ladies' and gentlemen's baths, billiards, lawn tennis, croquet; best wines, spirits, and malt liquors ; charges very moderate. Also the " Belmont," at Belmont.

ROUTE : By rail from Sydney or Newcastle to Cockle Creek, thence steamer to Toronto (4m.)

LAUNCESTON, TASMANIA, the principal town in the north of the colony, on the river Tamar, about 40 miles from its mouth ; it is surrounded by hills, the scenery is romantic, and the climate is very dry and healthy. The mean annual temperature is 55° F., and the mean daily range 20° F. ; the total rainfall in 1886 amounted to 30 inches, with 119 wet days. Shooting ; fishing ; boating. Hospital ; Post and Telegraph Office ; Mechanics' Institute ; Baths ; Musical Union; Academy of Music; Coursing, Racing, Cricket, Rowing, &c., Clubs; Town Park; Garden Crescent; Racecourse.

EXCURSIONS : Windmill Hill and Cataract Hill, both affording charming views ; " Corra Linn" (6½m.), a romantic gorge, through which the North Esk rushes over a series of cataracts ; " The Dam," a place where an artificial lake is formed for the purpose of supplying the town with water ; " Clarke's Ford," an old crossing-place of the river (4m.), surrounded by pretty scenery ; the " Devil's Punch Bowl," (3m.), a cleft in a green-stone precipice, through which the rains find their way to the ground ; the " Cataract Gorge," with precipices on each side, fully 400 feet high ; Rosevear's Point (12m.) ; " Brady's Look-out "; Dilston.

DOCTORS : Drs. W. Cotterell, H. C. Hallowes, W. G. Maddox, R. W. Murphy, L. G. Thomson, W. R. Stewart.

HOTELS : The "Criterion," the "Launceston," the "Globe," the "Brisbane," the "City," the "Post Office ; " also a Coffee Palace.

LAWSON, NEW SOUTH WALES, 2,399 feet above sea-level, 58 miles (by rail) W. from Sydney. Much resorted to by invalids, who can here without fatigue enjoy the mountain scenery, and the pure, invigorating air. Post and Telegraph Office.

EXCURSIONS : Adelina Falls (two of 40 feet descent, one of 60, and one of 70 feet), and the Junction Falls, all on the south side of the line ; Dante's Glen, and three other waterfalls' on the northern side—one of 40 feet, one of 90, and one with a descent of 120 feet ; the Wentworth Falls.

HOTELS : The "Blue Mountain Inn," the "Sanatorium."

LILYDALE, VICTORIA, 24 miles (by rail) E. from Melbourne, picturesquely situated on the Olinda creek, in a vine-growing district ; the surrounding country is very mountainous. The average annual rainfall is 32 inches. Post and Telegraph Office ; Mechanics' Institute ; Rechabite Hall.

EXCURSIONS : Dandenong Ranges ; Burt's Hill, near Croydon, commanding magnificent views (5m.) ; Fernshawe ; Coranderak Aboriginal Station ; Warburton ; the famous vineyards of St. Hubert's and Yering.

DOCTOR : Dr. A. V. Henderson.

HOTELS : The "Crown," the "Lilydale," the "Commercial," the "Olinda."

LITTLE RIVER, VICTORIA, 108 feet above sea-level, 30 miles (by rail) S.W. from Melbourne, in a district consisting of elevated plains, and abounding in springs of fresh water of a mineral taste ; the surrounding scenery is beautiful and picturesque. Good shooting (hares, rabbits, wild turkey, black swan, wild duck, &c.) Post and Telegraph Office.

EXCURSIONS : The You Yangs mountains, rising abruptly from the surrounding plains (4m.) ; Station Peak, 1,154 feet in shape like a gigantic pyramid, from the summit of which a magnificent view may be obtained.

HOTELS : The " Little River," the " Rothwell."

LORNE, VICTORIA, 115 miles S.W. of Melbourne, a favourite watering-place on the south coast, beautifully situated on the Erskine river, at Loutit bay, well sheltered by the lofty Otway range. Fine beach ; lovely scenery ; the climate is mild and equable. The mean annual temperature is 58° F. ; the average annual rainfall is 30·4 inches. Pier ; sea-bathing ; fishing ; shooting ; boating. Post and Telegraph Office ; Public Library ; Public Park.

EXCURSIONS : Erskine Falls (4m.) ; Falls of the Apsley, in the heart of the forest (8m.) ; the " Sanctuary ; " the Rapids.

SPECIAL INDICATIONS : Phthisis, Asthma, Liver Complaints.

SEASON : Throughout the year.

DOCTOR : Dr. Thos. Barker.

HOTELS: " Mountjoy's Temperance," Anderson's " Grand Pacific," " Lorne Family."

ROUTE : By rail to Birregurra (83m.), thence coach (24m.), or by steamer direct.

MACEDON, VICTORIA, 1,660 feet above sea-level, 44 miles (by rail) N.W. from Melbourne, with UPPER MACEDON, from 2,200 to 3,000 feet above sea-level, 3 miles from the railway station, favourite health resorts, beautifully situated in a heavily timbered district. The surrounding country is mountainous, the scenery very romantic, and the climate is unrivalled for salubrity. The mean annual temperature at Macedon is 53° F., and at Upper Macedon (3,000 feet level) 48·2° F. The average annual rainfall is 35·7 inches. Excellent fruits of all kinds are raised. State Nursery, having a handsome lake alongside. Post and Telegraph Office.

EXCURSIONS : Mount Macedon, 3,324 feet (3m.) ; the " Camel's Hump " (6m.) ; Hanging Rock ; there are also several picturesque waterfalls and fern-tree gullies in the vicinity ; the Coliban Falls, a romantic spot, near Trentham (14m.)

HOTELS : The " Victorian Alps," close to the Railway

station ; the "State Nursery"; "Burnett's Family." At UPPER MACEDON—The "Waterfalls;" also Mrs. Gracie's, Mrs. Smart's, and Mrs. Morrison's boarding-houses.

Dr. D. Turner, of Melbourne, has favoured the author of this guide with the following description of Mount Macedon as a health resort :—"Mount Macedon, which has been steadily gaining in popularity for some years past as a health resort, is situated 43 miles north of Melbourne, the main line of railway to Sandhurst and Echuca, passing by its base. By express train it is only an hour's travelling distance from the metropolis. The highest peak of the mountain is about 3,400 feet above the level of the sea. This is one of the highest points of the Victorian coast range.

"The climate during the summer months is cool and bracing, prevailing winds being from the south. The mean temperature during the summer and autumn months is about 53° F. In other words Mt. Macedon is 4° cooler than the city of Edinburgh in summer time. Of course there are days at Macedon, which are hotter than the summer days at Edinburgh ; it is the superior coolness of the nights at Macedon which brings down the average of the temperature. The mean temperature of Melbourne in summer time is 63° F., so that the city is 10° hotter than Macedon. The rainfall at Macedon is generally supposed to be much greater than it is in Melbourne, but as a matter of fact, in summer there is scarcely any appreciable difference between the two places in this respect. The Macedon climate is bracing and tonic, and on most constitutions it has a stimulating effect.

"Of late years a revolution has taken place with regard to the climatic treatment of consumption. Formerly it was held that cold was injurious to consumptives. Now it has been placed beyond all possibility of doubt that a climate with a pure, cold, and rarefied atmosphere is by far the most suitable for the prevention and cure of consumption. Such a climate can only be obtained at high altitudes. There are higher places than Macedon in Victoria, but the close proximity of the locality to the metropolis, and its easy accessibility by rail, ensure that when its benefits are fully appreciated it will be the sanatorium of Victoria. The fact of its having been recently chosen as a summer residence for His Excellency the Governor is a proof of its growing estimation in public favour.

The railway returns show that the passenger traffic to Macedon has more than doubled within the last three years.

"The accommodation for visitors at Macedon, still leaves something to be desired, but it is improving every year. There are now four boarding-houses, and one hotel seeking the public custom; and great advances are expected to be made in this direction ere long. The soil is free from damp, and even after a heavy fall of rain, it is dry in a few hours. The mountain sides abound in streams of running water of the purest quality. The scenery is varied and picturesque, the different views to be obtained from the top of the range, can hardly be surpassed in Australia. There are numerous fern-gullies, and places for pleasant rambles, and the Mount is within walking distance of the natural phenomenon known as the 'Hanging Rock.' Several of the Melbourne medical men have made Mount Macedon summer quarters for their families; they are constantly travelling backwards and forwards, and there is a permanent resident medical practitioner (Dr. G. H. Salter) at Gisborne, three or four miles distant from the Mount."

MANLY, New South Wales, the most popular watering place of the colony, situated at the head of North Harbour, 9 miles (by steamer) N.E. from Sydney. The mean annual temperature is 61° F., and the mean daily range 16° F. The average annual amount of rainfall is 48 inches. Fine sandy beaches, both on the ocean and harbour sides; pier; sea-bathing, hot salt-water baths; fishing; yachting; Ivanhoe Park; Aquarium. Post and Telegraph Office.

Excursions: Narrabeen Lagoon, a picturesque spot (bathing, fishing, boating) 7m.; Pittwater (14m.)

Doctor: Dr. W. H. Tibbits.

Hotels: The "Pier," the "Steyne," the "Clarendon," the "Ivanhoe."

Boarding-houses: Mrs. Maguire's "Bay View," Esplanade, where visitors are well cared for; Mrs. Watkins, Mrs. Sutton's, Miss Phillips', Mrs. Walker's, Mrs. Sargent's.

MANOORA, South Australia, 1,283 feet above sea-level, 75 miles (by rail) N. from Adelaide, and 40 miles from the coast, on the River Gilbert, in a wheat-growing district;

the surrounding scenery is very pretty.   Post and Telegraph Office ; Institute.

HOTELS : The "Manoora," the "Burton."

MARULAN, NEW SOUTH WALES, 2,105 feet above sea-level, 114 miles (by rail) S. from Sydney.   Scenery wild and magnificent.   Wallabies and kangaroos are numerous.   Post and Telegraph Office.

HOTELS : The "Royal," the "Terminus."

MASTERTON (PROV. WELLINGTON), NEW ZEALAND, 71 miles (by rail) N.E. from Wellington, situated on a plain, in an agricultural and grazing district.   Public Park, with two bathing sheds.   Post and Telegraph Office ;   District Hospital ;   Public Library and reading-room ;   Literary Institute ;   Theatre Royal ;   Masonic, Oddfellows, and Forresters' Halls, Cricket Club.

There are a number of cold medicinal springs in the district, the principal ones are :—

1. PAHUA, a cold spring belonging to the class of saline waters, especially interesting from the large proportion of Iodine which it contains.

Analysis (in grains per gallon).—Chloride of Sodium, 1303·329grs. ; Chloride of Potassium, 0·501gr. ; Chloride of Magnesium, 34·960grs. ; Chloride of Calcium, 120·885grs. ; Iodine of Magnesium, 0·582gr. ; Bromide of Magnesium, traces ; Sulphate of Lime, 3·026grs. ; Phosphate of Alumina, 0·641gr. ; Phosphate of Iron, traces ; Phosphate of Lime, 0.430gr. ; Bicarbonate of Lime, 6.451grs. ; Silica, 1.696gr. ; Iodine, free 1·595gr. ; total, 1474·096 grains in one gallon, or 184·2 solid grains of mineral matter in one pint.   The total quantity of Iodine to the gallon (free and combined) is 2·127grs.

2. WALLINGFORD, a cold saline water containing 10·4grs., of mineral matter in one pint.   Reaction, acidic.

3. BURTON's SPRING, contains in addition to Iodine, traces of Arsenic.

4. AKITEO *(a)* SPRING, is a strong saline water, of an alkaline character, containing Iodides and Bromides.   The total quantity of mineral matter in one pint is 62·4 solid grains.

5. AKITEO *(b)* SPRING, an aerated chalybeate water, of sulphurous character, containing 4·8 solid grains of mineral matter in one pint. It is similar to the acidulated ferruginous waters of Recoaro (Prov. Vicenza, Lombardy), and Pyrmont (Waldeck, Germany), and would be valuable as a tonic, especially, in female diseases, anæmia, chlorosis, intestinal and stomachic catarrhs, scrofula, &c.

Temperature of all these springs is 60° F., or below.

EXCURSIONS : Kuripuni, a suburb 1 mile (by rail), surrounded by splendid scenery ; the romantic Manawatu Gorge, a cleft in the Ruahine mountains, between Woodville and Palmerston, with its wild and beautiful scenery.

HOTELS : The " Prince of Wales," the " Royal," the " Star," the " Empire," the " Occidental," the " Club."

MELTON, VICTORIA, 23 miles (by rail) N.W. from Melbourne, on the Toolern-Toolern creek, sheltered by well-timbered ranges ; the climate is very mild. Surrounding scenery is varied and romantic. Post and Telegraph Office.

SPECIAL INDICATIONS : Pulmonary Affections.

EXCURSIONS: Mount Cotterill, and Mount Koroit (4m.) ; Djerriwarrh Creek (4m.)

HOTELS : The " Raglan," the " Royal," the " Golden Fleece," " Minn's."

MEREWORTH, NEW SOUTH WALES, near Berrima, 2,300 feet above sea-level, 90 miles S. of Sydney, and 80 miles from the coast, prettily situated. The country is undulating and lightly timbered. Cold, strongly ferruginous waters.

EXCURSIONS : *See* MOSS VALE.

DOCTOR : Dr. G. P. Lambert, from Berrima (1½m.)

HOTEL : Mrs. Warren's boarding-house, where visitors will find good accommodation.

ROUTE : By rail to Moss Vale, thence by Mr. Warren's conveyance (4m).

MITTAGONG (OR NATTAI), NEW SOUTH WALES, 2,069 feet above sea-level, 77 miles (by rail) S. from Sydney, and 28 miles from the coast. The scenery is of a most picturesque and romantic character. The annual average rainfall is 20·35 inches, with 63 wet days. Cold ferruginous waters ; one of the numerous chalybeate springs, situated a short distance from the town, flows into a small well, bricked round for the convenience of invalids. Post and Telegraph Office.

EXCURSIONS : " The Gib," a cliff in the neighbourhood, so called from a fancied resemblance to the rock at Gibraltar ; Joadja Kerosene Shale Mine (reached by the Company's tramway, 16m.) ; Bowral ; Berrima ; Moss Vale.

DOCTOR : Dr. W. Middleton.

HOTELS : The " Nattai," " Hilder's," " Murphy's," " Sheather's ; " also Massingham's, Bedford's, and Waite's boarding-houses.

MOAMA, NEW SOUTH WALES.—*See* ECHUCA.

MORDIALLOC, VICTORIA, 17 miles (by rail) S.E. from Melbourne, a favourite watering-place on the shores of Port Phillip Bay. The average annual rainfall is 26·9 inches. Park ; esplanade ; pier ; fine beach ; excellent fishing ; shooting (quail, wild duck, black swan) ; boating. Post and Telegraph Office.

DOCTOR : Dr. H. W. S. Verity, from Cheltenham (4m.)

HOTELS : " Rennison's," " Bloxsidge's."

MORNINGTON (OR SCHNAPPER POINT), VICTORIA, 33 miles S. of Melbourne, a beautiful watering place on the S.E. coast of Port Phillip. Dry temperature, mild winter. The average annual rainfall is 35·9 inches. Sea-bathing ; sea-fishing ; shooting (rabbits). Public Park ; Race-course ; Athenæum. Post and Telegraph Office.

SPECIAL INDICATIONS : Phthisis, Rheumatism.

SEASON : December to April.

DOCTOR : Dr. F. L. Hooper, who makes a specialty of obstetrics and diseases of children.

HOTELS : The " Royal," " Cricketer's Arms," " Tanti," " Kirkpatrick's," " Mornington House."

ROUTE : By rail to Frankston, (27m.), thence coach (8m.) ; or in summer by steamer.

MORWELL, Victoria, 283 feet above sea-level, 89 miles (by rail) E. from Melbourne, and 30 miles from the coast, pleasantly situated on the Morwell river, surrounded by high, heavily-timbered ranges. The scenery is highly picturesque, and the air pure, and salubrious. Good shooting and fishing. Post and Telegraph Office,

HOTEL : The " Morwell Inn."

MOSS VALE, New South Wales, 2,205 feet above sea-level, 86 miles (by rail) S. from Sydney, and 31 miles from the coast. The climate is bracing. The mean maximum temperature in the shade in 1885 was 64·3° F., the mean minimum temperature 48·4° F., and the mean temperature 56·4° F. The average annual rainfall is 40·63 inches, with 111 wet days. The scenery is pretty and interesting ; the immediate neighbourhood abounds in verdant valleys, grassy slopes, and open forest land. Post and Telegraph Office.

EXCURSIONS : The Fitzroy Falls, a series of waterfalls, the upper one with a descent of 400 feet, the middle one of 200 feet, and a third fall of upwards of 200 feet ; Berrima ; Sutton Forest ; Burrawang ; Robertson ; the Kangaroo Valley ; Mount Look-out.

DOCTORS : Drs. H. M. Madden, A. E. J. Barcroft.

HOTELS : " Elm Court," the principal hotel, noted for the excellence of its appointments ; the " Royal " is a well-conducted hotel.

MOTUEKA (Prov. Nelson), New Zealand, at a slight elevation above sea-level, 16 miles (by steamer) N.W. from Nelson, on the northern coast of the South or Middle Island, a small village, the centre of an agricultural and fruit-growing district, prettily situated about one mile from the western shores of Blind Bay, and ½ mile from the Motueka river. Behind are ranges of mountains, some 6,000 feet high, with stalactite and moa caves, which are easily accessible. The scenery is beautiful and varied. The climate is almost perfect ; it is dry, equable, and bracing ; the summer is delightfully cool on account of the regular sea-breezes ; the winter is cold, but dry, with calm cloudless days. Sea-bathing ; shooting ; fishing ; boating ; yachting.

Post and Telegraph Office ; Literary Institute ; Musical Society.

SPECIAL INDICATIONS : Phthisis in every stage ; Asthma ; Chronic Bronchitis ; also suitable for Convalescents.

SEASON : During the summer months.

DOCTOR : Dr. H. O. B. Deck, who, if sufficient inducement offered, would build a suitable sanatorium for invalids.

HOTELS : The " Motueka " ; the " Swan " ; also Yorke's accommodation house at Reivaka, pleasantly situated at the ' foot of the mountains, about 4 miles from Motueka.

ROUTE : From Nelson by steamer direct (16m.) ; or from Nelson by rail to Richmond (8m.), thence coach (24m.)

MOUNT BARKER, SOUTH AUSTRALIA, 1,049 feet above sea-level, 34½ miles (by rail) S.E. from Adelaide, and 22 miles from the coast, a favourite summer resort at the foot of Mt. Barker, in a fine agricultural district ; the vine and fruit are largely cultivated. The surrounding country is mountainous and very picturesque. The climate is bracing, though rather variable. The mean annual temperature is 56° F., and the mean annual amount of rainfall 30 inches. Post and Telegraph Office ; Institute.

EXCURSIONS : Mt. Barker, 2,300 feet high (3m.) ; Nairne (4m.) ; Habndorf (4m.) ; Little Hampton (1m.)

DOCTOR : Dr. L. W. Bickle.

HOTELS : The " Mount Barker," " Gray's Inn," " Temperance."

MOUNT BRYAN, SOUTH AUSTRALIA, 1,701 feet above sea-level, 110 miles (by rail) N. from Adelaide, in a wheat-growing and grazing district. The surrounding country is undulating. Post Office.

EXCURSION : Mt Bryan, 3,000ft. high.

HOTEL : The "Mount Bryan."

MOUNT LOFTY, (WITH CRAFERS, AND STIRLING EAST), SOUTH AUSTRALIA, 1,611 feet above sea-level, 19 miles (by rail) S.E. from Adelaide, favourite summer resorts at the foot of Mount Lofty. The surrounding scenery is very beautiful, and the climate bracing.   The mean annual amount of rainfall is nearly 43 inches.   English fruits are extensively grown.   Post and Telegraph Office ; Institute.

EXCURSION : Mt. Lofty, 2,400ft. high, commanding magnificent views.

DOCTOR : Dr. D. A. McLachlan (Stirling East).

HOTELS : The " Crafers," the " Half-way."

MOUNT MACEDON, VICTORIA.—*See* MACEDON.

MOUNT PERRY, OR TENNINGERING, QUEENS-LAND, 2,500 feet above sea-level, 200 miles N.W. of Brisbane, and 60 miles from the coast, situated at the foot of Mt. Perry, in a pastoral, and gold—and copper-mining district.   The surrounding country is mountainous and the scenery extremely beautiful.   The climate is fairly dry and very salubrious. English fruits are grown here.   There are a number of highly mineralized springs in the district, containing iron, magnesia, and soda, and having a temperature of from 65° F. to 75° F. Hospital ; Post and Telegraph Office ; School of Arts.

SPECIAL INDICATIONS : Chest Diseases, especially Asthma, Bronchitis, Pleurisy ; also for Convalescents.

HOTELS : The " Royal," the " Commercial," the " Terminus."

ROUTE : By steamer to Bundaberg, thence rail (66m.)

MOUNT VICTORIA, NEW SOUTH WALES, 3,490 feet above sea-level, 77 miles (by rail) W. from Sydney, and 61 miles from the coast, in the centre of the most famous sights of the Blue Mountains ; noted for its dry, and bracing atmosphere and the grandeur of its scenery ; during the summer season a very favourite place of resort for invalids. · The mean maximum temperature in the shade in 1885 was 62·7° F., the mean minimum temperature 46·5° F., and the mean temperature 53° F.   The average annual rainfall is 35·44 inches, with 91 wet days.   Post and Telegraph Office.

EXCURSIONS : Mt. Piddington ; the Fairy Dell ; the " Engineer's Cascade " ; Mt. Wilson, 3,580 feet ; the Little Zig-zag ; " Govett's Leap " ; Blackheath ; the Great Zig-zag ; Lithgow Valley ; Kanimbla Valley ; Katoomba Falls ;

the Fairy Bower ; Cox's Cave and Waterfall ; Mt. Victoria Pass ; Jenolan Caves (30m.)

SPECIAL INDICATIONS : General Debility, Nervous Affections, Liver Complaints.

SEASON : From October to April.

DOCTOR : Dr. E. H. Morgan.

HOTELS : The "Imperial" is the principal hotel, and one of the largest out of Sydney, it contains 70 rooms and can accommodate 80 people ; Mrs. Perry's hotel and the " Royal " are both comfortable, well-appointed hotels, situated in close proximity to the station. There are several well-conducted private establishments, the principal one being the " Manor House," which is favourably situated ; the " Waratah House," with superior accommodation.

MURRURUNDI, NEW SOUTH WALES, 1,546 feet above sea-level, 192 miles N. of Sydney, and 94 miles from the coast, beautifully situated at the foot of the Liverpool range of mountains. The scenery is picturesque and mountainous ; fine, bright and dry climate. The mean maximum temperature in the shade in 1885 was 71·5° F., the mean minimum temperature 52·7° F., and the mean temperature 62·1° F. ; the average annual rainfall is 30·35 inches, with 64 wet days ; cool summer evenings. There are numerous vineyards in the district. Shooting (turkey, duck, kangaroo, &c.). Post and Telegraph Office ; Hospital ; School of Arts.

EXCURSIONS : The " Rocks ; " Mount Murrulla (3½m.) ; Timor Caves ; Temple Court (1m.) ; Mt. Wingen, or the " Burning Mountain," 2,000 feet high (14m.), much resorted to for asthma.

SPECIAL INDICATIONS : Pulmonary Complaints, especially Asthma.

SEASON : Throughout the year.

DOCTOR : Dr. R. Bell.

HOTELS : The " Royal," the " White Hart," the " Commercial.

ROUTE : By steamer to Newcastle, thence by rail (120m.), or by rail direct.

E

NAPIER, New Zealand, the chief town of Hawke's Bay, picturesquely situated on Scinde Island (a peninsula), on the east coast of the North Island, about 7 miles from the southern end of the bay, in a fine grazing and timber-growing district. The climate is mild, dry, and tolerably equable ; the mean temperature in winter is 49·10° F., in spring 57·74° F., in summer 66·20° F., and in autumn 57·02° F. ; the mean annual temperature is 58·3° F ; the mean daily range 17·46° F., and the average annual amount of rainfall 36 inches, and in this respect Napier holds an intermediate position between Torquay (Devonshire), and Funchal (Madeira). The soil is porous and dries quickly after rain. Shooting (wild duck, pheasants) ; sea-fishing ; boating ; yachting. Clive-square Park ; Recreation Ground, Carlyle-street. Hospital ; Post and Telegraph Office. Athenæum ; Theatre Royal ; Gaiety Theatre ; Clarendon and Hawke's Bay Clubs.

EXCURSIONS : Taradale (4m.) ; Meanee (5m.) ; Petane, situated in a lovely valley, to the north-west of the inner harbour ; Clive (7m.) ; Hastings (12m.)

MONOGRAPH : Napier as a Health Resort for Pulmonary Invalids. By W. I. Spencer, M.R.C.S. Napier: R. C. Harding, 1885.

SPECIAL INDICATIONS : Chronic Bronchitis, Phthisis, Asthma, and other Pulmonary Affections.

SEASON : From April to Christmas.

DOCTORS : Drs. W. I. Spencer, E. Menzies, J. S. Caro, T. C. Moore.

HOTELS : The " Masonic," the " Criterion," the " Clarendon Club," the " Empire," the " Exchange," the " Royal," the " Star," the " Provincial."

ROUTE : By steamer.

NASEBY (Prov. Otago), New Zealand, 1,900 feet above sea-level, 92 miles N.W. of Dunedin, at the foot of Mount Ida, in a gold-mining district. Climate very bracing and healthy. Hospital ; Post and Telegraph Office ; Athenæum, with library ; Masonic Hall ; Jockey Club.

EXCURSION : Mount Ida, 5,600 feet, one of the highest mountains in Otago.

SEASON : From September to April.

DOCTOR : Dr. J. Whitton.

HOTELS : The "Victoria," the "Empire," the "Criterion," the "Royal."

ROUTE : From Dunedin by rail to Palmerston (41m.), thence coach.

NATTAI, NEW SOUTH WALES. *See* MITTAGONG.

NELSON, NEW ZEALAND, picturesquely situated on the south-eastern shores of Blind Bay, on the north coast of the South Island, in a grazing and hop-growing district. It is famed for the salubrity of its climate, which is one of the finest in the world ; it is often described as a place "where everlasting spring abides." The mean temperature in winter is 46·58° F., in spring 54·50° F., in summer 62·78° F., in autumn 55·76° F. ; the mean annual temperature is 54·86° F., and the mean daily range 20·16° F. The average annual amount of rainfall is 62 inches. The surrounding scenery is mountainous. Hospital ; Post and Telegraph Office ; Literary Institute ; Museum ; Theatre Royal ; Masonic Hall ; Provincial Hall ; Nelson Club ; Harmonic Society.

EXCURSIONS : Drive to the Waterworks ; Dun Mountains ; Zig-zag Hill, commanding a grand view of Nelson ; the Lighthouse, and Boulder-bank (by boat).

SPECIAL INDICATIONS : Pulmonary Complaints, especially Phthisis.

SEASON : Throughout the year.

DOCTORS : Drs. J. Hudson, W. J. Mackie, B. Locking, L. Boor, A. Coleman, G. H. Cressy.

HOTELS : The "Masonic," the "Trafalgar," the "Nelson," the "Commercial," "Panama House," the "Claremont House," the "Warwick House."

ROUTE : By steamer.

NEW BRIGHTON, NEW SOUTH WALES. *See* "LADY ROBINSON'S BEACH."

NEW BRIGHTON (CANTERBURY), NEW ZEALAND, a seaside resort of Christchurch.   Sea-bathing ; fishing ; boating.

HOTEL : "Patterson's."

ROUTE : By coach.

NEW NORFOLK, TASMANIA, 100 feet above sea-level, 21 miles (by steamer or rail) N.W. from Hobart, and 23 miles from the coast, prettily situated on the river Derwent, in a fine hop and fruit-growing district.   The total rainfall in 1886 amounted to 21½ inches, with 128 wet days. Shooting ; fishing.   Post and Telegraph Office ; Public Library.

EXCURSION : The Salmon and Trout Ponds on the River Plenty (7m).

HOTELS : The "Star and Garter," the "Bush" with large garden.

NEWPORT, NEW SOUTH WALES.   *See* "PITTWATER."

OATLANDS, TASMANIA, 1,337 feet above sea-level, 51 miles (by rail via Parattah) N. from Hobart, and 32 miles from the coast ; a handsome town, picturesquely situated on the highlands.   The mean annual temperature is 51° F., and the daily range 22° F.   The total rainfall in 1886 amounted to 23 inches, with 91 wet days.   Fishing ; shooting.   Post and Telegraph Office ; Public Library.

EXCURSIONS : Lake Tiberias, good fishing (eels) ; Table Mountain, 3,596 feet high ; Lakes Sorell and Crescent (wild ducks).

SPECIAL INDICATIONS : General   Debility,   Nervous Affections.

DOCTOR : Dr. G. E. Butler.

HOTELS : The "Oatlands," the "Wilmot Arms."

OHAEAWAI (BAY OF ISLANDS), NEW ZEALAND, 115 miles (overland), and 146 miles by steamer (via Russell) N. from Auckland.   The district is one of the fairest and love-liest spots in the whole of New Zealand.   The mean temperature in the shade in winter is 53·06° F., in spring 58·28° F., in summer 66·56° F., and in autumn 61·52° F. ; the mean annual temperature is 59·90° F.; the mean maximum temperature during the hottest month is 89·10° F., and the mean minimum temperature during the coldest month 31·82° F.; the mean daily range is 16·38° F. The mean annual amount of rainfall is 58·132 inches. Good shooting (pheasants, &c.) Post and Telegraph Office. In this district, 17 miles W. of Russell, are situated a group of hot springs, extending over an area of five square miles, used as baths, the waters of which are acidic, depositing sulphur and alum on cooling. Silica is only deposited as a granular sediment. These springs are chiefly interesting from their being accompanied by an escape of mercurial vapour which deposits cinnabar and metallic mercury. Their medicinal action is tonic and chalybeate, and having a specific alterative action in skin diseases.

Analysis (in grains per gallon).—Protoxide of Iron, 2·23grs.; Lime, 5·97grs.; Magnesia, 1·15gr.; Silica, 3·10grs.; Sulphuric Acid, 13·60grs.; Hydrochloric Acid, 66·91grs.; Sulphuretted Hydrogen, traces; Fixed Alkalies, 41·66grs.; Ammonia, traces; total 134·62 grains in one gallon, or 16·8 solid grains of mineral matter per pint.

Temperature.—From 60° F. to 116° F.

SPECIAL INDICATIONS : Skin Diseases, Rheumatism, Syphilitic Affections.

EXCURSIONS : Kawa Kawa township and coal-mine ; Manganese Mines, affording a magnificent panoramic view of the Bay ; Keri Keri river, with waterfall and old mission station ; the White Hall and Treaty Obelisk at Waitangi, opposite Russell ; Waitangi waterfall ; Whangaroa, 35 miles by steamer N. of Russell.

HOTEL : Goffe's accommodation-house.

OHINEMUTU (WITH ROTORUA), NEW ZEALAND, 962 feet above sea-level, 172 miles S.E. of Auckland, on the southern shores of Lake Rotorua, the centre of the famous thermal springs, and within easy reach of the numerous natural wonders and beautiful scenery of the lake district. A powerful smell of sulphur pervades the atmosphere. Post and Telegraph Office ; Hospital and Bath-pavilion at Rotorua ;

artistically laid out walks and drives, also lawn-tennis and bowling-greens, at Rotorua.

MONOGRAPHS.—1. Medical Guide to the Mineral Waters of Rotorua, by T. Hope Lewis, M.R.C.S. Eng., L.S.A. Lond., of Auckland, late Government Resident Medical Officer at Rotorua.   Auckland : H. Brett, 1885.

2. The Thermal Springs, Rotorua, New Zealand.   Hints on cases likely to benefit by treatment thereat.   By Alfred Ginders, M.D., Resident Medical Officer, Rotorua.   Wellington : G. Didsbury, Government Printer, 1885.

3. New Zealand Thermal Springs Districts.   Papers relating to the sale of the township of Rotorua with maps and plans of the district and township ; together with information relating to the hot-springs districts, and a report on the mineral waters.   Wellington : G. Didsbury, Government Printer, 1882.

The following springs are those which have the most valuable properties, and whose therapeutic action is best known :—

1. TE PUPUNITANGA, or "THE PRIEST'S BATH," at Rotorua, only a few feet from the lake's edge ; the water is strongly acidic and aluminous, depositing flocculent sulphur on the bed and sides of the bath ; reaction, acid.   There are four large public baths or pascinas (each 16 by 12 feet), two for each sex, with fourteen comfortable private dressing rooms attached, and provided with cold freshwater showers, and hot or tepid douches ; also two private baths (each 6 by 6 feet) for special cases.   It is considered the finest and most curative bath in the southern hemisphere.

Analysis (in grains per gallon) : Sulphate of Soda, 19·24grs. ; Sulphate of Potash, traces ; Sulphate of Lime, 7·41grs. ; Sulphate of Magnesia, 3·08grs. ; Sulphate of Alumina, 21·67grs. ; Sulphate of Iron, 1·24gr. ; Sulphuric Acid, 22·12grs. ; Hydrochloric Acid, 3·65grs. ; Silica, 18·41grs. ; total, 96·77grs. ; also Sulphuretted Hydrogen, 2·98grs., and Carbonic Acid gas, 2·16grs.

Temperature.—From 98° F. to 106° F. ; average 99° F

SPECIAL INDICATIONS : Gout, Dyspepsia, Sciatica, Skin Diseases, Disorders of the Liver, Sexual Impotence, Cold Feet, Amenorrhœa, Dropsy.

2. WHANGAPIPIRO, or "MADAME RACHEL's BATH," at Rotorua, saline waters of exquisite softness, with silicates, have the power of applying a gloss to the skin, which is due to the large quantity of silicates that they contain ; reaction, alkaline. There are two open-air baths (17 feet by 14 feet), one for each sex, and also single baths inside the house.

Analysis (in grains per gallon): Chloride of Sodium, 69·48grs.; Chloride of Potassium, 3·41grs.; Chloride of Lithium, traces ; Sulphate of Soda, 11·80grs. ; Silicate of Soda, 18·21grs. ; Silicate of Lime, 4·24grs. ; Silicate of Magnesia, 1·09gr. ; Iron and Alumina Oxides, 2·41grs. ; Silica, 5·87grs. ; total 116·46grs. in one gallon ; also Carbonic Acid gas, 3·79grs.

Temperature.—Formerly 174° F., but rose to 194° F. after eruption in June, 1886.

SPECIAL INDICATIONS : Diseases of the Skin, especially Psoriasis. *By internal administration* (whereby an increase in the elimination of urea and uric acid is produced) in Rheumatism, Gout, and certain forms of Dyspepsia.

3. ORUAWHATA, or "THE BLUE BATH," within the Rotorua Hospital grounds, a large reservoir, built of concrete, 36 feet by 20 feet, provided with hot and cold water douches and showers ; this water is of saline character with silicates.

Analysis (in grains per gallon).—Chloride of Sodium, 60·44grs. ; Chloride of Magnesium, 1·04grs. ; Sulphate of Lime, 5·48grs. ; Silicate of Magnesia, 0·32gr. ; Silicate of Soda, 8·38grs. ; Silicate of Iron oxide, 1·42gr. ; Silica, 14·20grs. ; total, 91·28grs. in one gallon. Sulphuretted Hydrogen, 5·52grs. ; Carbonic Acid, 2·21grs.

Temperature.—140° F.

SPECIAL INDICATIONS : Almost identical with the fore-going spring—(Whangapipiro).

4. CAMERON's BATH (known as Laughing-gas bath), within the Rotorua Sanatorium Reserve, a quarter-mile from the bath-pavilion, on the shores of Lake Rotorua, at a point

called Te Kauwhanga. It is a muddy pool 20 feet in diameter, with a constant discharge of gas (sulphuretted hydrogen), which, when inhaled, causes faintness and great excitement of the vascular and respiratory functions. The pool has no outflow ; the water is a dirty chocolate colour, hepatic, feebly saline, and has a persistent acid reaction and offensive odour. Bathing in the spring itself is to be deprecated.

Analysis (in grains per gallon) : Sulphate of Soda, 44·54grs. ; Chloride of Potassium, 1·67gr. ; Chloride of Sodium, 12·04grs ; Chloride of Calcium, 5·22grs. ; Chloride of Magnesium, 1·28gr. ; Chloride of Aluminium, 0·62gr. ; Silica, 9·22grs. ; Hydrochloric Acid, 5·92grs. ; total, 80·51grs. in one gallon. Sulphuretted Hydrogen, 4·42grs. ; Carbonic Acid, 1·96gr.

Temperature.—109° F. to 115° F.

5. THE PAINKILLER BATH, situated at Te Kauwhanga, resembles the above water (No. 4), but it is a little more saline and hepatic ; it is one of the most valuable sulphurous springs in the Reserve. The water has a distinct acid reaction, has an offensive odour, and deposits a brownish sediment on being boiled. This bath is reported to have great curative properties ; after using it, it is advisable to wash the body in the adjoining lake.

Analysis : Chloride of Sodium, 46·42grs. ; Chloride of Potassium, 1·71gr. ; Chloride of Calcium, 2·66grs. ; Chloride of Magnesium, 1·47gr. ; Chloride of Iron and Aluminium, 4·22grs. ; Sulphate of Soda, 29·14grs. ; Hydrochloric Acid, 6·84grs. ; Silica, 18·02grs. ; total 110·48grs. in one gallon. Sulphuretted Hydrogen, 4·84grs.

Temperature.—204° F.

6. THE COFFEE POT, also situated at Te Kauwhanga, a small mud spring, 8 feet in diameter ; the water is thick, brown, and muddy, covered with an oily slime, in fact, of a most uninviting appearance ; it has a persistent acid reaction and an offensive odour ; hepatic and feebly saline.

Analysis : Silica, 13·86grs. ; Sulphate of Soda, 23·71grs. ; Chloride of Potassium, 0·77gr. ; Chloride of Aluminium,

1·46gr. ; Chloride of Calcium, 2·04grs. ; Chloride of Magnesium, 1·62gr. ; Chloride of Iron, 1·47gr. ; Hydrochloric Acid, 7·66grs. ; Sulphuric Acid, 7·60grs. ; total, 60·19grs. in one gallon. Sulphuretted Hydrogen, 3·19grs.

Temperature.—80° F. to 100° F.

SPECIAL INDICATIONS of the last three baths (Nos. 4, 5, and 6) : Chronic Rheumatism and Gout Chronic Rheumatoid Arthritis, Cutaneous Diseases.

7. HINEMARU (" Stonewall Jackson " or "McHugh's Bath "), situated in the Rotorua Sanatorium Reserve. The water is of a yellowish colour, it is of a saline character, with silicates ; reaction, alkaline.

Analysis : Chloride of Sodium, 93·46grs. ; Chloride of Potassium, 4·69grs. ; Chloride of Lithium, traces ; Sulphate of Soda, 2·76grs. ; Mono-silicate of Soda, 6·41grs. ; Silicate of Lime, 2·89grs. ; Silicate of Magnesia, 1·02gr. ; Iron and Aluminium oxides, 2·10grs. ; Silica, 8·29grs. ; total, 121·62 grains in one gallon.

Temperature.—From 98° F. to 118° F.

SPECIAL INDICATIONS : Cutaneous Diseases, Rheumatism : if filtered, suitable for internal administration in atonic dyspepsia and the uratic diathesis (dose, one tumbler thrice daily between meals).

8. WAIHUNUHUNUKURI (a) or the " Clear Bath," at Lake House Hotel, Ohinemutu. Character of water, feebly saline, with excess of silica. Reaction, distinctly alkaline when concentrated.

Analysis : Chloride of Sodium, 22·42grs. ; Chloride of Potassium, 1·19gr. ; Chloride of Lithium, traces ; Sulphate of Soda, 8·16grs. ; Mono-silicate of Soda, 6·62grs. ; Mono-Silicate of Lime, 7·84grs. ; Mono-silicate of Magnesium, 1·26gr. ; Iron oxides, 0·41gr. ; Alumina, 0·62gr. ; Silica, in excess, 10·34grs. ; total, 58·86grs. in one gallon.

Temperature.—130° F. to 170° F.

SPECIAL INDICATIONS : Useful in the same class of cases as No. 2. (Madame Rachel's Bath.)

9. WAIHUNUHUNUKURI (*b*) or the "Muddy Bath," at Lake House Hotel, Ohinemutu. Character of water, ferruginous, with excess of silica. Reaction, acid.

Analysis: Sulphate of Soda, 22·44grs. ; Sulphate of Potash, 0·62gr. ; Sulphate of Lime, 9·81grs. ; Sulphate of Magnesia, 1·82gr. ; Sulphate of Iron, 12·66grs. ; Suphuric Acid, 18·49grs. ; Hydrochloric Acid, 7·66grs. ; Silica, 18·06grs. ; total, 91·56grs. in one gallon.

Temperature.—150° F.

SPECIAL INDICATIONS : In similar cases as No. 1 (The Priest's Bath), and, in addition, in Anæmia and Chlorosis. .

10. WAIKITE, at Morrison's Rotorua Hotel, Ohinemutu, a clear bath, water feebly saline. Reaction, alkaline in the cold.

Analysis : Chloride of Sodium, 39·64grs. ; Chloride of Potassium, 2·75grs. ; Chloride of Lithium, traces ; Sulphate of Soda, 4·20grs. ; Sulphate of Lime, 6·14grs. ; Silicate of Lime, 8·01grs. ; Silicate of Magnesia, 2·20grs. ; Iron Oxides, with a little Alumina, 5·14grs. ; Silica, 7·67grs. ; total, 75·75grs. in one gallon.

Temperature.—120° F.

SPECIAL INDICATIONS : Useful in the same class of cases as No 2 (Madame Rachel's Bath).

11. SCOTT's BATH, at the Palace Hotel, Ohinemutu. A clear bath, water feebly saline, with silicates. Reaction, alkaline.

Analysis : Chloride of Sodium, 39·44grs. ; Chloride of Potassium, 1·91gr. ; Chloride of Lithium, traces ; Sulphate of Soda, 13·82grs. ; Mono-silicate of Lime, 1·42gr. ; Mono-silicate of Magnesia, 0·69gr. ; Mono-silicate of Soda, 16·03grs. ; Alumina and Iron, 0·62gr. ; Silica, 2·85grs. ; total, 76·78grs. in one gallon.

Temperature.—116° F.

12. TE KOUTU (Tapui Te Koutu), or Graham's Farm Bath, about a mile from Ohinemutu, a large pool, 60 to 80 feet deep. Thick masses of slimy, confervoid plants line the

bottom of the pool. The water is clear, colourless, and highly silicious, with an alkaline reaction.

Analysis : Silicate of Soda, 32·12grs. ; Mono-silicate of Lime, 1·62gr. ; Mono-silicate of Magnesia, 0·40gr. ; Mono-silicate of Iron, 0·67gr. ; Sulphate of Soda, 7·06grs. ; Chloride of Potassium, 0·97gr. ; Chloride of Sodium, 29·94grs.; Phosphate of Alumina, traces; total, 72·78grs. in one gallon. Excess of Silica over what is required to pass these bases at mono-silicates is 5·55.

Temperature.—Usually from 90° F. to 100° F., with westerly or southerly winds ; but if the wind changes to north or east, the water rises 4 feet in level, and the temperature increases to 180° F., with a strong outflow.

SPECIAL INDICATIONS : Psoriasis; also in Rheumatic and Gouty Affections, due to the specific action of silicates in promoting the discharge of uric acid from the system.

13. TURIKORE, or the "SPOUT BATH," at Whakare-warewa, 2¾ miles from Ohinemutu. A warm waterfall which drains from a large pond 300 yards long, the reservoir of a number of boiling springs of constant activity and a stream of cold water from another source. The water is of a dirty-brown colour, and is in great repute among the Maoris for the cure of all cutaneous diseases, rheumatism, lumbago, sciatica, and kidney complaints ; it is of a sulphurous character and has a faintly acid reaction, which changes to alkaline on boiling the water.

Analysis : Silicate of Soda, 16·32grs. ; Silicate of Lime, 1·61gr. ; Silicate of Magnesia, 1·14gr. ; Silicate of Iron, 0·39gr. ; Sulphate of Soda, 13·47grs. ; Chloride Potassium, 1·24gr. ; Chloride of Sodium, 53·61grs.; Phosphate of Alumina, traces ; total, 87·78grs. in one gallon.

Temperature.—96° F. to 120° F.

SPECIAL INDICATIONS : Cutaneous Diseases, Lumbago, Chronic Rheumatism, Local Palsy of Muscles.

14. KOROTEOTEO, or the "OIL BATH," at Whakare-warewa, a strong boiling spring, surrounded by beautiful sulphur incrustations, throwing a powerful jet to a height of 20 feet. The water is distinctly alkaline or slightly caustic.

Analysis : Mono-silicate of Soda, 2·08grs.; Mono-silicate of Lime, 3·16grs.; Mono-silicate of Magnesia, 0·76gr. ; Mono-silicate of Iron, 0·85gr. ; Sulphate of Soda, 7·49grs. ; Chloride of Potassium, 1·46gr.: Chloride of Sodium, 66·34grs. ; Chloride of Lithium, traces ; Silica, free, 22·40grs. ; Phosphate of Alumina, traces ; total, 104·54grs. in one gallon.

Temperature.—214° F.

SPECIAL INDICATIONS : Cutaneous Diseases ; and internally in cases of acid dyspepsia.

15. THE ALUM BATH, near Whakarewarewa ; it has an acid reaction, and contains sulphate of alumina.

SPECIAL INDICATIONS : By the combined internal and external use in Hæmorrhoids, General Debility, Abdominal Congestion (dose, one tumblerful twice daily).

16. "JACK'S BATH," or SULPHUR POOL, at Arikikapakapa' 2 miles from Ohinemutu, a clear bath with a strong outflow· depositing sulphur, and surrounded by a great number of other baths and mud volcanoes. Character of water, acidic. Reaction, acid.

Analysis : Sulphate of Soda, 9·69grs.; Sulphate of Potash, 0·74gr.; Sulphate of Lime, 3·44grs. ; Sulphate of Magnesia, 1·82gr.; Sulphate of Iron, 3·40grs.; Sulphate of\ Alumina, 1·61gr. ; Sulphuric Acid, 12·84grs. ; Hydrochloric Acid, 3·78grs. ; Silica, 9·44grs.; total, 46·76grs. in one gallon. Sulphuretted Hydrogen, 2·76grs. per gallon.

Temperature.—160° F.

SPECIAL INDICATIONS : Said to have powerful curative properties, in action similar to the Priest's Bath (No. 1.)

17. THE " MUD BATH," at Arikikapakapa, a warm muddy hole, having a scum floating on the surface, and in composition similar to the preceding one, but having an excess of silica. Water acidic. Reaction, acid.

Analysis : Sulphate of Soda and Potash, 24·62grs. ; Sulphate of Lime, 8·23grs. ; Sulphate of Magnesia, 2.71grs.; Sulphate of Alumina, 4·02grs. ; Sulphuric Acid, 10·08grs. ; Hydrochloric Acid, 7·72grs. ; Silica, 16·25grs. ; total,

73·63grs. in one gallon. Sulphuretted Hydrogen, 0·86gr. per gallon.

Temperature.—98° F.

SPECIAL INDICATIONS : Principally used in the treatment of chronic and obstinate rheumatic pains.

18. Te Kute, the "Great Spring" (sulphurous), at Tihitary, near Lake Rotoiti, 10½ miles from Ohinemutu, a large, furiously boiling pool, continuously emitting dense volumes of steam. The water is of a muddy-brown colour, and contains a large proportion of sulphuretted hydrogen.

Analysis : Sulphate of Potash, 0·59gr. ; Sulphate of Soda, 12·66grs. ; Sulphate of Alumina, 11·22grs. ; Sulphate of Lime, 1·01gr. ; Sulphate of Magnesia, 0·69gr. ; Sulphate of Iron, 1·73gr. ; Phosphoric Acid, traces ; Sulphuric Acid, free, 0·77gr. ; Hydrochloric Acid, free, 1·63gr. ; Sulphuretted Hydrogen, 5·74grs. ; Silica, 12·40grs. ; total, 48·44grs. in one gallon.

Temperature.—Varying from 100° F. to 212° F. in various parts.

SPECIAL INDICATIONS : Wonderfully efficacious in cases of Chronic Rheumatism, both muscular and articular ; also in Sciatica, and parasitic diseases of the skin.

19. Te Mimi, at Okakahi, near Rotoiti Lake, a hot waterfall, the water of which is of an acidic character ; it is the overflow from a number of hot sulphurous springs on a high-level above Tikitere, and only differs from the preceding "Great Spring" in being more dilute, and having a larger portion of sulphuric acid and less sulphuretted hydrogen.

Analysis : Sulphate of Potash, 0·13gr. ; Sulphate of Soda, 4·78grs. ; Sulphate of Alumina, traces ; Sulphate of Lime, 2·04grs. ; Sulphate of Magnesia, 0·93gr. ; Sulphate of Iron, 0·23gr. ; Phosphate of Alumina, traces ; Sulphuric Acid, free, 12·48grs. ; Hydrochloric Acid, 3·82grs. ; Sulphuretted Hydrogen, 0·98gr. ; Silica, 4·12grs. ; total, 29·51grs. in one gallon.

Temperature.—90° F. to 112° F.

SPECIAL INDICATIONS : In action similiar to the preceding spring (No. 18).

20. Sulphur Bay Spring, at Arikikapakapa, on the edge of Lake Rotorua, formed by innumerable small jets forced up through the sand, having a disagreeable odour. This bath is reported to have a powerful action on the skin, owing no doubt to the large quantity of sulphuric acid it contains.

Analysis : Silica, 10·08grs. ; Sulphate of Soda, 8·37grs. ; Sulphate of Potash, 0·07gr. ; Sulphate of Alumina, traces ; Sulphate of Lime, 2·50grs. ; Sulphate of Magnesia, 0·93gr. ; Sulphate of Iron, 2·68grs. ; Phosphate of Alumina, traces ; Hydrochloric Acid, free, 0·86gr. ; Sulphuretted Hydrogen, 1·01gr. ; Sulphuric Acid, free, 18·02grs. ; total, 44·52grs. in one gallon.

Temperature.—90° F. to 100° F.

Special Indications : Cutaneous Diseases, Disorders of the Liver.

21. Perekari, or Sulphur Point Boiling-Pool, 1½ mile from Ohinemutu, a boiling pool in a sand-spit near the lake, in which the water is discoloured, and has a very offensive smell. Reaction, strongly acid.

Analysis : Silica, 18·17grs. ; Sulphate of Soda, 26·75grs. ; Sulphate of Alumina, traces ; Sulphate of Lime, 2·45grs. ; Sulphate of Magnesia, 1·86gr. ; Sulphate of Iron, 0·76gr. ; Chloride of Potassium, 0·63gr. ; Phosphate of Alumina, traces ; Hydrochloric Acid, free, 5·38grs. ; total, 56·00grs. in one gallon.

Temperature.—130° F. to 150° F.

22. Kuirau or Washing Spring, at Ohinemutu, on the shores of Rotorua Lake, where a strong stream flows from a number of hot springs, which cover an extent of about 30 acres. The water has an alkaline reaction, and is so soft that clothes can be washed in it without the use of soap.

Analysis : Silicate of Soda, 2·57grs. ; Silicate of Lime, 0·34gr. ; Silicate of Magnesia, 0·12gr. ; Silicate of Iron, 0·31gr. ; Silica, 18·42grs. ; Sulphate of Soda, 10·31grs. ; Chloride of Sodium, 45·70grs. ; Chloride of Potassium, 2·08grs. ; Phosphate of Alumina, traces ; total, 79·85grs. in one gallon.

Temperature.—136° F. to 156° F.

SPECIAL INDICATIONS : Useful in Rheumatic Affections, especially in Gouty constitutions.

23. MANUPIRUA, on the south-east shore of Rotoiti, a beautifully clear pool 20 feet in diameter, at the foot of a high pumice cliff on the shore of the lake. The water is clear with a bluish tinge, harsh to the touch, and deposits sulphur. This pool has a strong outflow of 40 or 50 gallons per minute.

Analysis : Silicate of Lime, 1·51gr. ; Silicate of Magnesia, 0·77gr. ; Silicate of Iron, 0·99gr. ; Silica, 8·53grs. ; Sulphate of Soda, 11·50grs. ; Sulphate of Lime, 2·43grs. ; Chloride of Sodium, 6·25grs. ; Chloride of Potassium, 0·47gr. ; total, 32·45grs. in one gallon.

Temperature.—107° F. to 110° F.

SPECIAL INDICATIONS : Valuable in Rheumatic Affections, and Chronic Psoriasis.

24. OTUKAPUARANGI, the " Pink Terrace," of Rotomahana, reported to have been destroyed during the eruption in June, 1886. The terrace had been built up round a great circular pool, 180 feet in diameter, from which there is a great outflow of clear, bright water, of a sulphurous character, depositing silicious sinter, of a delicate pink tint in large quantities. Reaction, faintly acid.

Analysis (before the eruption in 1886) : Silicate of Lime, 1·91gr. ; Silicate of Magnesia, 1·16gr. ; Chloride of Potassium, 1·05gr. ; Chloride of Sodium, 93·55grs. ; Sulphate of Lime, 10·96grs. ; Phosphate of Alumina, 0·54gr. ; Silica, 43·95grs. ; Iron Oxides, traces ; total, 153·12grs. in one gallon.

Temperature.—204· F. to 208° F.

25. TE TARATA, the " White Terrace," of Rotomahana, reported to have been destroyed during the eruption in June, 1886. This is a true geyser, having a large crater-shaped basin, 90 feet in diameter. The basin is emptied by an explosive effort, which throws the water to a height of 40 feet, emptying the basin which again fills up rapidly. The water has a deep azure blue colour, deposits silicious sinter as it cools, and has an alkaline reaction.

Analysis (before the eruption) : Silicate of Soda, 68·48grs. ; Mono-silicate of Lime, 1·62gr. ; Mono-silicate of Magnesia, 0·53gr. ; Mono-silicate of Iron, 0·51gr. ; Sulphate of Soda, 7·84grs. ; Chloride of Potassium, 2·57grs.; Chloride of Sodium, 62·61grs. ; Phosphate of Alumina and Lithium,· traces ; total, 144·16grs. in one gallon.

Temperature.—210° F.

OBJECTS OF INTEREST : The native village of Ohine-mutu ; the Boiling Springs ; the pleasure-ground at the Sanatorium.

EXCURSIONS : The Ngae Mission Station (7m. N.E.) ; the romantic island of Mokoia, with Hinemoa's bath, in Rotorua Lake (by boat) ; Lake Rotoiti, and the native village of Tapuaeharuru ; Lake Rotokawau, and the fiercely-boiling springs of Tikitere (10m. N.E.) ; Lake Rotomauiahia ; the remarkable geysers of Whakarewarewa (3m. S.) ; Lakes Okataina, Okareka, Tikitapu, and Rotokakahi ; Tarawera Lake and Beach ; Waitangi Falls ; the native village of Ariki ; Te Tarata hot-springs ; the remarkable Mt. Tarawera (1,964 feet high), with its three summits. (*Note.*—The native village Wairoa, and the famous White and Pink Terraces at Rotomahana were destroyed by the eruption of Mt. Tarawera, in June, 1886.)

DOCTOR : Dr. A. Ginders, Government Resident Medical Officer at Rotorua Sanatorium.

HOTELS : The " Lake House," with a splendid view of Lake Rotorua and the island of Mokoia ; the " Palace ;" " Morrison's " ; also the " Rotorua Temperance," close to the Government baths, Rotorua, and the " Geyser Hotel," at Whakarewarewa.

NOTE.—Patients desirous of residing elsewhere for the benefit of certain baths, can rent the whares of the Maoris and live amongst them at a cost of from 25s. to 35s. per week.

ROUTE : From Auckland by rail to Oxford, thence by coach ; or from Napier by coach via Taupo (150m.); or from Tauranga by coach (about 50m.)

ONEHUNGA (PROV. AUCKLAND), NEW ZEALAND, 8 miles (by rail) S. from Auckland, the port of Manukau harbour, on the west coast of the North Island. Climate mild and salubrious. Sea-bathing ; fishing ; boating. Post and Telegraph Office ; Free Library ; Public Hall ; Masonic Hall.

EXCURSIONS : *See* AUCKLAND.

DOCTORS : Drs. W. G. Scott, W. R. Erson.

HOTELS : The " Royal," the " Manukau," the " Exchange," the " Railway Terminus."

ONETAPU, NEW ZEALAND, at the sources of the Waikato and Whangaehu rivers, a powerful saline and ferruginous spring, which issues at the base of Mount Ruapehu, to the south of Lake Taupo, so strongly charged with sulphate of iron and alumina, as to taint the water of the latter river from its source to the sea, a distance of 70 miles. It is only one of the many mineral springs which occur in the still active volcanic district of Tongariro. It contains 58·0grs. of mineral matter per pint.

Temperature.—70° F.

ROUTE : From Napier.

ORAKEIKORAKO (PROV. AUCKLAND), NEW ZEALAND, 30 miles S. of Ohinemutu, and 22 miles N. of Taupo, a Maori settlement on the left side of the Waikato river, in a wild and lonely, though picturesque and romantic district.

1. THE ALUM CAVE SPRING, a hole some 30 to 40 feet deep, at the bottom of which is a pool of clear blue water, of a sulphurous character, strongly impregnated with alum and other mineral substances.

Analysis (in grains per gallon).—Salts, soluble in water, principally Alkaline Chlorines, 24·12grs.; Salts, soluble in acids, principally Sulphate of Lime, 3·84grs. ; Silica, 28·51grs. ; total salts, 56·47grs. ; loss by ignition, 3·24grs. ; reaction, slightly acid ; mineral matters per pint, 7·1gr.

Temperature.—60° F.

2. ORAKEIKORAKO SPRING, a large geyser, the waters of which are acidic.

Analysis (in grains per gallon) : Salts, soluble in water, 64·72grs. ; Salts, soluble in acids, 1·63gr.; Silica, 18·51grs. ;

F

total salts, 84·86grs. ; loss by ignition, 12·97grs. ; reaction faintly acid ; mineral matters per pint, 10·6grs.

Temperature.—From 90° F. to 106° F.

ROUTE : From Auckland by rail to Oxford, thence coach via Ohinemutu ; or from Napier by coach via Taupo.

ORANGE, NEW SOUTH WALES, 2,891 feet above sea-level, 192 miles (by rail) W. from Sydney, and 124 miles from the coast, an important inland town, noted for its bracing climate. The mean maximum temperature in the shade in 1885, was 65·7° F., the mean minimum temperature 44·2° F., and the mean temperature 55° F. The average annual rainfall is 36·49 inches, with 103 wet days. Hospital ; Post and Telegraph Office ; School of Arts.

DOCTORS : Drs. C. F. Coxwell, G. Goode, C. W. Heinemann, G. Proudfoot.

HOTELS : The " Royal," " Great Western," " Occidental," " Club House," " Telegraph."

OTAHUHU (PROV. AUCKLAND), NEW ZEALAND, 9 miles (by rail) S. from Auckland, pleasantly situated on the Manukau Harbour, on the west coast of the North Island. Climate very mild and salubrious ; surrounding scenery very picturesque. Post and Telegraph Office ; Public Library ; Temperance Hall.

EXCURSIONS : Sylvia Park, 740 acres, the establishment of the New Zealand Stud and Pedigree Company ; Onehunga ; Auckland.

HOTELS : The " Criterion," the " Star."

PEMBROKE (OTAGO), NEW ZEALAND, 1,040 feet above sea-level, 176 miles N.W. of Dunedin, a little village on the shores of the famous Lake Wanaka. The climate is very salubrious, and the surrounding scenery is wild and romantic. Post and Telegraph Office.

EXCURSIONS : By steamboat round Lake Wanaka ; Glendhu (10m.) ; Mount Iron (4m.), commanding splendid views ; Mount Grandview ; Brown's Bay, and head of Clutha River (4m.) ; Lake Hawea (6m.)

HOTELS : The " Wanaka," the " Commercial," and the " Hawea " close to the shores of Lake Hawea.

ROUTE : From Dunedin by rail to Lawrence (60m.), thence coach via Cromwell (116m.) ; or from Invercargill by rail to Kingston (87m.), thence by steamboat across Lake Wakatipu to Queenstown, thence by coach, via Arrowtown and Cromwell (71m.)

PENGUIN, TASMANIA, 92 miles N.W. of Launceston, a sea-side resort on the northern coast of the island, in a fine agricultural district. The climate is very salubrious. Sea-bathing ; fishing ; shooting ; boating. Post and Telegraph Office.

DOCTOR : Dr. J. McCall, from Ulverstone (7m.)

HOTEL : " Taylor's," also Sullock's boarding-house.

ROUTE : By steamer direct ; or by rail from Launceston to Formby (82m.), thence coach (20m.)

PETERSBURG, SOUTH AUSTRALIA, 1,746 feet above sea-level, 154 miles (by rail) N. from Adelaide, and 48 miles from the coast. The climate is very dry ; the total rainfall in 1882 was only 11 inches. Post and Telegraph Office.

HOTELS : The " Petersburg," the " Junction."

PHILLIP ISLAND, VICTORIA. *See* COWES.

PIALBA, QUEENSLAND, 22 miles N. of Maryborough, a favourite watering-place prettily situated on the shore of Hervey Bay. Bracing climate ; fine beach, abundance of oysters ; good fishing ; shooting. Post and Telegraph Office.

EXCURSION : Torquay-by-the-Sea, a small watering place (1½m.)

SPECIAL INDICATIONS : General Debility, Incipient Phthisis, Chronic Bronchial Catarrh.

HOTELS : The " Pialba," the " Point Vernon."

ROUTE : By coach from Maryborough.

PICTON, NEW SOUTH WALES, 549 feet above sea-level, 53 miles by rail S. from Sydney, and 21 miles from the coast, a favourite health resort, prettily situated in a valley.

Climate healthy. The mean annual rainfall is 23·35 inches, with 100 wet days. The mean maximum temperature in the shade in 1885 was 71·9° F., the mean minimum temperature 50·3° F., and the mean temperature 61·1° F. Goodlet's Home for Consumptives. Post and Telegraph Office.

EXCURSIONS : Burragorong ; Vault Hill ; Fern Valley ; Picton Lakes (6m.)

DOCTOR : Dr. F. G. Dalton.

HOTELS : The "Royal ;" "Great Southern Railway" ; also Mrs. O'Neil's boarding-house.

PITTWATER, NEW SOUTH WALES, 19 miles N. of Sydney, a charming district, beautifully situated at the head of Pittwater, on the south-west side of Broken Bay, the estuary of the picturesque Hawkesbury river. The country is undulating, and the scenery lovely, the climate is mild and balmy ; it is well-sheltered from all winds. This district has been described as the future sanatorium of the colony. Excellent fishing ; shooting ; sea-bathing ; boating, sailing. Post Office, at Bayview.

DOCTOR : Dr. W. H. Tibbits, from Manly.

HOTELS : The " Rock Lily," near Monavale, is a well-kept hostelry ; the " Newport," at Newport ; Bayview boarding house, at Newport.

EXCURSION : Lyx Cascade, a very romantic spot, 4 miles from the Rock Lily hotel.

ROUTE : By steamer to Manly, thence coach (14m.)

PORTARLINGTON, VICTORIA, 65 miles S.W. of Melbourne, a watering-place on Port Phillip Bay. The country is undulating, and the surrounding scenery is beautiful. Fine esplanade along the beach ; sea-baths ; ·jetty ; public gardens ; fishing ; boating. Post and Telegraph Office ; Mechanics' Institute.

EXCURSION : Drysdale, and Clifton mineral springs.

HOTELS : The " Bayview," the " Family."

ROUTE : By rail to Drysdale, thence coach (6m.) ; or by steamer direct.

PORT ELLIOT, South Australia, 77 miles (by rail) S. from Adelaide, a favourite watering place on the northern shore of Encounter Bay, in a wheat-growing district. The surrounding country is undulating. The mean annual amount of rainfall is 21 inches. Sea-bathing ; fishing ; boating. Post and Telegraph Office ; Institute.

EXCURSION : Port Victor (4½m.)

HOTELS : The " Royal," the " Railway," the " Port Elliot."

PORTLAND, Victoria, 40 feet above sea-level, 272 miles by rail, and 225 miles by steamer S.W. from Melbourne, situated on the coast, standing on high ground, overlooking the bay. The neighbourhood is thickly timbered, especially to the north, where the Nine-mile Forest lies, and the surrounding country is elevated ; the coast landscape is magnificent. The climate is mild and the air pure and salubrious. The winter is rather wet ; the heat in summer is tempered by sea-breezes. The temperature at Portland is higher than at any other place on the coast, due to the neighbourhood of warm ocean currents ; the mean temperature in January is 67° F. ; in April, 63° F. ; in July, 53° F. ; in October, 60° F. ; and in December, 64° F. ; the mean annual temperature is 56·7° F. The average annual rainfall is 33 inches. Sandy beaches ; sea-baths ; sea and river fishing ; shooting (kangaroo, plover, &c.) ; yachting ; boating. Post and Telegraph Office ; Benevolent Asylum ; Mechanics' Institute ; Masonic Hall ; Portland Club ; Botanic Gardens ; two jetties.

EXCURSIONS : Lady Julia Percy Island, a breeding place for seals (20m.) ; Bridgewater, a dairy-farming village on Cape Bridgewater (12m.) ; a walk along the Belfast Road to the Surrey River.

SPECIAL INDICATIONS : General Debility, Scrofula, Phthisis.

SEASON : During the summer months.

DOCTORS : Drs. J. S. Levis, H. E. Brewer.

HOTELS : "Mac's," a large and commanding edifice, overlooking the bay ; " Richmond House," an excellent hotel, delightfully situated ; the " London," much used by sporting men ; the " Club," the " Britannia," the " Commercial," the " Builder's Arms."

PORT LINCOLN, South Australia, 210 miles (by steamer) W. from Adelaide, beautifully situated on the south-east coast of Eyre's Peninsula, in a pastoral district. The scenery is charming ; the climate is most suitable for chest complaints ; the nights are always cool, and the mean annual amount of rainfall is 20 inches. Sea-bathing ; fishing ; boating ; jetty, 700 feet long. Post and Telegraph Office ; Casualty Hospital ; Institute.

OBJECT OF INTEREST : Flinders' Monument, erected by Lady Franklin.

EXCURSION : The Poonindie Aboriginal Station.

SEASON : During the summer months.

DOCTOR : Dr. G. P. Atkins.

HOTELS : The " Pier," the " Port Lincoln," the " Northern," the " Temperance."

PORT MACQUARIE, New South Wales, 49 feet above sea-level, 240 miles (by steamer) N. from Sydney, picturesquely situated on the sea-coast, on the south side of the river Hastings, in a timber, maize, and vine-growing district. The scenery is very fine. The climate is mild and balmy, similar to that of Lisbon. The mean maximum temperature in 1885 was 74·2° F., the mean minimum temperature 56 2° F., and the mean temperature 65·2° F. The average annual rainfall is nearly 58 inches, with 114 rainy days in the year. Sea-bathing ; fishing ; boating. Post and Telegraph Office.

EXCURSION : Camden Haven (26m.)

SPECIAL INDICATIONS : Bronchial Affections.

DOCTOR : Dr. W. S. Cortis.

HOTELS : The " Royal," the " Star " ; also Cavanagh's and Hinton's boarding-houses.

PORTSEA, Victoria, 37 miles (by steamer) S. from Melbourne, a much frequented watering-place on the east side of Port Phillip Heads, has a lovely aspect facing the bay along a sandy beach. Further inland is wild bush, the haunt of

rabbits and kangaroos.   Back Beach (2m.) ;   Ocean Park ;
Nepean Rotunda, used for theatrical entertainments ; sea-
bathing ; fishing; shooting.   Post and Telegraph Office.

OBJECTS OF INTEREST : The " London Bridge Caves," a
great natural curiosity.

EXCURSIONS :   Cape Schanck and its lighthouse ; Pulpit
Rock and St. Paul's, with a view of the Barwon Heads, and
the Cape Otway Ranges.

HOTELS :   The   " Nepean," affording every comfort, with
fine grounds for picnics ; the " Portsea."   .

PORT VICTOR, SOUTH AUSTRALIA.   *See* VICTOR
HARBOUR.

PURIRI (PROV. AUCKLAND), NEW ZEALAND, 9 miles
(by river steamer or conveyance) S.E. from Grahamstown,
(Thames), near the Waihou river.   A cold effervescent water
having valuable properties, from the presence of a large percentage of alkaline-carbonates ; it is bottled both as still and
aerated water, and is coming into repute as an antilithic
aperient, and would probably be useful in cases of acid
dyspepsia, and in disorders of the kidney and bladder.   In
chemical properties it approaches very closely to Fachingen
waters, some of the strongest alkaline waters in Germany,
which is largely exported.

Analysis (in grains per gallon) : Chloride of Sodium,
21·938grs.; Iodide of Magnesia, traces ; Sulphate of Soda,
0·940gr. ; Sulphate of Potash, 4·938grs. ; Carbonate of Iron,
traces ; Bicarbonate of Lime, 28·506grs.; Bicarbonate of
Magnesia, 25·625grs.; Bicarbonate of Soda, 452·393grs. ;
Bicarbonate of Lithia, traces ; Silica, 2·772grs.; Phosphoric
Acid, not determined ; total, 537·112 grains in one gallon,
or 67·1 solid grains of mineral matters per pint.

Temperature.—60° F.

EXCURSIONS : Thames Gold-mines ; by river steamer to
Ohinemuri ; the " Great Kauri Tree," 46 feet in girth ;
Totara Pah ; Kauaeranga Valley.

HOTEL : " Garrett's."

QUEENSCLIFF, VICTORIA, 60 miles (by steamer) S.
from Melbourne, one of the principal watering-places of

Victoria, at the entrance of Port Phillip Bay. Air very pure. Excellent sea-baths ; sandy beach ; fine pier ; fishing ; boating ; shooting on Swan Island and Duck Island. Post and Telegraph Office ; Mechanics' Institute ; Forester's Hall, used for concerts.

OBJECTS OF INTEREST : Two lighthouses ; fortifications.

SPECIAL INDICATIONS : Nervous Affections, Liver Complaints ; also for Convalescents.

SEASON : November to April.

HOTELS : The " Royal," the " Victoria," the " Esplanade," " Adman's."

QUEENSTOWN (OTAGO), NEW ZEALAND, 1,070 feet above sea-level, 110 miles N.W. of Invercargill, and 55 miles from the coast, very picturesquely situated on the northern shores of Lake Wakatipu. The surrounding mountain scenery is of extreme grandeur and beauty. The climate is very invigorating ; the mean annual temperature is 51° F., the difference between the coldest and the warmest months is 21° F., and the average annual amount of rainfall 50 inches. Abundant shooting and fishing. Post and Telegraph Office ; Hospital at Frankton ; Athenæum, with reading-room ; Theatre ; the Park, a pleasant resort, with walks and seats, commanding a fine view of the lake ; the " Esplanade," which runs along the shore of Queenstown Bay ; " Rowell's Garden."

EXCURSIONS : Shotover Gorge (2m.) ; Frankton (4m.) ; Kawarau Falls ; Arrowtown (12m.) ; Advance Peak, 5,740 feet high ; Lake Hayes, grand fishing ; the " Remarkables," a range of bare rugged mountains (7,688 feet high) ; Wedge Peak ; Mount Ben Lomond, and Mount Bowen (6m.), commanding magnificent views ; the head of Lake Wakatipu (by steamer), with Kinloch and Glenorchy (two villages) ; Diamond Lake ; Paradise Flat ; the celebrated glaciers of Mount Earnslaw ; Lennox Falls ; Mount Alfred ; Mount Judah ; Lake Harris (4,000 feet above sea-level) ; Rere Lake, a favourite resort for picnic parties.

SPECIAL INDICATIONS : Pulmonary Diseases, Bronchitis, Nervous Affections, Disorders of Digestion.

HOTELS : " Eichardt's," " Queen's Arm's," the " Prince of Wales," the " Mountaineer " ; also Mr. Birley's, at Glenorchy ; Mr. Bryant's, at Kinloch (at the head of the lake).

ROUTE : From Invercargill by rail to Kingston (87m.), thence by steamer across the lake ; or from Dunedin by rail to Lawrence (60m.), thence coach (136m.)

QUIRINDI, NEW SOUTH WALES, 1,278 feet above sea-level, 217 miles N. of Sydney, and 115 miles from the coast, situated on the Quirindi Creek, in an extremely fertile district ; there are numerous vineyards in the district. Very fine scenery, and mild, dry climate ; the mean maximum temperature in the shade in 1885 was 79·7° F., the mean minimum temperature 54·1° F., and the mean temperature 66·9° F. ; the average annual rainfall is 23·44 inches, with 60 rainy days. Good shooting ; Post and Telegraph Office.

SPECIAL INDICATIONS : Pulmonary Affections, especially Asthma.

SEASON : From October to April.

HOTELS : The " Terminus," the " Commercial," the " Bank," " Whitaker's."

ROUTE : By steamer to Newcastle, thence rail (144m.) ; or by rail direct.

RICHMOND, Tasmania, 50 feet above sea-level, 15 miles N.E. of Hobart, and 19 miles from the coast, beautifully situated on the Coal river. The total rainfall in 1886 amounted to 21 inches, with 139 wet days. Fishing ; shooting. Post and Telegraph Office ; Public Library.

DOCTOR : Dr. C. Turner.

HOTEL : The " Bridge."

ROUTE : By coach direct ; or by rail to Campania (27m.), thence coach (5m.)

RIVERTON (SOUTHLAND), NEW ZEALAND, 26 miles (by rail) W. from Invercargill, a rising summer resort, picturesquely situated on the coast, at the mouth of Jacob's River, in a rich dairy-farming district. The mean temperature in winter is 42° F. ; in spring, 51° F. ; in summer,

58° F., and in autumn, 50° F. The mean annual temperature is 50° F.; the mean daily range 20° F.; and the average annual rainfall is 50 inches. Sea-bathing; fishing; boating. Post and Telegraph Office; Hospital.

HOTELS : The " Commercial," the " Great Western," the " Globe," the " Railway," the " County."

ROBE, SOUTH AUSTRALIA, 208 miles (by steamer) S.E. from Adelaide, a seaside resort, situated on the southern shores of Guichen Bay, amidst a dreary country of sand-hills, but the coast scenery is picturesque, and the climate salubrious. The mean annual temperature is 58° F., and the mean annual rainfall 25 inches. Fine jetty 1,000 feet long, forming a favourite promenade.; sandy beach; sea-bathing; fishing. Post and Telegraph Office; Literary Institute.

EXCURSIONS : Lake Robe (3m.); Lake Eliza (4m.); Lakes St. Clair and Hawdon; Mt. Benson (3m.)

HOTELS : The " Robe," the " Criterion," the " Caledonian."

ROCK FLAT, NEW SOUTH WALES, 267 miles S. of Sydney, and 55 miles from the coast, on Rock Flat Creek, in a pastoral district, 10 miles from Cooma, on the road to Bombala. Post Receiving Office.

A very powerful cold effervescent mineral spring, leased to Mr. James Armstrong, is here situated.

Analysis (in grains per gallon): 49·845grs. of soluble solids, chiefly Carbonate of Soda, and Chloride of Sodium, with small quantities of Salts of Potassa; 65·870grs. of insoluble solids, chiefly Carbonate of Lime; and 17·600grs. of solids, volatile at red heat; or a total of 133·315grs. of solid matter in one gallon. Also 2·67grs. of Chlorine, and traces of Sal Ammonia.

ROUTE : By rail to Michelago, thence coach via Cooma.

ROMA, QUEENSLAND, 978 feet above sea-level, 317 miles (by rail) N.W. from Brisbane, and 260 miles from the coast, the principal town in the Western District; vine and oranges are extensively grown; fine climate; the average annual amount of rainfall is 38 inches ; Hospital ; School of Arts ; Post and Telegraph Office.

SPECIAL INDICATIONS : Phthisis.

DOCTORS : Drs. G. Comyn, J. L. Cuppaidge.

HOTELS : The "Club," the "School of Arts," the "Queen's Arms," the "Victoria," the "Commercial," the "Royal Mail."

ROSS, TASMANIA, 600 feet above sea-level. 83 miles (by rail) N. from Hobart, and 50 miles (by rail) S.E. from Launceston, and 30 miles from the coast ; a pretty township, beautifully situated on the Macquarie River, and one of the healthiest spots on the island ; good shooting. Post and Telegraph Office.

DOCTOR : Dr. H. J. Byrne.

HOTEL : The "Ross."

ROTORUA, NEW ZEALAND, on the southern shores of Lake Rotorua, immediately to the south-east of the celebrated ancient Maori village of Ohinemutu, the centre of the famous Hot Springs District. For detailed description, analyses, temperature, and special indications of a large number of the surrounding springs see "Ohinemutu."

Dr. A. Ginders, Medical Superintendent of the Sanatorium at Rotorua, has favoured the author of this guide with the following sketch of the Climate and Bathing facilities at Rotorua :—

"Rotorua is 990 feet above the sea-level. The nearest seaport town is Tauranga, distant about 42 miles. The climate of Rotorua is drier and more bracing than that of the coast. The heat of Summer is free from the moist oppressiveness that characterises that of Auckland and other coast towns. The mean temperature for the four seasons is as follows :—Spring, 53° F. ; Summer, 66° F. ; Autumn, 57° F. ; and Winter, 45° F. The relative moisture of the atmosphere (complete saturation = 100) is, for Spring, 74 ; Summer, 66 ; Autumn, 67 ; and Winter, 74. The average annual rainfall is 53 inches, and the number of days on which rain falls 150. Auckland has 20 inches less rain and 15 more rainy days. The daily range of temperature is greatest

in Summer and least in Winter. The nights in the hottest
Summer weather are invariably cool, and mosquitoes are unknown. The mean daily range of temperature is, for Spring,
21 F°. ; Summer, 28° F. ; Autumn, 23° F. ; and Winter, 20°
F. A climate better adapted to the necessities of the class of
patients visiting this health resort could not be desired. They
are, as a rule, persons in fairly vigorous health, in whom it is
desirable to maintain the normal power of adaptation and resistance to climatic changes. A climate in which the same
conditions prevailed for long periods of the year would fail to
secure this end ; but one in which the various factors of temperature, moisture, light, electricity, wind, and atmospheric
pressure are subject to moderate variations is in every way the
kind of climate to be desired. The bathing season is from
October to April ; the least agreeable months are July,
August, and September, but the invalid is virtually indepen-
dent of the weather, as ample boarding accommodation exists
close to the Baths. Although the Hot Springs of Rotorua
are very numerous and varied in their physical and chemical
character, Dr. Ginders, the Medical Superintendent of the
Sanatorium, believes they may be divided, for all practical
medical purposes, into two classes—those which have a stimu-
lant action on the nervous and vascular apparatus of the skin,
and those whose action is sedative. The former category
comprises the acid sulphurous waters, and the latter the alkaline and silicious. The Springs are used almost exclusively
for bathing purposes, the only water taken to any extent internally is the alkaline silicious water of the Rachel Spring,
which is mildly antilithic and useful in the uric acid diathesis.
A very valuable saline acidulous and chalybeate has recently
been discovered, which is likely to become very popular. The
Bathing Pavilions are comfortably fitted with every necessary
appliance, and the waters are supplied to large public piscinæ,
private baths, douches and showers, in which temperature is
regulated as required. Rheumatism and Cutaneous diseases
form 75°/₀ of the cases treated at this Sanatorium ; but the
waters prove beneficial in Neuralgias, Internal Congestions,
and certain forms of Paralysis. Electrical treatment is carried
out extensively in connection with the Baths, which greatly
adds to its efficiency by diminishing the resistance of the skin
and causing it to be more readily permeated by the current."

ROTTNEST, WESTERN AUSTRALIA, is an island about 7½ miles in length by 2½ miles in breadth, situated 12 miles from Fremantle, at the entrance of the port. It is used as a penal establishment for aboriginal prisoners, who are working on a reproductive farm ; the marine residence of the Governor is also on the island ; it contains several salt lakes, two of them very shallow, and from these a large quantity of bay salt has been collected every year since 1869. The brine contains from 20 to 25 per cent. of Chloride of Sodium, with some Sulphate of Lime and Magnesia. An analysis of the salt showed that in 100 parts of it there were 95·9 parts of pure Chloride of Sodium, 1·6 part of Chloride of Magnesium and Calcium ; traces of Sulphates, and 2·5 parts of moisture. Some part of the lakes could be set apart for Brine baths, such as are established at Arnstadt (near Weimar) and at Wittekind (near Halle), in Germany, which are much sought after in scrofulous diseases.

ROUTE : By steamer from Fremantle.

RYLSTONE, NEW SOUTH WALES, 1,993 feet above sea-level, 158 miles (by rail) N.W. from Sydney, and 95 miles from the coast. The climate is dry and extremely healthy, while in its neighbourhood are many charming views of valley, mountains, and of the Cudgegong River. The average annual rainfall is 24·22 inches, with 56 wet days. Post and Telegraph Office ; three hotels.

SPECIAL INDICATIONS : Pulmonary Affections.

DOCTOR : Dr. A. W. Bateman.

ST. HELEN'S (GEORGE'S BAY), TASMANIA, 80 miles E. of Launceston, a very favourite summer resort and watering-place at the head of a completely landlocked bay, noted for the purity of the atmosphere and the great salubrity of its climate ; scenery extremely picturesque. Grand fishing (flounders, bream, perch, flatheads) ; shooting (black swan, teal, ducks, pelicans, snipe) ; boating. Post and Telegraph Office.

EXCURSIONS : Scamander River (6m.) ; Falmouth ; " Diana's Basin," a charming salt-water lake ; Truganini's Throne (8m.) ; the Leda Falls (7m.).

HOTELS : The " Telegraph ;" the " Union."

Route : By rail from Launceston via Corners to St. Mary's, thence coach.

ST. KILDA (OTAGO), New Zealand, a fashionable watering-place and suburb of Dunedin, picturesquely situated on Tomahawk Bay. Fine ocean beach, fully a mile long ; sea-baths.

Objects of Interest : The Cliffs ; Lawyer's Head, with battery.

Hotels : The " Grand Pacific ;" the " Ocean Beach ;" the " St. Kilda ;" the " London ;" the " Pioneer."

Route : By tram from Dunedin (fare 3d.)

ST. KILDA, Victoria, 3 miles S. of Melbourne, a very fashionable watering-place, beautifully situated on the eastern shores of Hobson's Bay. Climate mild and salubrious. Sandy beach ; sea-baths ; hot salt-water baths ; fishing, boating, and yachting. Long Pier, provided with seats ; the Esplanade, a wide and beautifully-kept roadway along the sea-beach, is the most favourite promenade ; Public Park, with lake ; Public Library ; Assembly Hall ; Post and Telegraph Office.

Doctors : Drs. W. B. Rankin, R. Power, J. C. Johnston, E. L. Simmons, G. Annand.

Hotels : The " Esplanade," commanding a magnificent view of the Bay, has accommodation of the highest class ; the " George," a first-class family hotel, of ample accommodation : the " Prince of Wales," a first-class and roomy hotel ; the " Royal," an old-established and excellently-kept house ; " Morgan's Family," a large and comfortable hotel ; " Buck's Head," a comfortable and convenient house ; the " Village Belle ;" the " Greyhound ;" the " Victoria ;" the " Junction ;" the " Corner ;" the " St. Kilda Family."

Route : By rail, car, or 'bus.

SALE, Victoria, 32 feet above sea-level, 128 miles (by rail) E. from Melbourne, and 18 miles from the coast, the largest and most important town in Gippsland, the garden of Australia, one of the most attractive parts of the Australian colonies, noted for its magnificent scenery. The climate is fairly dry ; the average annual rainfall is 25·4 inches. Grand shooting (kangaroos, wallabies, quail, black swan, wild duck, teal, &c.) ; fishing ; boating. Post and Telegraph Office ; Mechanics' Institute ; Hospital ; Town Hall, fitted with a stage for concerts, &c. ; the Victoria, Oddfellows', Temperance, and Freemasons' Halls ; Artesian Baths, the water of which being of one temperature all the year round ; Botanic Gardens ; Race-course.

EXCURSIONS : Wellington ; Lake Victoria ; Lake King ; Ramahyuck, an aboriginal station on the Avon river (15m.)

DOCTOR : Dr. J. A. Reid.

HOTELS : The " Criterion," the " Club," the " Albion," the " Royal Exchange," the " Prince of Wales," the " Adelphi," the " Star."

SALISBURY, SOUTH AUSTRALIA, 110 feet above sea-level, 12½ miles (by rail) N. from Adelaide, on the Little Para river, in a fruit and vine-growing district. The surrounding country consists of mountains and plains. Post and Telegraph Office ; Assembly Room.

EXCURSIONS : St. Kilda sea-beach (7m.) ; Smithfield (6m.)

DOCTOR : Dr. C. E. Thompson.

HOTELS : The " Governor Macdonnell ;" the " Salisbury ;" the " Railway."

SANDGATE, QUEENSLAND, 13 miles (by rail) N. from Brisbane, a much frequented watering-place, pleasantly situated on the shores of Moreton Bay. Sea-baths ; fishing ; boating ; jetty. Post and Telegraph Office.

EXCURSIONS : Brighton ; Shorncliffe.

DOCTOR : Dr. C. L. Cunningham.

HOTELS : The " Sandgate ;" the " Osborne ;" the " Seaview ;" the " Musgrave ;" and the " Royal " at Brighton.

SANDHURST, VICTORIA, 758 feet above sea-level, 101 miles (by rail) N.W. from Melbourne, an important gold-mining town on Bendigo Creek, in a vine-growing district ; the surrounding country is undulating. Climate beautiful in winter, suitable for invalids suffering from any disease, especially asthmatical cases. The mean temperature in

January is 70° F., in April 59° F., in July 45° F., in October 57° F., and in December 67° F. The mean annual temperature is 58·6° F.; the average annual rainfall is 21·6 inches. Hospital, Post and Telegraph Office ; Mechanics' Institute ; Free Library ; Theatre Royal ; Race-course ; Museum ; Botanic Gardens (3½m.) ; Rosalind Park, facing the main street (Pall Mall), is a favourite place of resort in summer ; Weeroona Lake, an artificial sheet of water, covering 16 acres, surrounded by Pleasure Grounds ; Skating Rink.

EXCURSIONS : The celebrated vineyards of Strathfieldsaye (6m.) ; Eaglehawk (3m.) ; the various gold mines ; Epsom Pottery (4m.)

DOCTORS : Drs. E. Hinchcliffe, P. H. MacGillivray, O. Penfold, Boyd.

HOTELS : The " Shamrock," a very extensive and well-conducted house, affording accommodation for 100 visitors ; the " City Family," a roomy and well-conducted house ; the " Metropolitan," a well-known, first-class house, roomy and comfortable ; the " Freemasons' ; " " Niagara ; " " Albert ; " " Black Swan ; " " Commercial ; " " Victoria ; " " Post Office."

SCHNAPPER POINT, VICTORIA.—*See* MORNINGTON.

SCONE, NEW SOUTH WALES, 680 feet above sea-level, 167 miles N. of Sydney, and 78 miles from the coast, pleasantly situated on the Kingdon Ponds, bears a high character for healthiness. The climate is warm in summer, and agreeable in winter. The average annual rainfall is 21·71 inches, with 51 wet days. The mean maximum temperature in the shade in 1885 was 74·5° F., the mean minimum temperature 52·6° F., and the mean temperature 63·6° F. Grand mountain scenery. Hospital ; Post and Telegraph Office.

EXCURSIONS: Flat Rock, a very romantic and picturesque spot (6m.) ; Mount Wingen, a burning mountain (10m.), much resorted to for asthma.

SPECIAL INDICATIONS : Pulmonary Affections, especially Asthma.

DOCTOR : Dr. F. C. Stevenson.

Hotels : The " Golden Fleece ; " " Belmore ; " " Crown and Anchor ; " " Willow Tree."

Route : By steamer to Newcastle, thence by rail (96m.) ; or by rail direct.

SEMAPHORE (with LARGS BAY), South Australia, 9½ miles (by rail) N.W. from Adelaide, one of the principal watering places on the shores of St. Vincent's Gulf. Sea-bathing; fishing; boating ; jetty, 1,800 feet long, forming a favourite promenade. Post and Telegraph Office ; Literary Institute.

Excursion : Port Glanville Batteries (1m.)

Doctor : Dr. J. S. Mackintosh, residing at Glanville (¾m.)

Hotels : The " Semaphore ; " the " Jetty ; " the " Largs Bay ; " and at Glanville—the " Botanic ; " the " York."

SINGLETON, New South Wales, 136 feet above sea-level, 123 miles N. of Sydney, and 40 miles from the coast, a pretty town on the Hunter River, celebrated for its vine-yards (the Bebeah and Greenwood). The average annual rainfall is 22·46 inches, with 85 wet days. The mean maximum temperature in the shade in 1885 was 75·5° F., the mean minimum temperature 57° F., and the mean temperature 66·3° F. Three reserves—Burdekin Park, Victoria Square, and Redbounberry Park. Hospital ; Post and Telegraph Office ; Mechanics' Institute.

Excursion : Mount Royal.

Doctors : Drs. A. S. Bowman, R. Read.

Hotels : The " Caledonian," " Royal," " Commercial," " Union," " Woolpack," " Agricultural," " Northumberland."

Route : By steamer to Newcastle, thence by rail (49m.) ; or by rail direct.

SOMERVILLE, Victoria, 35 miles S.E. of Melbourne, near Western Port Bay, in a fruit-growing and dairy-farming district, sheltered from hot winds, and noted for its salubrity. Post-office ; Race-course at Baxter's Flat.

Excursions : Mount Eliza (4m.) ; Hastings (7m.)

Route : By rail to Frankston, thence coach (7m.)

G

SORRENTO, Victoria, 40 miles (by steamer) from Melbourne, the most fashionable watering-place on the S.E. coast of Port Phillip, near the Heads.   Climate exhilarating; mean temperature about 60° F.   Sea-bathing ; fishing ; ocean beach.   The Queen's Walk to Jubilee Point, an easy track from the back beach, amphitheatre to the headland immediately under the conspicuous mountain St. Paul.   Post and Telegraph Office ; Mechanics' Institute ; Sanatorium for Consumptives.   ·

SPECIAL INDICATIONS.—Pulmonary Affections, excepting Asthma.

SEASON : From November to April.

DOCTOR : Dr. F. W. Elsner, from Richmond (during the summer months only).

HOTELS : The " Sorrento," " Continental," " Morningston."

SOUTHPORT, Queensland, 46 miles S.E. of Brisbane, a favourite watering-place on the coast, at the mouth of the Nerang River, surrounded by magnificent scenery.   The total rainfall in 1884 was 82 inches, with 79 wet days. Sea-baths ; hot salt-water baths ; beach ; fine jetty, 800 feet long ; fishing ; boating ; shooting.   Post and Telegraph Office ; School of Arts ; Music Hall.

EXCURSIONS : Deepwater Point (Central Southport) ; Labrador (3m.) ;   Sugar Plantations (3m.) ;   Stradbroke Island ; Burleigh Heads (12m.), a pleasant drive along the beach.

SPECIAL INDICATIONS : All Chest Diseases.

SEASON : Throughout the year.

DOCTOR : Dr. J. Howlin.

HOTELS : The " European," the " Pacific," the " Southport," the " Queen's Arms," the " Woodlands," the " Ocean View House ;" the " Labrador," at Labrador ; the " Grand," at Deepwater Point ; and the " Burleigh Heads," at Burleigh Heads.   Also, Eversden's Boarding-house.

ROUTE : By rail to Beenleigh (24m.), thence coach ; or by steamer direct.

SPRINGWOOD, New South Wales, 1,216 feet above sea-level, 42 miles (by rail) W. from Sydney ; a favourite resort, said to be one of the finest places for all kinds of ferns, pleasantly situated on the slopes of the Blue Mountains. The climate is equable, exhilarating, and dry ; fresh and cool in summer, and not too cold in winter. The annual rainfall is 31 inches, with 107 wet days. The mean maximum temperature in 1885 was 68·9° F. ; the mean minimum temperature 51·9° F. ; and the mean temperature 60·4° F. Post and Telegraph Office.

Excursions : "The Valley," (1m.) ; Fitzgerald's Gully ; Flying Fox Gully, with pretty waterfalls ; Clear Water Gully (bathing) ; Madeline Glen, near Station.

Hotels: "The Royal," "Martyn's"; also "Chatsworth," a superior private boarding-house.

STANTHORPE, Queensland, 2,656 feet above sea-level, 207 miles (by rail) S.W. from Brisbane, and 90 miles from the coast, near the southern border, in a mineral district. The climate is dry and very invigorating. The days are warm, but the evenings are always cool. The total rainfall in 1884 was 18 inches, with 62 wet days. The surrounding country is mountainous, and the scenery is grand and beautiful. Hospital ; Post and Telegraph Office.

Special Indications : Phthisis, and all diseases requiring a bracing climate.

Doctor : Dr. A. Orton.

Hotels : The " Melbourne," the " Commercial," " Farley's."

STRATFORD, Victoria, 139 miles E. of Melbourne, situated on the River Avon, in a pastoral and agricultural district, near one of the most lovely stretches of water in Victoria, abounding with perch. The surrounding country is flat for a distance of 12 miles ; the climate is rather variable ; the mean annual temperature is 56·8° F. ; the average annual rainfall is 26·4 inches ; fishing ; shooting ; boating. Post and Telegraph Office ; Mechanic's Institute.

Adjacent to the township is a mineral spring of a saline character. The water is very clear, palatable to taste, and free from odour; reaction, neutral. It is very similar to the cold sulphate and saline waters of Hunyadi-Janos, near Buda Pesth (Hungary), although the amount of minerals is not so large. A tumblerful has exactly the same aperient effect as a wine-glassful of Hunyadi-Janos.

Analysis (in grains per pint) : Potassium Sulphate, 0.016 gr. ; Sodium sulphate, 0·673gr. ; Magnesium Sulphate, 0·641 gr. ; Calcium Sulphate, 0·086gr.; Sodium Chloride, 3·476grs.; Magnesium Chloride, 0·568gr. ; total, 5·460grs of solid matter per pint. Also traces of Alumina, Bromine, Iodine, Free and Albuminoid Ammonia, and Organic Matter. *Bacteriological examination* : In 10 days no result ; absence of germs.

SPECIFIC GRAVITY : 1005.

SPECIAL INDICATIONS : Affections of Digestive Organs and Liver, Gout.

DOCTORS : Dr. J. A. Reid, from Sale (11½m.), Dr. W. H. Brown, from Maffra (5m.)

EXCURSIONS : The Gippsland Lakes ; Ramahyuck, an aboriginal station on the Avon River ; Sale.

HOTELS : The "Stratford," the "Swan," the "Shakespeare."

ROUTE : By rail to Sale, thence coach (11½m.) ; or by steamer to Gippsland Lakes and River Avon, within 3 miles of Stratford.

SUMNER (CANTERBURY), NEW ZEALAND, a favourite watering-place, picturesquely situated 8 miles S.W. of Christchurch. The mean annual temperature is 52·88° F., the mean daily range, 17·10° F., and the average annual amount of rainfall 26 inches. Sea-bathing ; fishing; boating. Post Office ; Deaf and Dumb Institution. Near the village is a cave where a large quantity of Moa remains were found.

HOTELS : "Roper's," "Morton's."

ROUTE : By tram to Heathcote Bridge, thence 'bus.

SUMNER LAKE (CANTERBURY), NEW ZEALAND, 60 miles N.W. from Christchurch. There are some springs of a saline character at the distance of a few miles from the Lake.

The water contains only 2·3grs. of mineral matters per pint, hardly sufficient to entitle it to rank as a mineral water.

Temperature : 93° F.

ROUTE : By rail to Waikari (50m.), thence conveyance.

SUNBURY, VICTORIA, 702 feet above sea-level, 24 miles (by rail) N.W. from Melbourne, on Jackson's Creek, famous for its splendid vineyards and orchards. The country is elevated, interspersed with beautiful flats ; the scenery is very romantic and picturesque. The climate is dry and very healthy. The average annual rainfall is 21 inches ; the mean annual temperature, 55·7° F. Good rabbit and hare shooting ; fly fishing. Post and Telegraph Office.

OBJECTS OF INTEREST : The artificial lake and pleasure grounds of Rupertswood, the country residence of Sir W. J. Clarke.

EXCURSIONS : Mount Holden (or Mount Lyon), and Bald Hill, both covered with flourishing vineyards (1½m.)

SPECIAL INDICATIONS : Consumption, General and Nervous Debility.

SEASON : All the year round.

DOCTOR : Dr. T. Hodgson.

HOTELS : The " Rupertswood," the " Sir John Franklin." Also, Mrs. Thompson's private boarding-house.

SUTTON FOREST, NEW SOUTH WALES, 2,200 feet above sea-level, 89 miles S. of Sydney, and 30 miles from the coast. A favourite summer retreat, prettily situated ; the country is gently undulating. The average annual rainfall is 24·11 inches, with 65 wet days. Contains several villa residences, including the Governor's summer residence. Post and Telegraph Office.

EXCURSIONS : See Moss Vale.

HOTELS : The " Royal," " Commercial."

ROUTE : By rail to Moss Vale, thence conveyance (3m.)

SWANSEA, TASMANIA, 90 miles N.E. of Hobart, a rising watering-place on the shores of Oyster Bay, on the east coast of the Island. The climate is dry, equable and bracing. The total rainfall in 1886 amounted to 31 inches, with 56 wet days.   Beautiful scenery ; sandy beaches, 9 miles long ; sea and fresh-water baths ; fishing (both sea and river); shooting (black swan, duck, kangaroo, &c.) ; boating.   Post and Telegraph Office ; Public Library.

SPECIAL INDICATIONS : For Convalescents, Liver Complaints, General Debility, Bronchitis.

SEASON : From September to April.

DOCTOR : Dr. A. G. E. Naylor.

HOTEL : The " Pier," (C. E. Hurry, proprietor.)

ROUTE : From Hobart by coach via Richmond, or by steamer direct ; from Launceston by rail to Avoca, thence coach.

TANUNDA, SOUTH AUSTRALIA, 42 miles N.E. of Adelaide, and 34 miles from the coast, situated on the North Para River, at the foot of the Barossa Ranges, in a vine-growing district.   The surrounding country is mountainous, with large undulating plains.   The mean annual amount of rainfall is nearly 22 inches.   Post and Telegraph Office ; Institute.

EXCURSION : The " Käiserstuhl " (a mountain) 3m.

DOCTOR : Dr. C. A. Altmann.

HOTELS : The " Tanunda ;" the " Victoria."

ROUTE : By rail to Gawler, thence coach (17m.)

TAPUAEHARURU, NEW ZEALAND.—*See* TAUPO.

TARAWERA (HAWKE'S BAY), NEW ZEALAND, 50 miles N.W. of Napier, and 50 miles S.E. of Taupo, a small township in the narrow valley of the River Waipunga.   The district is very rough and broken, with grand mountain and forest scenery.   Post and Telegraph Office.   Here is situated the Tarawera Spring ; the waters of this spring are of a saline character, and very similar to the cold sulphurous soda waters of Labassère (Dep. Hautes Pyrénées), France.

Analysis (in grains per gallon) : Chlorine, with Bromine traces, 40·497grs.; Iodine, ·714gr.; Sulphuric Acid, 2·150grs.; Silica, 2·221grs. ; Carbonic Acid, traces ; Alumina, ·621gr. ; Iron, 1·049 gr.; Lime, 2·036grs.; Magnesia, ·492gr.; Potash,

3·681grs. ; Soda, 46·495grs. ; Lithia, traces ; total, 99·956grs. in one gallon, or 12·5 solid grains of mineral matters per pint.

Temperature : 130° F.

SPECIAL INDICATIONS : Pulmonary, Laryngeal and Bronchial affections.

EXCURSION : Tatarakina Mountain (2m.)

HOTEL : Brown's Accommodation House.

ROUTE : By coach from Taupo or Napier.

TAUPO (OR TAPUAEHARURU), NEW ZEALAND, 1,500 feet above sea-level, 224 miles S E. of Auckland, and 100 miles N.W. of Napier, on the right bank of the Waikato, at the north-east end of Lake Taupo, the centre of the hot springs of the Taupo district. Post and Telegraph Office ; Large wooden hall fitted up with a stage. The following waters are all from the neighbourhood of Taupo Lake, and are characterised by having iodine present as a usual constituent, an important element which is wanting in almost all the other hot springs of New Zealand. In general character they are saline and faintly acid, and are suitable for internal and external use, as alteratives in scorbutic and tubercular diseases, also in chronic nervous affections and cutaneous eruptions. There are a great number of springs in this district, all remarkable for their mineral and other properties. The principal ones are:—

(1.) THE TARAWERA SPRING.—*See* TARAWERA.

(2.) THE PARKES' SPRING, a cold, carbonated and slightly effervescent alkaline spring, having a composition similar to the Alkali-Muriatic, Iodide, and Bromine' waters of Luhatschowitz, in Moravia.

Analysis (in grains per gallon).—Chlorine, with Bromine traces, 56·076grs. ; Iodine, 1·012gr. ; Sulphuric Acid, 2·156grs.; Silica, 16·752grs. ; Carbonic Acid (in a combined form), 35·751grs., besides a quantity of this acid in a free state ; Lime, 1·994gr. ; Magnesia, ·613gr. ; Potash, 5·675grs. ; Soda, 80·710grs. ; Lithia, traces. Total : 200·789grs. in one gallon, or 25·1 solid grains of mineral matters per pint.

Temperature : 60° F.

SPECIAL INDICATIONS : Chronic Mucous Inflammations of the Respiratory, Digestive, and Urinary Organs; Hæmorrhoids, Congested Liver.

(3.)   CROW'S NEST SPRING, at Ruahine, the waters of which are of a saline character.

Analysis (in grains per gallon).—Salts, soluble in water, principally Alkaline Chlorides, 127·62grs. ; Salts, soluble in acid, principally Sulphate of Lime, 9·62grs.; Silica, 0·25grs.; total salts, 143·49grs.   Loss by ignition, 4·61grs. ; reaction, alkaline ; mineral matters per pint, 19·2grs.

Temperature : 170° F., being the same as that of Carlsbad Sprudel.

(4.)   RUAHINE SPRING : Saline waters, with faintly acid reaction.

Analysis (in grains per gallon).—Salts, soluble in water, 138·07grs.; Salts, soluble in acid, 4·21grs.; Silica, 10·03grs. ; total salts, 152·31grs. ; loss by ignition 3·09grs. ; mineral matters per pint, 19·1grs.

Temperature.—190° F.

(5)   ORAKEIKORAKO SPRING.—*See* ORAKEIKORAKO.

(6.)   ALUM CAVE SPRING.—*See* ORAKEIKORAKO.

(7.)   McMURRAY'S BATH, the waters of which are of a sulphurous character.

Analysis (in grains per gallon).—Salts, soluble in water, 8·13grs. ; Salts, soluble in acids, 9·24grs. ; Silica, 15·75grs. ; total salts, 33·12grs.; loss by ignition, 1·52gr. ; reaction, slightly acid ; mineral matters per pint, 4·2grs.

Temperature.—126° F.

(8.)   WAIPAKAHI SPRING, the waters of which have a sulphurous character.

Analysis.—Salts, soluble in water, 6·16grs ; Salts, soluble in acids, 3·08grs. ; Silica, 12·33grs. ; total salts, 21·57grs. in one gallon ; loss by ignition, 4·65grs. ; reaction, slightly acid ; mineral matters per pint, 2·8grs.

Temperature.—From 98° F. to 120° F.

(9.) TE HUKAHUKA SPRING (Wairakei Geysers), the waters of which are of a sulphurous character.

Analysis.—Salts, soluble in water, 3·09grs.; Salts, soluble in acids, 4·62grs. ; Silica, 6·10grs. ; total salts, 13·81grs. in one gallon ; loss by ignition, 3·08grs. ; reaction, slightly acid ; mineral matters per pint, 1·8gr.

Temperature.—116° F.

(10.) OTUMUHIKA [a] SPRING ; the waters of this spring are of a sulphurous nature.

Analysis.—Salts, soluble in water, 5·28grs.; Salts, soluble in acids, ·74gr. ; Silica, 7·86 grs. ; total salts, 13·88grs. in one gallon, or 1·5 gr. of mineral matters per pint ; loss by ignition, 3·47grs. per gallon ; reaction, faintly acid.

Temperature.—From 100° F. to 150° F.

(11.) OTUMUHIKA [b] SPRING, the waters of which are of a sulphurous character.

Analysis.—Salts, soluble in water, 13·88grs. ; Salts, soluble in acids, 4·31grs. ; Silica, 9·25grs. ; total salts, 27·44 grains in one gallon ; loss by ignition, 3·08grs. ; reaction, faintly acid ; mineral matters per pint, 3·4grs.

Temperature : 150° F.

(12.) OTUMUHIKA [c] SPRING, the waters of which have a sulphurous character.

Analysis.—Salts, soluble in water, 3·85grs.; Salts, soluble in acids, 1·69gr. ; Silica, 2·94grs. ; total salts, 8·48grs. in one gallon ; loss by ignition, 1·54gr. ; reaction, faintly acid ; mineral matters per pint, 1·2gr.

Temperature.—78° F.

(13.) OTUMUHIKA [d] SPRING (Acacia), contains 3·9grs. of mineral matters per pint ; reaction, feebly alkaline.

Temperature.—136° F.

(14.) ROTOKAWA, OR BLACK WATER SPRING, contains 17·8grs. of mineral matters per pint ; reaction, acidic.

Temperature.—192° F.

(15.) ROTOKAWA, OR YELLOW WATER SPRING, contains 22grs. of mineral matters per pint ; reaction, acidic.

Temperature.—152° F.

(16.) PIROIRORI, OR WHITE WATER, at Wairakei, contains 1·8gr. of mineral matters per pint ; reaction, alkaline.

Temperature.—112° F.

(17.) MCPHERSON'S SPRING, at Lofley's Gully, contains 1·9gr. of mineral matters per pint ; reaction, feebly alkaline.

Temperature.—96° F.

(18.) THE COLD STREAM, at Lofley's Gully, contains 1·3gr. of mineral matters per pint ; reaction, feebly alkaline.

Temperature.—76° F,

(19.) THE WARM STREAM, at Lofley's Gully, contains 2·8grs of mineral matters per pint ; reaction, feebly alkaline.

Temperature.—114° F.

(20.) KOKOWAI SPRING, at Lofley's Gully, is a feebly saline water, and contains 2grs. of mineral matters per pint.

Temperature.—104° F.

(21.) A. C. BATH, No. 1, at Waipahihi, is a water of a chlorinated saline character, and contains 4·7grs. of mineral matters per pint.

Temperature.—110° F,

(22.) A. C. BATH, No. 2, at Waipahihi, is of a saline character and contains 5·7grs. of mineral matters per pint.

Temperature : 146° F.

. (23.) TEA-TREE SPRING, at Waipahihi, an alkaline silicious water, containing much Silicic Acid, but changing rapidly on exposure to the atmosphere, and becoming alkaline.   Mineral matters per pint, 13·4grs.

Temperature : 170° F.

(24.) WAIPAHIHI STREAM, a saline water, containing 8·6 grs. of mineral matters per pint.

Temperature : 98° F.

EXCURSIONS : Mount Tauhara, an isolated wood-covered mountain, 3,000 feet high (4m.); Maori settlement on left bank of Waikato river ; Glen Lofley and Lofley's Baths (1½m.); the celebrated Crow's Nest Geyser, a raised funnel of silica, 10 feet high, presenting the appearance of a bird's nest (1m.) ; near the Crow's Nest is " The Witches' Cauldron," a large boiling spring, covered with a dense cloud of steam ; the " Big Ben," one of the most remarkable boiling red clay springs in the district ; the Huka Falls and Wairakei Geysers (6m.); the famous " Steam Hammer ;" the Tuhuatahi and Terekereke Geysers ; Karapiti, the famous fumarole ; Rotokawa (Bitter Lake), with extensive sulphur deposits, 8 miles N.E., swarming with water fowls ; Lake Taupo, or Moana, 1,250 feet above sea-level, measures 24 miles by 18 miles ; Tokano, a settlement at the southern end of the lake ; Tongariro (6,500 ft.), a volcano, 12 miles S. of the lake ; Ruapehu (9,000 ft.), 16 miles further south.

HOTELS : The " Lake," being the most frequented ; the " Taupo ;" the " Geyser," at Wairakei ; " Lofley's," at Glen Lofley. There is also a hotel at Tokano.

ROUTE : By coach from Napier ; or from Auckland by rail to Oxford, thence coach via Ohinemutu.

TE AROHA (PROV. AUCKLAND), NEW ZEALAND, 350 feet above sea-level, 126 miles by rail (special railway carriages are provided for invalids) S.E. from Auckland, and 36 miles by steamer or coach from Thames, a gold-mining township on the Thames river, at the base of Mt. Te Aroha. The climate is equable, dry, and salubrious. The scenery is exceedingly interesting. Post and Telegraph Office ; Public Library and Reading-room; Domain (40 acres), with Pleasure Grounds and Tennis Courts. There are a number of springs situated in the centre of the township, 18 in all, of which 15 are hot or tepid, also seven bath-houses, all of which are most comfortably fitted up, and leave nothing to be desired as regards privacy or cleanliness ; also a large building containing private single baths, and a summer house with fountain, providing the mineral water for internal use. These baths are open from 6 a.m. to 10 p m. The waters, which are used both externally and internally, are, with the exception of the sulphur spring (No. 16), saline and feebly alkaline, and strongly charged with carbonic acid gas, which is constantly escaping from the springs in large quantities, rendering them effervescent and pleasant. These springs are very similar to those of Vichy (France), Ems (Germany), and Bilin (near Teplitz, Bohemia), and are stated to possess curative properties of a most extraordinary character.

BATH No. 1 (9ft. 10in. x 7ft.) is very much used, and is set apart for females ; the water is clear and colourless.

Analysis (in grains per gallon) : Bicarbonate of Soda, 461·56grs. ; Chloride of Sodium, 60·25grs ; Chloride of Potassium, 1·72gr. ; Sulphate of Soda, 38·32grs. ; Carbonate of Lime, 10·77grs. ; Carbonate of Magnesia, 6·86grs. ; Silica, 7·56grs. ; Alumina and Iron Oxide, traces,—or a total of 586·99grs. of mineral matters in one gallon.

Temperature : 102° F.

BATH No. 2 (9ft. 7in. x 3ft. 5in.) is famous for relieving persons suffering from rheumatism ; a large building with waiting and dressing rooms attached.

Analysis (in grains per gallon) : Bicarbonate of Soda, 426·29grs. ; Chloride of Sodium, 60·45grs. ; Chloride of Potassium, 1·90gr. ; Sulphate of Soda, 32·67grs. ; Carbonate of Lime, 7·12grs. ; Carbonate of Magnesia, 4·21grs. ; Silica, 7·12grs. ; Alumina and Iron Oxide, traces,—or a total of 539·76grs. of mineral matters in one gallon.

Temperature : 112° F.

BATH No. 3 (14ft. x 10ft.) is a reservoir of hot, clear, and colourless water, which supplies eight private single baths in a building 200ft distant from it ; this reservoir contains altogether about 15,000 gallons of water.

Analysis (in grains per gallon) : Bicarbonate of Soda, 429·19grs. ; Chloride of Sodium, 60·51grs. ; Sulphate of Soda, 32·82grs. ; Carbonate of Lime, 7·24grs. ; Carbonate of Magnesia, 4·20grs. ; Silica, 7·21grs. ; Alumina, Iron Oxide, and Potassium, traces,—or a total of 541·17grs. of mineral matters in one gallon.

Temperature : From 90° F. to 112° F.

BATH No. 4 (11ft. x 9ft.) is largely used, and has a building erected over the spring; the water is of a pale yellow colour.

Analysis (in grains per gallon) : Bicarbonate of Soda, 246·49grs.; Chloride of Sodium, 34·24grs.; Sulphate of Soda, 19·16grs. ; Carbonate of Lime, 4·62grs. ; Carbonate of Magnesia, 2·14grs.; Silica, 5·17grs.; also traces of Alumina, Iron Oxide, and Potassium; or a total of 311·82grs. of mineral matters in one gallon.

Temperature : 92° F.

BATH No. 5 (6ft. 7in. x 5ft. 8in) is largely used, and has a building erected over the spring, the water of which is clear and colourless.

Analysis (in grains per gallon) : Bicarbonate of Soda, 476·58grs. ; Chloride of Sodium, 68·77grs. ; Sulphate of Soda, 36·92grs. ; Carbonate of Lime, 6·91grs. ; Carbonate of Magnesia, 3·15grs. ; Silica, 6·10grs. ; also traces of Alumina, Iron Oxide, and Potassium ;—total, 598·43grs. of mineral matters in one gallon.

Temperature : 100° F.

BATH No. 6 (4ft. x 9ft.) is largely used, and has a good building erected over the spring, the water of which is clear and colourless.

Analysis (in grains per gallon) : Bicarbonate of Soda, 499·75grs. ; Chloride of Sodium, 66·23grs. ; Sulphate of Soda, 35·14grs ; Carbonate of Lime, 7·12grs. ; Carbonate of Magnesia, 2·99grs.; Silica, 7·14grs.; also traces of Alumina, Iron Oxide, and Potassium ;—total, 618·37grs. of mineral matters in one gallon.

Temperature : 104° F.

BATH No. 7 (7ft. 6in. x 5ft.) is tepid and not much used, although built over.

Analysis (in grains per gallon) : Bicarbonate of Soda, 444·20grs. ; Chloride of Sodium, 67·13grs. ; Sulphate of Soda, 34·04grs.; Carbonate of Lime, 7·46grs. ; Carbonate of Magnesia, 4·34grs. ; Silica, 7·01grs.; also traces of Alumina,

Iron Oxide, and Potassium ;—total, 564·18grs. of mineral matters in one gallon.

Temperature : 86° F.

. SPRING No. 8 is known as the drinking fountain, the water, which is clear and colourless, is freely used by all those suffering from dyspepsia, etc., and affords great relief to many. The fountain is built over the spring, so that the water may be drawn from a tap.

Analysis (in grains per gallon) : Bicarbonate of Soda, 451·97grs. ; Chloride of Sodium, 66·14grs. ; Chloride of Potassium, 1·96grs. ; Sulphate of Soda, 32·91grs. ; Carbonate of Lime, 7·47grs. ; Carbonate of Magnesia, 4·21grs. ; Silica, 8·60grs. ; also traces of Alumina, and Iron Oxide ;— total, 573·26grs. of mineral matters in one gallon.

Temperature : 109° F.

SPRING No. 9.

Analysis (in grains per gallon) : Bicarbonate of Soda, 301·17grs. ; Chloride of Sodium, 41·29grs. ; Sulphate of Soda, 22·16grs. ; Carbonate of Lime, 4·94grs. ; Carbonate of Magnesia, 2·61grs. ; Silica, 6·44grs. ; also traces of Alumina, and Iron Oxide ;—total, 378·61grs. of mineral matters in one gallon.

Temperature : 112° F.

SPRING No. 10.

Analysis (in grains per gallon) : Bicarbonate of Soda, 276·19grs. ; Chloride of Sodium, 35·24grs. ; Sulphate of Soda, 19·19grs. ; Carbonate of Lime, 4·67grs. ; Carbonate of Magnesia, 2·31grs. ; Silica, 6grs. ; also traces of Alumina and Iron Oxide ;—total, 343·60grs. of mineral matters in one gallon.

Temperature : 96° F.

SPRING No. 11.

Analysis (in grains per gallon) : Bicarbonate of Soda, 261·44grs. ; Chloride of Sodium, 34·69grs. ; Sulphate of Soda, 20·12grs. ; Carbonate of Lime, 5·11grs. ; Carbonate of Magnesia, 2·56grs. ; Silica, 6·11grs. ; also traces of

Alumina and Iron Oxide ;—total, 330·03grs. of mineral matters in one gallon.

Temperature : 88° F.

SPRING No. 12.

Analysis (in grains per gallon): Bicarbonate of Soda, 300·97grs.; Chloride of Sodium, 41·66grs.; Sulphate of Soda, 22·96grs. ; Carbonate of Lime, 5·12grs. ; Carbonate of Magnesia, 2·99grs.; Silica, 7·11grs.; also traces of Alumina and Iron Oxide ;—total, 380·81grs. of mineral matters in one gallon.

Temperature : 88° F.

SPRING No. 13, the water of which has a pale yellow colour, is run into No. 5 Bath.

Analysis (in grains per gallon): Bicarbonate of Soda, 301·64grs. ; Chloride of Sodium, 40·67grs. ; Sulphate of Soda, 21·86grs. ; Carbonate of Lime, 6·11grs. ; Carbonate of Magnesia, 3·13grs. ; Silica, 6·86grs. ; also traces of Alumina and Iron Oxide ;—total, 380·27grs. of mineral matters in one gallon.

Temperature : 120° F.

SPRING No. 14, the water of which has a pale yellow colour, is run into the reservoir (No. 3).

Analysis (in grains per gallon): Bicarbonate of Soda, 321·64grs.; Chloride of Sodium, 42·61grs. ; Sulphate of Soda, 23·16grs. ; Carbonate of Lime, 7·14grs.; Carbonate of Magnesia, 3·49grs. ; Silica, 6·66grs. ; also traces of Alumina and Iron Oxide ;—total, 404·70grs. of mineral matters in one gallou.

Temperature : 122° F.

SPRING No. 15, the water of which is clear and colourless, and largely used for drinking.

Analysis (in grains per gallon): Bicarbonate of Soda, 331·76grs. ; Chloride of Sodium, 43·11grs. ; Sulphate of Soda, 22·16grs. ; Carbonate of Lime, 6·91grs. ; Carbonate of Magnesia, 3·61grs. ; Silica, 7·05grs.; also traces of Alumina and Iron Oxide ;—total, 414·60grs. of mineral matters in one gallon.

Temperature : 139° F.

SPRING No. 16, known as the "Sulphur Spring," is a cold spring of an acidic and hepatic character; sulphur is found in small quantities in the surrounding clay, and strong sulphuretted hydrogen gas is emitted.

Analysis (in grains per gallon) : Sulphate of Soda, 1·82gr. ; Sulphate of Lime, 0·61gr. ; Sulphate of Magnesia, 0·36gr. ; Sulphate of Alumina and Iron Oxides, 0·20gr. ; Silica, 7·04grs. ; Hydrochloric Acid, free, 1·11gr. ; Sulphuric Acid, 0·21gr. ;—total, 11·35grs. of mineral matters in one gallon.

SPRING No. 17 is a cold spring ; the water, which is used for bathing the eyes, is rather turbid, owing to the presence of precipitated sulphur.

Analysis (in grains per gallon) : Bicarbonate of Soda, 9·36grs. ; Chloride of Sodium, 2·71grs. ; Sulphate of Soda, 3·92grs. ; Carbonate of Lime, 0·64gr. ; Carbonate of Magnesia, 0·27gr. ; Silica, 4·21grs. ; — total, 21·11grs. of mineral matters in one gallon. Also 1·4gr. of Sulphuretted Hydrogen.

SPRING No. 18, is a cold soda water spring, clear and colourless.

Analysis (in grains per gallon) : Bicarbonate of Soda, 181·72grs. ; Chloride of Sodium, 16·12grs. ; Sulphate of Soda, 8·16grs. ; Carbonate of Lime, 1·97gr. ; Carbonate of Magnesia, 1·01gr. ; Silica, 13·14grs ; also traces of Alumina and Iron Oxide ;—total, 172·12grs. of mineral matters in one gallon.

(*Note.*—Lithia has been found wherever it has been tested for, but only as traces.)

SPECIAL INDICATIONS : Efficacious in Gouty and Rheumatic Affections, Chronic Dyspepsia, Disorders of the Urinary Organs, Cutaneous Diseases, Splenic and Hepatic Disorders, Diseases due to excess of acidity, Neuralgia, Sciatica.

SEASON : Throughout the year.

DOCTOR : Dr. A. F. Wright.

EXCURSIONS : Te Aroha Mountain, 3,200 feet high, commanding magnificent views ; Matamata ; Waitoa ; Shaftesbury ; also some very fine waterfalls.

HOTELS : The " Club ;" the " Palace ;" the " Hot Springs ;" also the " Waverley " boarding-house.

(A Company has been formed to establish a first-class Sanatorium at Te Aroha, immediately adjoining the Hot Springs Domain, which is expected to be completed in January, 1888 ; it will be replete with every comfort and convenience for invalids, and capable of accommodating from 15 to 20 visitors.)

TENNINGERING, QUEENSLAND.—*See* MOUNT PERRY.

TENTERFIELD, NEW SOUTH WALES, 2,827 feet above sea-level, 475 miles N. of Sydney, and 80 miles from the coast, beautifully situated on a plain, at the head of the river Dumaresq, surrounded by lofty hills. The scenery is magnificent, and the climate extremely salubrious. The average annual rainfall is 30·72 inches, with 72 wet days. The mean maximum temperature in the shade in 1885 was 75·3° F., the mean minimum temperature 46·4° F., and the mean temperature 60·9° F. Hospital ; Post and Telegraph Office ; School of Arts.

DOCTORS : Drs. T. H. Tennant, J. M. Warren.

HOTELS : The " Commercial;" " Royal;" " Court House;" " Great Northern;" " Criterion;" " Telegraph."

ROUTE : By steamer to Newcastle, thence rail (381m.) ; or by rail direct.

TIMARU (CANTERBURY), NEW ZEALAND, 100 miles (by rail) S.W. from Christchurch, and 130 miles (by rail) N. from Dunedin, an important and flourishing town, at the S.W. end of the Ninety Mile Beach, the shipping port of an extensive agricultural district. Hospital ; Post and Telegraph Office ; Mechanics' Institute ; Theatre Royal.

EXCURSION : Mt. Cook, with Alpine scenery and climate (by rail to Fairlie Creek, thence by conveyance via Lakes Tekapo, Pukaki, and Ohau).

HOTELS : The " Royal;" the " Club;" the " Clarendon;" the " Criterion;" the " Grosvenor;" the " Queen's;" the " Timaru;" the " Commercial."

DOCTORS : Drs. H. V. Drew, J. Ewart, R. B. Hogg.

H

TOOWOOMBA, QUEENSLAND, 1,921 feet above sea-level, 100 miles (by rail) W. from Brisbane, and 80 miles from the coast, the most important town on the western slope of the main range on the Darling Downs, the so-called "Garden of Queensland." The climate is very fine, cool and bracing; cool nights in summer; the winter is rather cold; the mean maximum temperature in summer is about 82° F. The total rainfall in 1884 was 29 inches, with 95 wet days. Vines and oranges are extensively grown. Hospital, Post and Telegraph Office, School of Arts, Theatre, Botanical Gardens.

SPECIAL INDICATIONS : General Debility, Convalescence from Fever and Ague.

SEASON : From October to April.

DOCTORS : Drs. S. Flood, E. Sheaf.

HOTELS : The "Royal;" the "White Horse;" the "Club;" the "Imperial;" the "Commercial;" the "Metropolitan;" "Hennessy's;" the "Queen's;" also Daneney's boarding-house.

TORQUAY, TASMANIA.—See FORMBY.

ULLADULLA, NEW SOUTH WALES, 159 miles (by steamer). S. from Sydney, a small watering-place on the coast, in a dairy-farming and vine-growing district. The country is undulating, and the scenery is varied and picturesque. The climate is warm and equable, and the heat in summer is tempered by sea-breezes; the temperature is fairly moist. The average annual rainfall is nearly 45 inches, with 112 wet days; the mean temperature is about 65° F., and frosts are almost unknown. Sea-bathing, boating, fishing, shooting. Post and Telegraph Office; School of Arts.

EXCURSIONS : Lake Burrill, Lake Conjola, Milton.

SPECIAL INDICATIONS : Pulmonary Affections.

SEASON : September to April.

DOCTOR : Dr. A. S. Ogg, at Milton (4m.)

HOTEL : The "Harbour View;" also Hughes' boarding-house.

ULVERSTONE, TASMANIA, 84 miles N.W. of Launceston, a rising sea-side resort at the mouth of the River Leven, on the north coast of the island, in a timber-growing district. The scenery is extremely picturesque, and the climate cannot be surpassed as regards salubrity, but it is not suitable for pulmonary affections. Sea-bathing; splendid sea and fresh water fishing (black-fish, herring, lobster, &c.); fair shooting; boating. Post and Telegraph Office; Public Library.

DOCTOR : Dr. J. McCall, proprietor of a very nice sanatorium with limited accommodation.

HOTELS : " Webb's ;" " Clark's."

ROUTE : By steamer direct ; or by rail from Launceston to Formby (82m.), thence coach (12m.)

VICTOR HARBOUR (OR PORT VICTOR), SOUTH AUSTRALIA, 81 miles (by rail) S. from Adelaide. a favourite seaside resort, pleasantly situated on the shores of Victor Harbour, a small bight of Encounter Bay. The surrounding country is somewhat mountainous. Jetty (three-quarters of a mile in length) across to Granite Island ; Breakwater, 1,000 feet in length. Sea-bathing ; fishing ; boating. Post and Telegraph Office.

DOCTOR : Dr. M. P. O'Leary.

HOTELS : The " Austral," the " Crown," the " Victor Harbour."

VICTORIA, TASMANIA, 20 feet above sea-level, 24 miles (by coach) S.W. from Hobart, pleasantly situated on the banks of the Huon river, surrounded by hills, in a hop and fruit-growing district ; the climate in summer is mild, balmy, and salubrious ; the scenery is exceedingly pretty. Post and Telegraph Office.

EXCURSIONS :—*See* FRANKLIN.

HOTEL : The " Picnic."

WAIKOUAITI, OR HAWKSBURY (PROV. OTAGO), NEW ZEALAND, 32 miles (by rail) N. from Dunedin, a much frequented watering-place on the east coast of the

South Island. Splendid sea-beach ; sea-bathing. Post and Telegraph Office ; Athenæum ; Oddfellows' Hall.

EXCURSION : Goodwood.

HOTELS : The " Golden Fleece," the " Railway Station."

WAIRAKEI (PROV. AUCKLAND), NEW ZEALAND.—*See* TAUPO.

WAIUKU (PROV. AUCKLAND), NEW ZEALAND, 40 miles S.E. of Auckland, on the southern shores of Manukau Harbour, in a dairy-farming and fruit-growing district. The climate is mild and salubrious, and the scenery charming. Post and Telegraph Office ; Public Hall.

HOTEL : " Sedgwick's."

ROUTE : From Auckland by rail to Onehunga (8m.), thence steamboat.

WAIWERA, NEW ZEALAND, 24 miles N. of Auckland, a much frequented watering-place with thermal springs, prettily situated on the western shore of Hauraki Gulf. The climate is warm, equable and dry. The surrounding scenery is magnificent. Sea-bathing ; fishing (mullet) ; shooting (pheasants); boating ; beach. Post and Telegraph Office.

The thermal springs here situated are of a weakly alkaline and saline character, and are extensively used as baths in rheumatic and dyspeptic complaints; used internally they have also a mild antilithic action. This water is bottled by A. Rayner, of Blenheim ; Thomson Bros., Dunedin ; and Milson & Co., Lyttelton.

Analysis (in grains per gallon) : Chloride of Sodium, 116·715grs. ; Chloride of Potassium, ·091gr. ; Chloride of Lithium, traces ; Iodide of Magnesium, traces ; Sulphate of Soda, ·383gr. ; Bicarbonate of Soda, 87·513grs. ; Bicarbonate of Lime, 10·692grs. ; Bicarbonate of Magnesia, ·954gr.; Bicarbonate of Iron, ·683gr. ; Alumina, traces ; Silica, 2·464grs. ; total, 219·495 grains in one gallon, or 17·7 solid grains of mineral matters per pint.

Temperature: 110° F.

SPECIAL INDICATIONS : Rheumatism, Gout, Dyspepsia, Spinal Diseases, Skin Diseases, Disorders of Kidney and Bladder.

SEASON : October to March.

DOCTOR : Dr. J. Campbell, from Warkworth (16m.)

EXCURSIONS : Caves (1m. S.) ; Puhoi, a German settlement and native village ; Mahurangi River and Harbour ; Island of Kawau (11m.), the property of Sir George Grey ; Matakana, a Maori stronghold.

HOTEL : " Graham's Waiwera," an excellent hotel, with spacious baths, affording most comfortable accommodation for invalids and visitors.

ROUTE : By steamer direct from Auckland ; or by ferryboat from Auckland to North Shore, thence coach.

WALCHA, NEW SOUTH WALES, 3,386 feet above sealevel, 309 miles N. of Sydney, and 85 miles from the coast, beautifully situated on the River Apsley, has a salubrious and bracing climate, combined with splendid scenery. The average annual rainfall is 26·37 inches, with 108 wet days. The mean maximum temperature in the shade in 1885 was 68·9° F., the mean minimum temperature 44·4° F., and the mean temperature 56·7° F. Post and Telegraph Office ; School of Arts.

EXCURSIONS : " Crawford's Nob ;" Apsley Waterfalls (700 feet deep).

DOCTORS : Drs. G. A. Boodle, C. U. D. Schrader.

HOTELS : The " Commercial ;" " Walcha ;" " Royal ;" " New England ;" " Apsley."

ROUTE : By steamer to Newcastle, thence rail to Walcha Road (222m.) ; or by rail direct to Walcha Road, thence coach (12m.).

WARBURTON, VICTORIA, 2,200 feet above sea-level, 44 miles E. of Melbourne. The scenery of the district, particularly of the neighbouring fern-tree gullies, is amongst the finest in Victoria. Climate mild and very salubrious, although rather moist in winter ; the average annual rainfall is 56·7 inches.   Fishing in the Yarra River ; shooting (deer, hares, wallaby, lyre-birds, wonga).   Post Office.

SPECIAL INDICATIONS : Chest complaints.

HOTEL : The " Warburton."

ROUTE : By rail to Lilydale (23m.), thence coach daily (2s.)

WARRNAMBOOL, VICTORIA, 170 miles S.W. of Melbourne, pleasantly situated on the shores of Lady Bay, the most important seaport of the colony next to Port Phillip ; noted for its salubrity, and frequently styled the " Ultima Thule of health "; climate mild and dry ; the average annual rainfall is 27·1 inches.   Sea-baths ; hot salt-water baths, said to be very effective in cases of rheumatism, sciatica, and nervous affections generally.   Shelly Beach ; Botanical Gardens ; Albert Park ; Victoria Park.; Friendly Societies' Park ; Hospital ; Mechanic's Institute ; Post and Telegraph Office ; Race-course.

EXCURSIONS : Hopkins' River (splendid fishing) ; Tower Hill, an extinct volcano, entirely surrounded by the Tower Lake (11m.) ; Bay of Islands, a marine picture of wild and fantastic beauty (26m.) ; Hopkins' Falls ; Emu Creek Falls; Aboriginal Station at Framlingham (18m.)

DOCTORS : Drs. T. F. Fleetwood, R. H. Harrington, H. L. Miller.

HOTELS : The " Commercial;" the " Western;" the " Victoria ;" the " Royal ;" the " Rising Sun ;" the " Caledonia ;" the " Princess Alexandra ;" the " Royal Exchange."

ROUTE : By steamer direct ; or by rail to Camperdown, thence coach.

WARWICK, QUEENSLAND, 1,497 feet above sea-level, 166 miles (by rail) S.W. from Brisbane, and 90 miles from the coast, on the River Condamine, near the southern border, one of the prettiest and healthiest inland towns of the colony. The climate is temperate and bracing, and unsurpassed for salubrity.   The average annual rainfall is 32 inches, with 70 wet days.   Vine and fruits are extensively grown.   Hospital ; Post and Telegraph Office ; School of Arts.

DOCTOR : Dr. W. J. Tilley.

HOTELS : The " Commercial ;" the " Cosmopolitan ;" the " Criterion ;" the " Royal ;" the " Australian ;" the " Bavarian ;" the " Queen's ;" the " Victoria ;" the " Rose ;" the " European."

WATSON'S BAY, NEW SOUTH WALES, 7 miles (by steamer) from Sydney, a favourite watering-place on South Head, at the entrance to Port Jackson, with high rocks in the background, affording splendid views all round. The mean maximum temperature in the shade during the hottest month is 82·5° F., and the mean minimum temperature during the coldest month 46·6° F., the mean annual temperature is 61·7° F., and the mean daily range 16·5° F. ; the average annual amount of rainfall is 48·286 inches, with 133 rainy days in the year. Sandy beach ; sea-bathing ; fishing ; boating. Post and Telegraph Office.

OBJECTS OF INTEREST : Fortifications ; the " Gap," where the " Dunbar " stranded ; two lighthouses.

DOCTOR : Dr. J. C. Sibley.

HOTELS : The " Pier ;" the " Gap ;" the " Signal."

WEDDERBURN, VICTORIA, 573 feet above sea-level, 150 miles by rail (to Wedderburn Road station) N.W. from Melbourne, the centre of a mining and farming district, situated on the Torpichen creek. The surrounding country is undulating, and covered with mallee and flowering shrubs. The climate is warm, equable, and very dry. The average annual rainfall is 20·6 inches. There are some vineyards in the district. Good shooting. Post and Telegraph Office ; Literary Institute.

SPECIAL INDICATIONS : Pulmonary Affections, principally Phthisis.

SEASON.— From April to October.

DOCTOR : Dr. P. Macvean.

HOTELS : The " Royal ;" the " Wedderburn ;" Mandeville's boarding-house.

WELLINGTON, NEW SOUTH WALES, 995 feet above sea-level, 248 miles (by rail) N.W. from Sydney, and 165 miles from the coast, very prettily situated on the banks of the

Macquarie river, at the foot of some high, heavily timbered hills ; well sheltered by ranges of mountains from the hot, dry winds in summer, and from the bleak winds in winter. The district is rich in mineral, pastoral, and agricultural resources ; the vine is largely cultivated. The scenery is exceedingly pretty, and the climate is dry, warm, and equable. The summer (from November to February) is hot, but the atmosphere is always particularly dry and clear ; during the remainder of the year the climate is exceedingly pleasant and exhilarating. The mean temperature in summer is 80° F., and in winter 60° F. ; the mean annual rainfall is 23 inches, with 49 wet days. The drinking water contains a large percentage of lime salts. Excellent fishing (bream, cat-fish, huge cod weighing up to 80lbs.) ; good shooting (hares, wallaby, kangaroo, quail, bronze-winged pigeon, wild turkey) ; boating. Hospital ; Post and Telegraph Office.

EXCURSIONS : The Wellington Caves (4m.), famed for their beauty, and interesting on account of the deposit of fossil bones found in them, especially of the extinct marsupial lion ; the " Meeting of the Waters " of the Macquarie and Bell rivers, near the town ; Mount Arthur, from which a splendid view of the river is obtained ; the beautiful drive up the valley of the Macquarie to an old chapel, a missionary outpost of early days ; the Gorge of the Curra creek.

SPECIAL INDICATIONS : All Chest Diseases, especially Consumption, Chronic Bronchitis, Asthma ; General and Nervous Debility ; Rheumatism is likewise benefitted.

SEASON : Throughout the year.

DOCTORS : Drs. Th. Barker, R. Rygate.

HOTELS : The " Royal;" the " Exchange;" the " Occidental;" the " Commercial;" the " Bridge;" the " Railway;" the " Telegraph;" the " Club."

WHAINGAROA (PROV. AUCKLAND), NEW ZEALAND, 100 miles S.W. of Auckland, on the shores of Whaingaroa Harbour. The climate is equable, rarely exceeding 80° F. in the shade in summer; the nights are always cool, ranging in summer between 50° F. and 60° F., and in winter from 40° F. to 60° F. Good fishing and shooting. Post and Telegraph Offices at Raglan and Waitetuna.

Within five miles of the head of Whaingaroa Harbour are numerous hot springs of a sulphurous character ; the Maoris have for ages used them at all seasons, and so great is their fame with the Maoris that they come from a distance of from 200 to 300 miles. These springs have not yet been analysed. Mr. J. K. McDonald is the chairman of the Whaingaroa Hot Springs Domain Board.

Temperature.—From 110° F. to 160° F.

SPECIAL INDICATIONS : Rheumatism, Cutaneous Diseases.

HOTELS : At Raglan—The " Temperance ;" the " Harbour View." At Waitetuna—The " Half-way." At Whaingaroa Springs—The " Hot Springs ;" also one of the best hydropathic establishments in New Zealand.

ROUTE : From Auckland, by rail to Onehunga, thence steamer to Raglan, thence boat ; or from Auckland, by rail to Hamilton, thence coach to Waitetuna.

WHANGAPE (WAIKATO), NEW ZEALAND, 224 miles S. from Auckland, a postal town, with a hot alkaline spring, having a composition similar to those of Puriri and Waiwera. It contains 6·0 solid grains of mineral matters per pint.

Temperature.—From 160° F. to 200° F.

ROUTE : From Auckland or Tauranga.

WHANGAREI (PROV. AUCKLAND), NEW ZEALAND, 75 miles (by steamer) N. from Auckland, beautifully situated on the Hoteo river, 15 miles from Whangarei Heads, in a fruit-growing district. Post and Telegraph Office ; Literary Institute, with Library; Good Templars' Hall. There are some aerated chalybeate medicinal springs in the district.

EXCURSIONS : Two large waterfalls ; fine Limestone Caves ; Kamo Coal Mines (4m.) ; Mangapai (14m.)

HOTELS : The " Whangarei ;" " Settlers'."

WHITE ISLAND, NEW ZEALAND, 60 miles (by occasional vessel) E. of Tauranga, a conical island in the Bay of Plenty, formed by the summit of an extinct volcanic mountain rising out of deep water, has an altitude of about 900 feet, and an area of about two square miles. The crater, the precipitous sides of which vary in height from 400 to 800 feet, with a circumference of a mile and a half, is occupied by a lake of strong mineral water, which is fed by intermittent geysers and boiling springs surrounding it. All these waters are intensely acid, and deposit sulphate of lime, while the accompanying vapours (which often reach a height of 10,000 feet, and never less than 2,000 feet,) form extensive deposits of pure sulphur. The first water is too powerful to be used medicinally in its natural state, as will be seen from the following analysis :—

1. *Analysis* (in grains per gallon) *of the White Island Lake Water.*—Sulphate of Iron, 1,163·980grs. ; Sulphate of Soda, 680·325grs. ; Sulphate of Potash, 297·124grs. ; Sulphate of Lime, 251·682grs. ; Sulphate of Magnesia, 66·312grs. ; Sulphate of Alumina, 87·668grs. ; Sesquichloride of Aluminum, 1,870·085grs. ; Silicious matters, 23·628grs. ; Hydrochloric acid, free, 10,409·589grs. Total, 14,850·393 grains in one gallon, or 1,850·8 solid grains of mineral matters per pint.

Temperature.—From 97° F. to 212° F.

2. *Analysis,* (in grains per gallon) *of the White Island Springs.*—Sulphate of Lime, 115·933grs. ; Sulphate of Soda, 9·240grs. ; Sulphate of Magnesia, 29·120grs. ; Sulphate of Potash, traces ; Sulphate of Protoxide of Iron, 23·573grs.; Sulphate of Alumina and Ammonia, traces ; Silicic Acid, free, 9·013grs. ; Sulphurous and Phosphoric Acids, traces ; Sulphuric Acid, free, 11·933grs. ; Hydrochloric Acid, free, 9·706 grs. Total, 208·518grs. in one gallon, or 26·1 solid grains of mineral matters per pint.

Temperature.—210° F.

WICKLIFFE BAY (Otago), New Zealand, situated at Cape Saunders. about 12 miles N.E. of Dunedin. The Wickliffe Bay Spring is of a saline character, and contains 34·6grs. of mineral matters in one pint.

Analysis (in grains per gallon).—Sulphuric Acid, combined, 39·3grs. ; Chlorides, 112grs. ; Magnesia, 18·3grs. ; Lime, 11·5grs. ; Alkalies, 83grs. ; Carbonic Acid, combined, 12·6grs.

WOLLONGONG, New South Wales, 67 feet above sea-level, 66 miles S. of Sydney, a sea-side health-resort, prettily situated on the coast, at the foot of Mount Keira, in a fine agricultural, coal-mining, and dairy-farming district, the centre of the far-famed Illawarra district, the garden of the colony. Grand and varied mountain and ocean scenery; splendid climate. The mean maximum temperature in the shade, in 1885, was 73·6° F. ; the mean minimum temperature 55·8° F., and the mean temperature, 64·8° F. The average annual rainfall is 38·52 inches, with 73 wet days. Sea-bathing, sandy beaches, fishing. Hospital, Post and Telegraph Office, School of Arts, Free Library, Temperance Hall, Protestant Hall, picturesque Government Reserves.

EXCURSIONS : Mount Keira (1,540 feet high), Illawarra Lakes (4m.), Bulli Pass (8m.), Dapto, Mount Kembla.

DOCTORS : Drs. T. W. Lee, J. Thompson.

HOTELS : The " Harp of Erin;" the " Cricketers' Arms;" the " Commercial;" the " Royal Alfred;" the " Freemasons';" the " Queen's;" the " Brighton."

ROUTE : By rail or steamer.

WOODEND, Victoria, 1,840 feet above sea-level, 49 miles (by rail) N.W. from Melbourne. The country is elevated and the scenery romantic. The climate is very salubrious. The average annual rainfall is 50 inches. Post and Telegraph Office ; Mechanics' Institute ; Race-course ; Botanical Gardens ; Reserve.

EXCURSIONS : The " Hanging Rock " (4m.) ; Mount Macedon (1½m.), with an everflowing spring of excellent water ; the Elephant, a lofty wooded hill ; the Coliban Falls, near Trentham (14m.)

HOTELS : The " Commercial ;" the " Victoria ;" the " Woodend."

WOODFORD, New South Wales, 2,191 feet above sea-level, 55 miles (by rail) W. from Sydney ; noted for its fine bracing atmosphere, which resembles that of the more elevated portions of the west of England.

HOTEL : The " Woodford."

WYNYARD, TASMANIA, 104 miles N.W. (by steamer) from Launceston; situated near Table Cape, on the north-west coast of the island. Grand forest and coast scenery; the climate is bracing and equable; sea-bathing; both sea and fresh-water fishing; shooting (quail). Post and Tele-graph Office, Public Library.

SPECIAL INDICATIONS : Nervous Affections. and for Con-valescents.

DOCTOR : Dr. A. W. Graham.

HOTELS : The " Courthouse ;" the " Commercial ;" the " Wynyard Coffee Palace."

YAMBA, NEW SOUTH WALES, about 200 feet above sea-level, 307 miles (by steamer) N.E. from Sydney; a favourite seaside resort of the residents of the Clarence River district, at the entrance of the Clarence, on the South Head overlooking the sea; about 48 miles from Grafton. The scenery is wild and romantic and the climate pleasant, but not suitable for pulmonary affections. Good sea-bathing; fishing; shooting. Post and Telegraph Office.

SPECIAL INDICATIONS : For Convalescents.

SEASON : Summer and spring.

DOCTOR : Dr. A. J. Hood, residing at Maclean.

HOTELS : The " Woolli ;" " Muirhead's Family ;" also Ryall's boarding-house.

YANGAN, QUEENSLAND, 1,699 feet above sea-level, 180 miles by rail (via Warwick) S.W. from Brisbane, situated on a permanent creek, in a beautiful valley surrounded by lofty hills. The climate is fine and bracing, with none of the ener-vating heat of lower levels. In the district there are a num-ber of springs strongly impregnated with iron. Fishing; shooting. Post Office. No hotels or boarding-houses estab-lished as yet.

SPECIAL INDICATIONS : Phthisis.

YARCOWIE, SOUTH AUSTRALIA, 1,712 feet above sea-level, 134 miles (by rail) N. from Adelaide, and 50 miles from the coast. The climate is very dry; the total rainfall in

1882 was only a little over 9 inches. Post and Telegraph Office.

HOTELS : The " Yarcowie ;" the " Commercial."

YEPPOON, QUEENSLAND, 40 miles (by coach) N.E. from Rockhampton, a rising watering-place on the Pacific coast, surrounded by wooded hills. The scenery is very pretty ; there are lovely fern-tree gullies, dells, forests, &c., also splendid views of the sea, dotted with numerous islands and rocks. The temperature is very equable. The heat of the summer is tempered by fresh and invigorating breezes from the sea, and the climate in autumn and spring is delightful. Fine sheltered beaches ; sea-bathing ; many cool shaded walks ; good fishing, both in the sea, and in Ross Creek (bream, whiting, flathead); duck shooting. Post Office.

EXCURSIONS : Adelaide Park, Sugar Plantation, Woodlands, Emu Park (12m.) ; *See* also Hewittville (Emu Park).

SPECIAL INDICATIONS : General Debility, Convalescence.

HOTELS : The " Yeppoon," situated close to the sea (for bathing purposes there is a covered shed for gentlemen close to the Yeppoon Hotel ; that for the ladies is about 300 yards to the north of it, near a shady nook at the rocks) ; the " Pacific ;" the " Sea View." (Furnished cottages can be rented at from 25s. to 30s. a week).

YONGALA, SOUTH AUSTRALIA, 1,689 feet above sea-level, 159 miles (by rail via Petersburg) N. from Adelaide, and 37 miles from the coast, in a wheat-growing district. The climate is dry and bracing ; the total rainfall in 1882 was nearly 12 inches. Post and Telegraph Office ; Institute.

HOTELS : The " Yongala ;" the " Globe."

III

CLASSIFICATION OF HEALTH RESORTS NAMED, ACCORDING TO THEIR RESPECTIVE COLONIES;

WITH REMARKS ON THE PHYSICAL ASPECTS OF THE VARIOUS COLONIES.

———◆———

NEW SOUTH WALES.

NEW SOUTH WALES is bounded on the north by Queensland, on the west by South Australia, on the south by Victoria, and on the east by the Pacific Ocean. The extreme latitudes are 28° 10′ and 37° 20′ S., and the extreme longitudes 141° and 153° 40′ E. It contains an area of 310,700 square miles, and a population of 1,070,000. Its metropolis is Sydney, and the other chief towns are—Newcastle, Maitland, Bathurst, Goulburn, Albury, and Parramatta.

HEALTH RESORTS.—Albury, Armidale, Bathurst, Belmont, Blackheath, Booroolong, Bowenfels, Bowral, Burradoo, Camden, Campbelltown, Chowder Bay, Coogee Bay, Crookwell, Dubbo, Eden, Glencoe, Glen Innes, Gosford, Goulburn, Guyra, Katoomba, Kiama, Kurrajong Heights, Lady Robinson's Beach, Lake Bathurst, Lake George, Lake Macquarie, Lawson, Manly, Marulan, Mereworth, Mittagong, Moama, Moss Vale, Mount Victoria, Murrurundi, Nattai, New Brighton, Newport, Orange, Picton, Pittwater, Port Macquarie, Quirindi, Rock Flat, Rylstone, Scone, Singleton, Springwood, Sutton Forest, Tenterfield, Ulladulla, Walcha, Watson's Bay, Wollongong, Woodford, Yamba.

MOUNTAINS.—A range of mountains, running parallel to the coast at an average distance of about thirty miles from it, divides New South Wales into two very unequal portions;

the maritime part, east of this range, is an undulating plain intersected by numerous streams, and the country west of the mountains is a considerable breadth of elevated table-lands which farther west sinks into vast plains. This great dividing range of mountains, though perfectly continuous, bears various local names, as the New England Range, on the north-east (highest point, Ben Lomond, 5,000 feet) ; the Liverpool Range, south of the last (highest point, Oxley's Peak, 4,500 feet) ; the Blue Mountain Range, to the west of Sydney, attaining a height of 4,040 feet ; the Muniong Range, a continuation of the Australian Alps of Victoria (highest point, Mount Kosciusko, 7,176 feet). There are also the Coast Ranges, three in number ; two Interior Ranges, near the western boundary of the colony, viz. :—The Grey Range (highest point, Mount Arrowsmith, 2,000 feet), and the Barrier Range (highest point, Mount Lyell, 2,000 feet).

VALLEYS AND PLAINS.—The Illawarra Valley, 50 miles long by 5 miles in breadth, surrounded in horse-shoe form by lofty heights, is a scene of great tropical beauty. The Liverpool Plains, in the northern part of the colony, cover an area of nearly 17,000 square miles ; the Monaro Plains, in the south-eastern part of the colony, forming an undulating plateau 70 miles in length and about 2,000 feet above sea-level ; the Jerry and Patrick's Plains, on the Hunter River ; the Yass Plains ; the Riverina, vast plains in the south-western part.

. RIVERS.—Nearly all the rivers of New South Wales take their rise in the Great Dividing Range, and may be divided into two groups—those which flow eastward into the ocean, and those that flow westward, and ultimately join the Murray River, or some of its numerous tributaries. The principal rivers, which receive the easterly flow, are the Hawkesbury, 330 miles ; the Hunter, 300 miles ;· the Shoalhaven, 260 miles ; the Clarence, 240 miles ; the Macleay, 190 miles ; the Richmond, 120 miles ; the Manning, 100 miles. The principal rivers on the western watershed are ·the Murray River, forming the southern boundary of New South Wales, and making its way to the coast of South Australia, with a length of 1,120 miles within the colony ; the Murrumbidgee, 1,350 miles ; the Darling, 1,160 miles ; the Lachlan, 700 miles. The chief affluents of these great streams are the Macquarie, 750 miles ; the Namoi, 600 miles; the Bogan, 450 miles; the Gwydir, 445 miles; the Castlereagh, 365 miles ; the Macintyre, 350 miles. .

LAKES.—The largest is Lake George, situated near Bungendore, at an elevation of 2,129 feet, being 25 miles long by 8 miles wide ; in its vicinity is Lake Bathurst, with an area of 8 square miles ; Lake Macquarie is an inlet of the sea, south of Newcastle, and Lake Illawarra is also an inlet of the sea, south of Wollongong.

NEW ZEALAND.

New Zealand consists of a group of islands in the South Pacific Ocean, lying between lat. 34° 12' and 47° 20' S., and extending diagonally between the extreme long. of 166° 30' and 178° 40' E. The two principal islands are the North Island and the South or Middle Island, and a third off the south coast of the South Island is called Stewart Island ; besides these there are the Chatham and Auckland Islands, and other groups belonging to the colony. The North Island is divided from the Middle or South by Cook's Strait, and the South Island from Stewart's by Foveaux Strait. The area of the whole group is about 104,403 square miles. The total population is 635,000, including about 42,000 Maoris. The North Island is divided into four provincial districts, viz. :—Auckland, Taranaki, Hawke's Bay, and Wellington. The South Island has five provincial districts—Nelson, Marlborough, Canterbury, Otago (with Southland), and Westland. Wellington is the capital of New Zealand and the seat of Government ; Auckland was the former capital, and the other chief towns on the North Island are—Napier, Thames, Wanganui, and New Plymouth. The principal towns on the South or Middle Island are—Dunedin, Christchurch, Nelson, Oamaru, Invercargill, Lyttelton, Timaru and Hokitika.

THE NORTH ISLAND.

HEALTH RESORTS.—Auckland, Devonport, Hutt, Masterton, Napier, Ohaeawai, Ohinemutu, Onehunga, Onetapu,

Orakeikorako, Otahuhu, Puriri, Rotorua, Tapuaeharuru, Tarawera, Taupo, Te Aroha, Wairakei, Waiuku, Waiwera, Whaingaroa, Whangape, Whangarei, White Island.

MOUNTAINS.—In the North Island the mountains occupy
one-tenth of the surface, and all the ranges are in direct continuation of those of the South Island. The highest mountains are Mount Ruapehu (9,100 feet) and Mount Tongariro
(6,500 feet), both of which lie south of Lake Taupo, nearly in
the centre of the Island ; and Mount Egmont (8,300
feet), near the western entrance of Cook Strait. The principal
ranges are the Tararua and Ruahine Ranges, in the province
of Wellington.

PLAINS.—The Waikato Plains, one of the finest districts
of the North Island. A number of other plains lie on the
western side of the island.

RIVERS.—The largest rivers are the Waikato ; the Waipa,
a tributary of the Waikato ; the Thames or Waihou, all three
flowing north ; and the Wanganui, the Hutt, and the Wairoa
Rivers flowing south.

LAKES.—Taupo, the largest lake, is situated in the centre
of the North Island, at an elevation of 1,250 feet above sea-
level ; it is 36 miles long by 25 miles in greatest breadth
The other lakes are Rotorua, Tarawera, Rotoiti, Rotomahana,
and several smaller ones.

THE SOUTH OR MIDDLE ISLAND.

HEALTH RESORTS.—Akaroa, Amberley, Clyde, Dunstan,
Gibbston, Goodwood, Hanmer Plains, Motueka, Naseby,
Nelson, New Brighton, Pembroke, Queenstown, Riverton,
St. Kilda, Sumner, Sumner Lake, Timaru, Waikouaiti,
Wickliffe Bay.

MOUNTAINS.—The western side of the South Island is
traversed in its entire length by a range of mountains known
as the Southern Alps ; it is crossed at intervals by low passes ;
the greatest height of the main range is 10,000 feet to 14,000
feet, and it has extensive snow-fields and glaciers. The
highest mountains are Mount Cook (Canterbury), 12,349
feet ; Mount Hochstetter, 11,200 feet ; Mount Earnslaw,
north-west of Lake Wakatipu, 9,165 feet ; Mount Arthur,

I

west of Nelson, 8,000 feet ; Mount Aspiring (Otago), 9,949 feet ; Mount Franklin (Prov. Nelson), 10,000 feet ; Mount Ida (Prov. Otago), 5,498 feet ; Mount Bathan's (Otago), 6,600 feet ; Mount Pisa (Otago), 6,246 feet ; &c., &c.

PLAINS,—The only extensive plains on the South Island are the Canterbury Plains, situated between the parallels of 43° and 45°.

RIVERS.—The largest rivers are the Clutha, Waiau, Taieri, Waitaki, Rakaia, Waimakariri, Rangitata, Hurunui, Clarence, Wairau, Buller, Motueka and Grey.

LAKES.—The lakes of the South Island are large and numerous.   The largest lake is Te Anau (38 miles long by 1 to 6 miles broad), 132 square miles in area and 694 feet elevation ; Wakatipu Lake is 50 miles long, with an area of 114 square miles and an elevation of 1,069 feet ; Lake Wanaka, 29 miles long, with an area of 75 square miles and an elevation of 974 feet ; Lake Manipori is 18 miles long, with an area of 50 square miles and an elevation of 597 feet ; Lake Hawea, 19 miles long, area 48 square miles, elevation 1,189 feet ; and Lake McKerrow,—all in the province of Otago ; Lakes Coleridge, Tekapo, and Ellesmere, in the province of Canterbury ; and Lake Brunner, in the province of Westland.

QUEENSLAND.

QUEENSLAND forms the North-Eastern portion of the Australian Continent. It lies between lat. 29° and 10° 45′ S., and long. 138° and 153° 30′ E.   The Pacific, Torres Straits, and Gulf of Carpentaria form the northern boundary ; the southern boundary is formed by New South Wales and South Australia ; on the west it is bounded by South Australia, and on the east by the Pacific Ocean.   It contains an area of 668,497 square miles, with a population of 365,000.   Brisbane is the metropolis, and the other chief towns are—Ipswich, Rockhampton, Gympie, Townsville, Maryborough, and Toowoomba.

HEALTH RESORTS.—Beenleigh, Bundaberg, Cambooya, Cleveland, Dalby, Dalveen, Emu Park, Gowrie Junction, Greenmount, Harlaxton, Hendon, Hewittville, Ipswich, Killarney, Mount Perry, Pialba, Roma, Sandgate, Southport, Stanthorpe, Tenningering, Toowoomba, Warwick, Yangan, Yeppoon.

MOUNTAINS.—Ranges of mountains, averaging from 2,000 to 3,000 feet high, run parallel with the coast, but at varying distances from it, throughout the whole of Queensland. The highest mountains are the Bellenden Ker peaks, in the north of the colony, south of Cairns, 4,200 feet : Mount Dalrymple, west of Bowen, 4,250 feet ; Mount Mitchell and Mount Lindsay, on the MacPherson range, near the southern border, 3,500 feet in height.

RIVERS.—The principal rivers are the Burnett, the Fitzroy, and the Burdekin, flowing into the Pacific ; the Flinders, the Albert, the Mitchell, the Gilbert, and the Norman, emptying themselves into the Gulf of Carpentaria ; the Victoria or Barcoo River flows through Cooper's Creek to Lake Eyre ; the Dumaresque, the Condamine or Balonne, and the Warrego, flowing towards the Darling.

SOUTH AUSTRALIA.

SOUTH AUSTRALIA embraces the whole central portion of the Continent. From the Great Bight to lat. 26° S. it lies between long. 129° to 141° E., and from lat. 26° S. to the Gulf of Carpentaria, between long. 129° to 138° E. It is thus bounded on the north and south by the Ocean, on the west by Western Australia, and on the east by Queensland, New South Wales, and Victoria. It contains an area of 903,690 square miles, and a population of 345,000, Its metropolis is Adelaide, and the other principal towns are— Port Adelaide, Glenelg, Kooringa, Mount Gambier, and Kapunda.

HEALTH RESORTS.—Aldgate, Angaston, Brighton, Clarendon, Echunga, Edithburgh, Glanville, Glenelg, Hallett, Henley Beach, Jamestown, Kooringa, Manoora, Mount Barker, Mount Bryan, Mount Lofty, Petersburg, Port Elliot, Port Lincoln, Port Victor, Robe, Salisbury, Semaphore, Tanunda, Victor Harbour, Yarcowie, Yongala.

MOUNTAINS.—The principal ranges are the Mount Lofty Range, commencing at Cape Jervis, and extending northwards (highest points, Mount Lofty and Mount Barker, each 2,330 feet) ; the Flinders Range, commencing at the north-eastern side of Spencer's Gulf and extending northwards (highest points, Mount Remarkable, 3,170 feet ; Mount Brown and Mount Arden, each 3,000 feet) ; the Gawler Range, to the south of Lake Gairdner (highest point, Mount Sturt, 2,000 feet) ; the Stuart Range, to the west of Lake Torrens.

RIVERS.—The only important river is the Murray, in the S.E., which after a course of nearly 1,500 miles through New South Wales and Victoria, enters South Australia at a distance of nearly 500 miles from its mouth. The Gawler, Torrens, Onkaparinga, and other streams flowing into St. Vincent's Gulf, are not of much importance.

LAKES.—Lake Gairdner, an immense salt lake, north of the Gawler Range, is 130 miles long and lies 366 feet above sea-level. Lake Torrens, 90 miles north of Spencer's Gulf, is another large salt lake, 115 miles long ; Lake Eyre, still further north, is also a salt lake. Lakes Alexandrina and Albert, forming the mouth of the Murray River, are sheets of fresh water. The Coorong, a back water of Lake Albert, runs parallel with the coast in a south-east direction for 90 miles.

TASMANIA.

TASMANIA is an island situated south of the eastern part of Australia, from which it is separated by Bass' Strait, 150 miles wide. It lies between lat. 40° 44' and 43° 39' S., and long. 144° 38' and 148° 24' E. It contains an area of 24,330 square miles, or 26,375 square miles including the other islands belonging to the colony. The total population is 145,000. Hobart is the capital, and Launceston is the chief town in the north of the island ; the other principal towns are—Beaconsfield, Longford, Westbury, and New Norfolk.

HEALTH RESORTS.—Campbell Town, Deloraine, Evandale, Formby, Franklin, George's Bay, Georgetown, Hobart, Kingston, Launceston, New Norfolk, Oatlands, Penguin, Richmond, Ross, St. Helen's, Swansea, Torquay, Ulverstone, Victoria, Wynyard.

Mountains.—There are two chains of mountains, the eastern and the western tiers, running through the island almost north and south. The highest mountains in the northern division of the eastern tier are Ben Lomond (5,010 feet), Mount Barrow (4,644 feet), Ben Nevis (3,910 feet), Mount Victoria (3,964 feet), Mount Arthur (3,895 feet). In the Central Division are the Table Mountain (4,736 feet), Miller's Bluff (3,977 feet) ; and in the southern division are Mount Wellington (4,166 feet), Mount Bonnet (4,131 feet), Adamson's Peak (4,017 feet), Mount La Perouse (3,800 feet). In the western tier are Mount Humboldt (5,520 feet), Cradle Mountain (5,069 feet), Mounts Field West and East (4,721 feet and 4,167 feet), Mount Rolland (4,047 feet), Mount Dundas (3,922 feet), and others.

Rivers.—The largest river is the Derwent, which enters the sea near Hobart, and its chief tributaries are the Ouse, Clyde, and Jordan. The Tamar is the most important river in the north-east, and its chief tributaries are the Esk, Macquarie, and Lake Rivers. Other considerable rivers are the Huon, forming a fine estuary in the south ; the Gordon and King Rivers flowing into Macquarie Harbour on the west coast ; the Pieman and Arthur Rivers to the north-west ; in the north are a number of streams, amongst them the Forth, the Mersey, and the Ringarooma ; on the east coast are the Swanport and Prosser Rivers, and in the south-east the Coal River.

Lakes.—The principal lakes are in the centre of the island. The largest are Great Lake with an area of 28,000 acres (3,820 feet above sea-level) ; Lake Sorell, 3,000 feet above sea-level ; Lake St. Clair, 3,239 feet above sea-level ; Lake Arthur ; Lake Echo ; Lake Tiberias, and others.

VICTORIA.

Victoria is the smallest division of Australia, and forms the extreme S.E. part of the Continent. It extends from lat. 34° to 39° S , and from long. 141° to 150° E. It is bounded on the north by the River Murray, which divides it from New South Wales, on the east by the Pacific, on the south by Bass' Straits, and on the west by the meridian of 141° E., which divides it from South Australia. It contains an area of 87,884 square miles, and a population of 1,060,000. Melbourne is its metropolis, and the other chief towns are—Ballarat, Sandhurst, Geelong, Stawell, Clunes, Echuca, Warrnambool, Maryborough, Kyneton, Hamilton, Ararat, and Beechworth.

HEALTH RESORTS.—Alexandra, Apollo Bay, Bairnsdale, Ballaarat, Ballan, Beechworth, Belfast, Brighton, Buninyong, Charlton, Clifton Springs, Coimadai, Cowes, Dandenong, Daylesford, Dromana, Drysdale, Echuca, Elphinstone, Fernshawe, Fern Tree Gully, Frankston, Healesville, Hepburn, Kyneton, Lilydale, Little River, Lorne, Macedon, Melton, Mordialloc, Mornington, Morwell, Phillip Island, Portarlington, Portland, Portsea, Queenscliff, St. Kilda, Sale, Sandhurst, Schnapper Point, Somerville, Sorrento, Stratford, Sunbury, Warburton, Warrnambool, Wedderburn, Woodend.

MOUNTAINS.—The principal range of mountains are the Australian Alps, in the east of the Colony (highest points, Mount Bogong, 6,508 feet ; Mount Hotham, 6,400 feet ; Mount Feathertop, 6,303 feet ; the Cobberas, 6,025 feet ; Mount Cope, 6,015 feet ; Mount Gibbo, 5,764 feet ; Mount Howitt, 5,715 feet; Buffalo Peak, 5,645 feet ; Twins, 5,575 feet ; Mount Benambra, 4,840 feet). A prolongation of the Australian Alps, called the Great Dividing Range, traverses Victoria from east to west, dividing it into two unequal parts. The range has various local names, as the Pyrenees, to the north-west of Ballarat (highest points, Ben Nevis and Mount Ararat) ; the Grampians, further west (highest point, Mount William, 5,400 feet). Other ranges are—the Strzelecki, to the north of Wilson's Promontory ; the Dandenong Ranges, to the south-east of Melbourne ; the Otway Ranges ; and the Sierra and the Victoria Ranges south of the Grampians.

RIVERS.—The most important river is the Murray, with a length of 1,300 miles within the colony, and its chief tributaries are the Goulburn (350 miles), the Mitta-Mitta (175 miles), the Ovens (140 miles), the Loddon (225 miles), and the Campaspe (150 miles). The Wimmera (220 miles), and the Avoca (163 miles), are lost in the lakes amongst the mallee scrub country of the north-west. The principal rivers on the southern watershed are the Snowy River, with a length of 120 miles within the colony ; the Tambo (85 miles); the

Latrobe (135 miles); the Yarra Yarra (150 miles), which enters the bay of Port Phillip at Melbourne ; the Barwon (70 miles), with its tributaries, the Moorabool and Leigh ; the Hopkins (150 miles), enters the sea at Warrnambool ; the Glenelg (280 miles), with its tributary, the Wannan (105 miles), enters the sea at the south-west corner of the colony.

LAKES.—Lake Corangamite, to the north of Cape Otway, is the largest salt lake, covering 57,000 acres ; not far from this is Lake Colac (fresh water), 6,600 acres ; Lake Burrumbeet (fresh water), 14 miles N.W. of Ballarat, covers 5,440 acres ; Lake Connewarre (salt), west of Queenscliff, covering 7,680 acres ; Lake Wendouree, adjoining Ballarat, of 600 acres in extent; Lakes Hindmarsh, Tyrrell, Albacutya, and others in the Wimmera district, are salt but not permanent lakes. The Gippsland lakes are Lake Wellington, with an area of 34,500 acres ; Lake Victoria, 28,500 acres ; and Lakes Reeve, King, and Tyers.

WESTERN AUSTRALIA.

WESTERN AUSTRALIA is formed by that portion of the continent situated to the west of long. 129° E., which divides it from South Australia ; on all the other sides it is bounded by the ocean. It lies between lat. 13° 44' and 35° S., and long. 129° to 113° E. It contains an area of about 1,060,000 square miles, and a population of 40,000. Perth is the metropolis, and the other chief towns are—Fremantle, York, Albany, and Geraldton.

HEALTH RESORTS.—Busselton, Rottnest.

MOUNTAINS.—The principal range of mountains is called the Darling Range, which runs about 20 miles from and parallel with the west coast, and extends from Cape d'Entrecasteaux, the south-west corner of the colony, to near the Murchison River, beyond Champion Bay (highest point, Mount William, 3,000 feet) ; the Stirling Range, north of King George Sound, in the south of the colony (highest point, Ellen's Peak) ; the Roe Range, to the west of Busselton ; the Herschell Range, the northern continuation of the Darling Range; and others.

RIVERS.—The principal rivers on the west coast, com-

mencing from the south, are the Blackwood, the Swan, the
Murchison, the Gascoyne ; on the north-west coast the Ash-
burton and the Fortescue ; and on the north coast the De
Grey river.

LAKES.—There are numerous lakes, but most of them are
salt and shallow ; the largest are Lakes Austin, Lefroy,
Moore, Barlee, Cow-cowing, Deborah, etc.

IV.

CLASSIFIED LIST OF HEALTH RESORTS NAMED, ACCORDING TO THEIR THERAPEUTIC INDICATIONS.

—————◆—————

The following order has been adhered to—

ABBREVIATIONS.—N.S.W., New South Wales ; N.Z., New Zealand ; Qu., Queensland ; S.A., South Australia ; Tas., Tasmania ; Vic., Victoria ; W.A., Western Australia.

* *The Mineral Springs of each class are arranged according to their strength ; the most powerful waters are mentioned first, and the feeble ones at the end of each class.*

1.—ACIDIC WATERS.

Waters containing an excess of Mineral Acids, such as Hydrochloric and Sulphuric Acid. These waters are useful in Gout, Dyspepsia, Sciatica, Skin Diseases, Liver Disorders, Sexual Impotence, Cold Feet, Amenorrhœa, &c.

HOT SPRINGS.—(1.) Ohaeawai (containing iron and being accompanied by an escape of mercurial vapour) ; (2.) The Priest's Bath, at Rotorua (*see* Ohinemutu, Spring No. 1) ; (3.) The Muddy Bath [Spring No. 9] at Ohinemutu (this spring is strongly charged with sulphate of iron) ; (4.) White Island, Spring No. 2 ; (5.) Sulphur Bay Spring, at Arikika-pakapa (*see* Ohinemutu, Spring No. 20) ; (6.) The Mud Bath, at Arikikapakapa (*see* Ohinemutu, Spring No. 17) ; (7.) Jack's Bath, at Arikikapakapa (*see* Ohinemutu, Spring No. 16) ; (8.) Te Mimi, at Okakahi (*see* Ohinemutu, Spring No. 19) ; (9.) Hanmer Plains, Spring No. 7 ; (10.) Perekari [Spring No. 21], near Ohinemutu ; (11.) Yellow Water Spring (*see* Taupo, Spring No. 15) ; (12.) Black Water Spring (*see* Taupo, Spring No. 14) ; (13.) Orakeikorako [Spring No. 2.] *Note.*—The " White Island " Lake Water also belongs to this class, but it is too powerful to be used medicinally in its natural state. (All these springs are situated in New Zealand.)

2.—MURIATED ALKALINE WATERS.

These waters contain, in addition to Carbonate and Bicarbonate of Soda, and Carbonic Acid, a considerable quantity of Chloride of Sodium. These waters have a special action on the lungs, chest, and nervous system ; taken internally, they render the urine alkaline, and cause the bowels to act freely. They are of value in affections of the Respiratory, Digestive, and Urinary Organs, and in all diseases due to excess of acidity ; if thermal, they are useful also in Rheumatic Affections.

COLD SPRINGS.—(1.) Puriri, N.Z.; (2.) Dubbo, N S.W.; (3.) Te Aroha, N.Z. (Spring No. 18) ; (4.) Rock Flat, N.S.W.

HOT SPRINGS.—(1.) Te Aroha, N.Z. (Springs Nos. 1 to 15) ; (2.) Waiwera, N.Z. ; (3.) Whangape, N.Z.

[NOTE.—The Editor of this Guide is not aware of the existence of any Simple Alkaline Water in the Australasian Colonies.]

3.—ALKALINE SILICEOUS WATERS.

Waters containing much Silicic Acid, but changing rapidly on exposure to the atmosphere, and becoming alkaline. They promote the discharge of uric acid from the system, and are useful in Rheumatic and Gouty Affections.

COLD SPRINGS.—Te Aroha, N.Z. (Springs Nos. 18 and 17) ; Hepburn, Vic.

HOT SPRINGS.—(1.) Madame Rachel's Bath, at Rotorua (*see* Ohinemutu, Spring No. 2) ; (2.) Te Koutu [Spring No. 12], near Ohinemutu ; (3.) The Oil Bath, at Whakarewarewa (*see* Ohinemutu, Spring No. 14) ; (4.) The Alum Cave Spring, at Orakeikorako ; (5.) The Clear Bath [Spring No. 8] at Ohinemutu ; (6.) The Blue Bath, at Rotorua (*see* Ohinemutu, Spring No. 3) ; (7.) The Washing Spring, on Rotorua Lake (*see* Ohinemutu, Spring No. 22) ; (8.) Scott's Bath [Spring No. 11] at Ohinemutu ; (9.) The Spout Bath, at Whakarewarewa (*see* Ohinemutu, Spring No. 13) ; (10.) Hinemaru, at Rotorua (*see* Ohinemutu, Spring No. 7) ; (11.) Waikite [Spring No. 10], at Ohinemutu ; (12.) Te Aroha, N.Z. [Springs 1 to 15] ; (13.) Tea-tree Spring, at Waipahihi, (*see* Taupo, Spring No. 23) ; (14.) Herberton, Qu.

4.—ALUMINOUS WATERS.

Waters strongly impregnated with alum ; they have a tonic and astringent action, and are useful in Hæmorrhoids, General Debility, Abdominal Congestion, etc.

Hot Springs.—(1) The Alum Bath, near Whakarewarewa (*see* Ohinemutu, Spring No. 15); (2) The Priest's Bath, at Rotorua (*see* Ohinemutu, Spring No. 1) ; (3) The Alum Cave Spring at Orakeikorako.

Cold.—Onetapu (this spring is also strongly charged with Sulphate of Iron).

5.—BITTER WATERS.

The principal ingredients are the Sulphates of Soda and Magnesia ; they have a purgative and diuretic action, and are useful in Diseases of the Digestive and Urinary Organs, Liver Complaints, Nervous Disorders, Corpulence, Headache, Giddiness, Dyspnœa, etc.

Stratford, Vic. ; Te Aroha, N. Z. (Spring No 16).

6.—BRINES.

These waters contain so large a quantity of Chloride of Sodium, that their chief use is for bathing ; scrofulous diseases especially are benefitted by them.

Rottnest, W.A.

(N.B.—A large proportion of the wells sunk in the interior of New South Wales, Queensland, and South Australia yield brackish water, many of them being of a pronounced briny character, and could be made use of as baths.)

[NOTE.—For *hot* salt-water and ordinary sea-baths see " Sea-side Health Resorts."]

7.—EARTHY, or CALCAREOUS WATERS.

These contain earthy substances, especially Sulphates and Carbonates of Lime and Magnesia. They are useful in Dyspepsia, Diseases of the Genito-urinary Organs, Chronic Bronchitis, Pulmonary Catarrh, Diarrhœa, Eczematous Skin Diseases, etc.

Ballan, Vic.; Amberley, N.Z.

8.—FERRUGINOUS, or CHALYBEATE WATERS.

These waters increase the red corpuscles and fibrine of the blood, they stimulate the nervous, circulating, and digestive organs, and are useful in all classes of diseases where tonic and invigorating medicines are required to assist blood formation, especially in Anæmia, and Chlorosis, also in Nervous Complaints, Debility of Muscles and Mucous Membranes, Stomachic and Intestinal Catarrh, all Female Complaints, etc.

(a.) ACIDULOUS CHALYBEATES.

This class of mineral waters contains Carbonate of the Protoxide of Iron, with Carbonate of Magnesium and Carbonic Acid.

Hepburn, Vic. ; Masterton, N.Z. (Spring No. 5.)

———

(b.) SALINE ACIDULOUS CHALYBEATES.

These waters, in addition to the above, contain Sulphates and Carbonates of Soda and Lime, and Chloride of Sodium.

Springs Nos. 4, 2, 1 and 3 at Clifton Springs (*see* Drysdale, Vic.) ; Amberley, N.Z. ; Ballan, Vic.

———

(c.) SULPHATE CHALYBEATES.

Waters strongly charged with Sulphate of Iron.

Cold. — Onetapu, N.Z. (contains also Sulphate of Alumina.)

Hot.—Waihunuhunukuri [Spring No. 9] at Ohinemutu.

———

(d.) UNDETERMINED CHALYBEATES.

Chalybeate Waters, of which no analyses could be obtained.

Mereworth, N.S.W. ; Mittagong, N.S.W. ; Mount Perry, Qu. ; Whangarei, N.Z.

9.—IODO-BROMATED MURIATED WATERS.

The principal ingredients in these springs are Chloride of Sodium, Iodide of Sodium, and Bromide of Magnesium. Taken internally, they increase the secretion of saliva, and stimulate the mucous membranes ; they are useful in Scrofulous Diseases, Female Diseases, Diseases of the Skin, Ears, Eyes, Respiratory Organs, Bones and Joints, and in Chronic Affections generally.

COLD.—The Parkes Spring (*see* Taupo, N.Z., Spring No. 2) ; The Pahua Spring (*see* Masterton, N.Z., Spring No. 1) ; Burton's Spring, contains also traces of Arsenic (*see* Masterton, N.Z., Spring No. 3.)

HOT.—Tarawera, N.Z.

10.—MERCURIAL WATERS.

Waters strongly charged with Mercury, and, therefore, should be efficacious in Hepatic and Syphilitic Affections.

Ohaeawai, N.Z. (both hot and cold.)

11.—MURIATED LITHIA WATERS.

Waters containing Lithium and Chloride of Sodium. Useful in Gout and kindred affections, Uric Acid Diathesis, Chronic Rheumatism, Gravel, Stone in the Bladder, etc. Traces of Lithium have been found in the following springs :—

COLD.—Dubbo, N.S.W. ; Puriri, N.Z. ; Taupo, N.Z., Spring No. 2.

HOT.—Hanmer Plains, N.Z., Springs Nos. 1 and 8 ; Herberton, Qu. ; Ohinemutu, N.Z., Springs Nos. 8, 10, 11 and 14 ; Tarawera, N.Z. ; Te Aroha, N.Z. ; Waiwera, N.Z.

12.—SALINE WATERS.

The characteristic element in these waters is the large amount of Chloride of Sodium which they contain. The *cold* waters of this class are admirably suited to Abdominal Congestions, Scrofula, Anæmia, Dyspepsia, Hæmorrhoids, etc. ; the *hot* waters are useful in Gout, Rheumatism, Scrofula, Affections of Mucous Membranes, etc.

COLD.—Masterton, N.Z., Springs Nos. 1, 2, and 4; Clifton Springs Nos. 4, 1, 3, and 2 (*see* Drysdale, Vic.) ; Stratford, Vic.

HOT.—(1) Crow's Nest Spring, at Ruahine (*see* Taupo, N.Z., Spring No. 3) ; (2) Ruahine Spring (*see* Taupo, Spring No. 4) ; (3) Waiwera, N.Z. ; (4) Wickliffe Bay, N.Z. ; (5) Hinemaru, at Rotorua (*see* Ohinemutu, N.Z., Spring No. 7) ; (6) Te Aroha N.Z. ; (7) Madame Rachel's Bath, at Rotorua (*see* Ohinemutu, Spring No. 2) ; (8) Otukapuarangi, at Rotomahana (*see* Ohinemutu, Spring No. 24) ; (9) Oruawhata, at Rotorua (*see* Ohinemutu, Spring No. 3) ; (10) Koroteoteo, at Whakarewarewa (*see* Ohinemutu, Spring No. 14) ; (11) Turikore, at Whakarewarewa (*see* Ohinemutu, Spring 13) ; (12) The Painkiller Bath, at Te Kauwhanga (*see* Ohinemutu, Spring 5) ; (13) Kuirau [Spring 22] at Ohinemutu ; (14) Waikite and Scott's Bath [Springs 10 and 11] at Ohinemutu ; (15) Hanmer Springs (*see* Hanmer Plains, N.Z.) ; (16) Herberton, Qu. ; *see* also Taupo, N.Z., Springs Nos. 20, 21, 22.

13.—SULPHUROUS OR HEPATIC WATERS.

These contain Sulphurous Acid, Sulphurets of Metals, and Sulphuretted Hydrogen, with a good deal of Chloride of Sodium. They accelerate the circulation and stimulate the nervous system ; they are very efficacious in all Skin Diseases, Rheumatism, Neuralgia, Paralysis, Neurosis, Scrofula, Gout, Congestion of Liver, Sciatica, Glandular Swellings, &c.

HOT.—Hanmer Springs, Nos. 8 and 1 (see Hanmer Plains, N.Z.) ; Ohinemutu, N.Z., Springs, Nos. 4, 5, 6, and 18 ; Orakeikorako, N.Z. ; Taupo, N.Z., Springs Nos. 7, 8, 9, 10, 11, 12 ; Whaingaroa, N.Z.

14.—THERMAL MUD BATHS.

Waters of a muddy character, which have proved useful in Chronic Rheumatism and Gout, Chronic Rheumatoid Arthritis, Cutaneous Diseases, &c.

Ohinemutu, N.Z., Springs Nos. 4, 5, 6, 9, 17, 18.

15.—INDIFFERENT THERMAL SPRINGS.

These waters contain but small quantities of mineral matters, and are chiefly remarkable for their high temperature. They are useful in relieving Nervous Affections, Gout and Chronic Rheumatism, Affections of the Respiratory Organs, &c.

Taupo, N.Z., Springs Nos. 8, 9, 10, 11, 12, 13, 16, 17, 19, 20. Also Sumner Lake, N.Z.

16.—UNDETERMINED WATERS.

Waters of which no analysis could be obtained—Coimadai, Vic. ; Gibbston, N.Z. (astringent) ; Little River, Vic.

17.—SEA-SIDE HEALTH RESORTS.

THE sea air and the air at the sea-side are influenced by the constant evaporation from the sea, and also by the temperature of the sea. Owing to these circumstances the sea air generally contains more moisture and is more equable in temperature, the summer being less hot and the winter less cold at the sea side than at inland places in the same latitude. A very important fact is the comparative purity of the sea-air from organic admixture and inorganic dust, while the presence of a greater or less amount of saline particles cannot be regarded as a disadvantage. The amount of ozone is greater ; that of carbonic acid smaller. A residence at the sea-side alone, without sea-bathing, produces on many constitutions all the effects which are usually ascribed to sea-bathing. The sea water itself (*aqua marina*) contains Chlorides of Sodium, Magnesium and Potassium; Sulphates of Lime, Soda and Magnesia; Carbonate of Lime, Bromide of Magnesium, Iodine, and various animal and vegetable bodies. It is of a cathartic nature and makes an excellent tonic bath.

The following sea-side health resorts may be chosen for the various Nervous Disorders, also for Insomnia, Anæmia, Scrofula, Impotence, Phthisis, Hysteria, Blennorhœa, Leucorrhœa, and other diseases:—

NEW SOUTH WALES.—Chowder Bay, Coogee Bay, Eden, Gosford, Kiama, Lady Robinson's Beach (New Brighton), Lake Macquarie, Manly, Pittwater, Port Macquarie, Ulladulla, Watson's Bay, Wollongong, Yamba.

NEW ZEALAND.—Akaroa, Auckland, Devonport, Goodwood, Motueka, Napier, Nelson, New Brighton, Onehunga, Otahuhu, Riverton, St. Kilda, Sumner, Timaru, Waikouaiti, Waiuku, Waiwera.

QUEENSLAND.—Cleveland, Emu Park (Hewittville), Pialba, Sandgate, Southport, Yeppoon.

SOUTH AUSTRALIA. — Brighton, Edithburgh, Glenelg, Henley Beach, Port Elliot, Port Lincoln, Robe, Semaphore, Victor Harbour.

TASMANIA.—Formby and Torquay, Georgetown, Kingston, Penguin, St. Helen's, Swansea, Ulverstone, Wynyard.

VICTORIA.—Apollo Bay, Belfast, Brighton, Cowes, Dromana, Frankston, Lorne, Mordialloc, Mornington, Portarlington, Portsea, Queenscliff, St. Kilda, Sorrento, Warrnambool.

WESTERN AUSTRALIA.—Busselton, Rottnest.

[NOTE.—Hot salt-water baths can be had at Manly, near Sydney, also at St. Kilda and Warrnambool (Victoria), and at Southport (Queensland); they cause an increased excretion of urine and urea, they stimulate the Nervous and Muscular Systems, and are very effective in Rheumatism, Sciatica, and Nervous Affections.]

18.—CLIMATIC HEALTH RESORTS.

ONE of the most important considerations with regard to climatic health-resorts is their comparative fitness for the

K

residence of invalids; their climates should admit of regular and daily exercise in the open air, so that the invalid may derive every advantage which this form of revulsion is capable of effecting; as all sudden changes of temperature interfere with exercise in the open air, the equability of temperature is essential. In recommending a change of air on account of ill-health, we should take into consideration not only the character of the disease, but the habits of the patient, and the peculiarities of the patient's constitution; also the resources of the health resort, and the character of the local hotels. In obstinate or chronic cases it will be advisable to furnish the patient with an introduction from the family physician to the resident doctor.

A change of air will be found useful in Phthisis, Bronchial Catarrh, Convalescence, Nervous and Chronic Debility, Uterine Diseases, Chlorosis, Laryngitis, and other Diseases.

Besides the sea-side health resorts enumerated above, the following inland places can be recommended :—

(a.) UNDER 1,000 FEET ABOVE SEA-LEVEL.

NEW SOUTH WALES.—Albury, Camden, Campbelltown, Moama, Picton, Scone, Wellington.

NEW ZEALAND.—Clyde,† Hutt,* Ohaeawai, Ohinemutu, Rotorua, Taupo, Whangarei.*

QUEENSLAND.—Beenleigh,* Bundaberg,* Ipswich, Roma.

SOUTH AUSTRALIA.—Echunga.

TASMANIA.—Campbelltown, Deloraine, Franklin,* Hobart,* Launceston, New Norfolk, Richmond, Ross, Victoria.

VICTORIA —Bairnsdale, Charlton, Dandenong, Drysdale,* Echuca, Fernshawe,† Ferntree Gully, Healesville, Little River, Melton, Morwell, Sale, Somerville,* Sunbury, Wedderburn.

* Situated in proximity to the sea.
† The height of these places could not be ascertained.

(b.) FROM 1,000 TO 1,500 FEET ABOVE SEA-LEVEL.

NEW SOUTH WALES.—Quirindi, Springwood.

NEW ZEALAND.—Pembroke, Queenstown.

QUEENSLAND.—Dalby, Hendon, Warwick.

SOUTH AUSTRALIA. — Aldgate, Jamestown, Manoora, Mount Barker.

TASMANIA.—Evandale, Oatlands.

VICTORIA.—Alexandra, Ballaarat, Elphinstone.

(c.) From 1,500 to 2,000 feet above sea-level.

NEW SOUTH WALES.—Kurrajong Heights, Murrurundi, Rylstone.

NEW ZEALAND.—Naseby.

QUEENSLAND.—Cambooya, Gowrie Junction, Greenmount, Killarney, Toowoomba, Yangan.

SOUTH AUSTRALIA.—Hallett, Kooringa, Mt. Bryan, Mt. Lofty, Petersburg, Yarcowie, Yongala.

VICTORIA.—Ballan, Beechworth, Buninyong, Kyneton, Macedon, Woodburn.

(d.) FROM 2,000 TO 2,500 FEET ABOVE SEA-LEVEL.

NEW SOUTH WALES.—Bathurst, Bowral, Burradoo, Goulburn, Lake Bathurst, Lake George, Lawson, Marulan, Mereworth, Mittagong, Moss Vale, Sutton Forest, Woodford.

QUEENSLAND.—Harlaxton, Herberton, Mt. Perry.

VICTORIA. — Daylesford, Hepburn, Upper Macedon, Warburton.

19.—HEALTH RESORTS AT A HIGH ALTITUDE.

MOUNTAIN air, which is generally pure, light, and exhilarating, will be found beneficial in the early stages of Phthisis (either incipient or threatened), also in Asthma, Pleurisy, Rhachitis, Nervous and Chronic Debility, Convalescence, Epilepsy, Hypochondriasis, Dyspepsia, Liver Complaints, and other diseases. But mountain air is distinctly disadvantageous in Heart Diseases, Emphysema, Hæmoptysis, Chronic Bronchitis, Chronic Rheumatism, and similar affections.

The following stations have been arranged according to their height above sea level, the highest stations being named first :—

Booroolong, N.S.W., 4,328 feet ; Guyra, N.S.W., 4,328 feet ; Glencoe, N.S.W., 3,794 feet ; Glen Innes, N.S.W., 3,518 feet ; Blackheath, N.S.W., 3,494 feet ; Mount Victoria, N.S.W., 3,490 feet ; Walcha, N.S.W., 3,386 feet; Katoomba, N.S.W., 3,349 feet ; Mount Macedon, Vic., 3,324 feet ; Armidale, N.S.W., 3,313 feet ; Upper Macedon, Vic., 3,000 feet ; Crookwell, N.S.W., 2,995 ; Bowenfels, N.S.W., 2,972 feet ; Dalveen, Qu., 2,906 feet; Orange, N.S.W., 2,891 feet; Tenterfield, N.S.W., 2,827 feet ; Stanthorpe, Qu., 2,656 feet.

20.—WINTER STATIONS.

USEFUL in Phthisis, Asthma, Bronchial Catarrh, Chronic Rheumatism, Gout, Hypochondriasis, Anæmia, Convalescents, Neurosis, etc. The following places or districts can be recommended as Winter Stations :—

Albury, N.S.W. ; Beenleigh, Qu. ; Bundaberg, Qu. ; Charlton, Vic. ; Cleveland, Qu. ; Echuca, Vic. ; Hewittville, Qu. ; Ipswich, Qu. ; Moama, N.S.W. ; Nelson, N.Z. ; Pialba, Qu. ; Roma, Qu. ; Rotorua, N.Z. ; Sandgate, Qu. ; Sandhurst, Vic. ; Southport, Qu. ; Wedderburn, Vic. ; Wellington, N.S.W. ; Yeppoon, Qu. ; the Riverina District, N.S.W. (*see* page 1), and the districts of Maranoa, Warrego, Mitchell, North and South Gregory, in the interior of Queensland (*see* page 6), also Messrs. Lionel Ching & Co.'s floating sanatorium (*see* special advertisement.)

21.—GRAPE CURE.

THE Grapes, containing nearly twenty-five per cent. of Sugar, tend to favour the accumulation of fat, and therefore, they are a pleasant substitute for cod-liver oil in the treatment of phthisis and other wasting diseases. In addition to climate, the Grape Cure *could* form the basis of treatment at the following places :—

Albury, N.S.W. ; Angaston, S.A. ; Busselton, W.A. ; Camden, N.S.W.; Clarendon, S.A.; Echuca, Vic.; Lilydale, Vic. ; Mount Barker, S.A. ; Murrurundi, N.S.W. ; Port Macquarie, N.S.W. ; Quirindi, N.S.W. ; Roma, Qu. ; Salisbury, S.A. ; Sandhurst, Vic.; Scone, N.S.W. ; Singleton, N.S.W.; Sunbury, Vic. ; Tanunda, S.A. ; Toowoomba, Qu. ; Warwick, Qu. ; Wellington, N.S.W.

22.—WHEY CURE.

THE Whey, a pleasant diluent, containing much milk-sugar, is the fluid part of milk which remains after the separation of the curd, the coagulum which separates from milk upon the addition of acid, rennet, or wine ; the whey may be from goats', ewes', or cows' milk. The Whey Cure has been recommended for Bronchial Catarrh, Laryngeal Affections, and for convalescents after acute inflammatory diseases. The whey should be taken in the early morning, from one to four pints, at a temperature of 105° F.

In addition to climate, the Whey Cure *could* form the basis of treatment at the following places :—

Akaroa, N.Z.; Bairnsdale, Vic. ; Bowral, N.S.W.; Eden, N.S.W.; Kiama, N.S.W.; Mittagong, N.S.W. ; Moss Vale, N.S.W.; Sale, Vic. ; Sutton Forest, N.S.W. ; Ulladulla, N.S.W.; Waiuku, N.Z. ; Wellington, N.S.W. ; Wollongong, N.S.W.

V

THE NEW ZEALAND THERMAL SPRINGS DISTRICTS.

REMARKS ON THE HOT-SPRINGS DISTRICTS, NORTH ISLAND.*

By the Hon. Sir W. Fox, K.C.M.G.

THE hot-spring country is well defined by Dr. Hochstetter as commencing at the northern base of Ruapehu and Tongariro Mountains, at the southern end of Lake Taupo, and .thence extending in a north-easterly direction, for a distance of about 150 miles, to White Island, in the Bay of Plenty, being for the whole distance about the same width as Taupo Lake, say twenty-five to thirty miles, and possibly fed by an underflow from that lake. A few springs not included in that area may be found in other parts of the Island, as at Tara-wera, fifty miles from Taupo, on the Napier Road, and at Mahurangi, in the country north of Auckland, and a few other localities. But these are insignificant in comparison with those which lie within the limits above defined.

There are some half-dozen sites in the country referred to in which the number of springs and other active volcanic agencies are so great as to afford almost unlimited facilities for the establishment of sanatory institutions, and it is to these that I wish to draw the particular attention of the Government. Before doing so, however, it may be well to distinguish the different forms in which the heated water and

---

* This and the following article have been reprinted, by kind permission of the Honorable the Colonial Secretary of New Zealand, from the pamphlet entitled "The New Zealand Thermal Springs Districts," published by the New Zealand Government in 1882.

steam emerge from the subterraneous reservoirs and appear on the surface.   They are classified by Hochstetter under three heads :   1. *Puias*, which are geysers continuously or inter-mittently active.   2. *Ngawhas*, which are inactive *puias*, emitting steam, but not throwing up columns of hot water. 3. *Waiarikis*, which signifies any sort of cistern of hot water suitable for bathing.   The lines of distinction are perhaps not always very well defined.   To these may be added mud vol-canoes, and numerous creeks and streams either entirely hot, or tepid, or cold with occasionally hot springs breaking into them and raising their temperature for several yards around. This feature also occurs in some of the lakes, as Rotorua and Rotomahana.

I will now proceed to describe the localities which, from their wealth of hot springs and fumaroles, appear more par-ticularly adapted for sanatory purposes and the establishment of hydropathic institutions.

Beginning at the southern extremity of the district above defined—that is, at the southern end of Lake Taupo—there is, at Tokaano, a very largely-developed group of active and quiescent springs.   The Native village which bears that name is erected in the midst of them, and they are used for the various purposes of bathing, cooking, and other domestic uses, by a population of two or three hundred souls.   The principal bath consists of a deep *ngawha* between two boiling *puias*—the two outer ones, above and below, being boiling hot, or nearly so, while the central one is of a temperature of not more than 100° to 110°, and therefore very pleasant for bath-ing.   Its heat can be increased or diminished at will by shut-ting off its connection with the upper *puia*, which is easily done with a sod or a bunch of fern leaves.   The bathing pool is about six yards in diameter, and its construction is con-venient and peculiar, consisting of a deep central channel which cannot be bottomed by diving, surrounded by a shelf of a yard or two wide, on which the water is only two or three feet deep. This affords accommodation both to the expert swimmer and to those who have not acquired that useful accomplishment.

A fine clear creek of cold water, five or six yards wide, runs through the settlement, on both shores of which are many *puias* and *ngawhas*, some violently boiling and others of various degrees of heat and ebullition. Some of these already mingle their waters with the cold creek, rendering it for a few yards a pleasant warm bath, and in many more places the hot and cold water could easily be led into each other, so as to provide an almost unlimited number of baths of any temperature which might be desired.

Tokaano has a special importance relating to the settlements of Whanganui and other places on the West Coast, from which it will be easily accessible when the road now under construction is finished. The bathing facilities, however, at present, can only be used in common with the Natives, who morning and evening resort to the principal bath in such numbers as often to completely fill it. If they should continue to occupy Tokaano, it would be necessary to utilize some of the other springs or cisterns in the neighbourhood for those who might prefer privacy to the communistic lavatory system of the Natives.

Besides the existence of great bathing facilities, Tokaano offers many other objects of interest to the tourist or valetudinarian. Yachting on the lake; excursions to the falls of Waihi, and the place of Te Heu Heu's sepulture beneath a vast landslip which engulphed his village and a large number of his people; the ascent of Tongariro, and possibly of Ruapehu (a feat not unworthy of the foremost members of the Alpine Club)—such features confer attractions on Tokaano which ought some day to establish it as one of the most favourite resorts of the district.

Leaving Tokaano, there are, I believe, no springs worthy of notice along the eastern shore of the lake till the northern end is reached at Tapuaeharuru, where the Waikato River, which flowed in near Tokaano, flows out again, much after the fashion of the Rhone through the Lake of Geneva—with this difference, however, that, while the blue colour of the Rhone has passed into a proverb, the waters of the Waikato are of an equally lucid and transparent green, unsullied by any trace of muddy deposit or milky tinge from the snow-water weepings of Ruapehu.

On the western banks of the Waikato, where it leaves the lake, stands on a jutting promontory an old Maori pa, with some rather fine but rapidly decaying remains of ornamental gateways and barge boards. On the eastern bank is the Constabulary barrack, and the surveyed site of a township, which consists at present of a single publichouse and store.

The bright waters of the lake—green, transparent, and cool, and the eddying stream of the Waikato, afford excellent opportunity for cold-water bathing, while at no great distance are hot springs which might be easily turned to account. Of these there are three principal groups:—

1. About two miles below Tapuaeharuru is a group of *puias* and *ngawhas*, the chief of which is an intermittent one known as the Crow's Nest. It occasionally throws up a column of hot water 10 or 15 feet high, but was formerly more energetic and may be so again. Close to it are several less violent but very hot *ngawhas*, close to the edge of the river, affording great facility for intermixing and regulation of temperature. A person once erected a bath here, with appliances for mixing the hot and cold water, but the number of bathers was not remunerative, and "Mac's bath," as it was called, has gone out of repair.

2. About half-a-mile eastward from the river is a small swampy flat, at the foot of an irregular cliff of 30 or 40 feet

high, through which flow two small streams of a yard or two
wide, one barely tepid, the other too hot to handle.   At the
point where the two unite a tolerably good bath has been
erected by John Loffley, formerly an A.B. sailor in Her
Majesty's Navy, who served in the Naval Brigade during the
Waikato war.   A dressing-room is annexed, and Loffley has
a small house in the neighbourhood, where he occasionally
receives an invalid boarder.   He has made attempts to clear
and plant the six or eight acres of adjacent swampy land, and
generally shows a creditable degree of energy in endeavouring,
with very limited means, to develop the hygienic resources of
the two streams over which he presides as a sort of river god.

3. At the distance of a mile-and-a-half from the Constabulary post and township, along the eastern shore of the lake,
a warm stream a yard or two wide crosses the road and me-
anders into the lake.   Following it inland by a Maori track
a narrow gorge is reached, in which the small stream expands
into two considerable pools, varying in depth from a few inches
to several feet.   They are both of considerable temperature,
and a favourite resort of neighbouring Natives, who, however,
are few in number.   These pools are not at present very
accessible, and their banks are encumbered with raupo and
rushes, presenting no very pleasant accommodation for bathers.
The water has also a dingy and unattractive hue; and, though
capable of containing many bathers at a time, would require a
good deal to be done to make the locality a place of general
resort.   The water, also, is probably much diluted and less
charged with alkaline and other medicinal substances.

Besides these three principal bathing-places, there are
numerous fumaroles and steam jets in the surrounding
country; one in particular near the coach road, which forms a
marked feature, and is, I conceive, the same described by
Hochstetter under the name of Karapiti.   This fumarole and
the surrounding fissures might probably be utilized as steam
baths.

Before passing on from Taupo I may observe that its northern end is not without some attractions for the excursionist,
though it does not present scenery of the highest class.   Some
writers (even Hochstetter) have expressed themselves in terms
of rapturous admiration of the scenery of this lake.   I cannot,
however, think that any one familiar with the more remarkable
lakes of the world, and even of those in New Zealand, such
as Whakatipu, Te Anau, Wanaka, and others, would assign
to Taupo a first place in lacustrine scenery.   It is undoubtedly
deficient in almost all the features which distinguish the most
admired lakes elsewhere.   Its shores are generally low, it has
few indentations, bays, or sandy coves, few rocky headlands,
jutting promontories, or overhanging precipices, and absolutely
no foliage on its banks or anywhere near.   Only one small
island diversifies its vast surface.   Nevertheless, it is a grand
sheet of bright transparent water, and a charming mirror for
the splendid atmospheric effects which form so picturesque a
feature of New Zealand scenery, particularly within reach of
such mighty rulers of the cloud-world as Ruapehu and Tongariro.   The scenery in connection with these mountains at the
south end of the lake has already been alluded to.   At the
northern end, within three miles of Tapuaeharuru, is the much
smaller Tauharu Mountain, which may be easily ascended in
a couple of hours, and which affords a sweeping bird's-eye
glance over the whole hot-spring and lake country as far as
the Bay of Plenty.   The lively stream of Waikato, with its
numerous rapids, occasional bold cliffs, and little wooded islets,
are also inviting objects for tourists.   The most remarkable
object of all, however, is the Huka Fall, which would be considered a fine one in any part of the world, though far exceeded
in size by many.   The river which immediately above is
about two chains wide, and of the exquisite transparent green
which distinguishes most rivers which flow from deep lakes
(and particularly the upper portion of the Waikato), after

brawling in rapids and eddying in reaches for a few miles, is suddenly pent in between perpendicular walls of rock some 50 or 60 feet high, and not ten paces apart. Between these the whole descending river rushes for a distance of two or three hundred yards, churned into a mass of snow-white foam, and roaring with the hoarse voice with which great cataracts are gifted, till, the confining walls suddenly receding, it shoots forth as if out of the barrel of a gigantic gun, and plunges in a solid white mass into a dark-green pool that lies waiting for it below at a depth of 50 feet perpendicular. A party of up-wards of seventy Whanganui Natives, on a visit to Taupo, are said to have challenged the resident natives of Tapuaeharuru to descend the Huka in canoes. The residents thought dis-cretion the better part of valour; but the Whanganuis, in a fit of bravado, made the attempt. Their canoe was sucked under the 'moment it reached the foaming gorge, and only one native who leaped ashore, was ever seen again.

The next group of springs worthy of notice is at Orakei-korako, about twenty miles down the Waikato River. It presents one of the most remarkable groups of hot springs and fumaroles in the Lake Country, or anywhere in the world, and is capable of varied adaptation to sanatory purposes. The banks of the river for several miles, both above and below, consist of steep and broken terraces, from every part of which, at a distance of only a few yards from each other, there burst out jets of steam or runlets of hot water. Hochstetter, when there, counted seventy-six steam jets at one glance of the eye, and at some seasons of the year more may be seen. The principal open *waiariki* or bath is a very remarkable one. It lies immediately beneath a Native village, which crests the high bank on the top of extensive old fortifications. A strong geyser, some 100 yards back from the river, has created a silicious terrace, called by the Natives Pahu Kowhatu, con-structed in much the same manner as those in Lake

Rotomahana, but of less extent and elevation, and less curiously carved or terraced. At the top of this structure, which is at right angles to the river, are three principal *puias* or *ngawhas*, much resembling those at Tokaano. The farthest from the river, which has been the parent of the whole terrace, is in a state of constant and violent ebullition, at a temperature of about 202° (Hochstetter). The next to it, the temperature being reduced to bearable heat, contains a most perfect natural " Sitz-bath," with elbow rests and a polished seat, let in as it were into the shallower and wider cistern which surrounds it. One peculiarity of this bath is that in a very few minutes of immersion it covers the body with a most exquisite varnish or coating, quite invisible to the eye, but as smooth as velvet, and which gives the bather the feeling of being the most " polished " person in the world. This I do not remember to have perceived in any other of the hot springs in which I have bathed. It was a sensation of Paradise to sit in this bath after a long and hot day's travel, watching the full moon rising above the craggy ridge of the lofty river banks, and gradually dispersing the dark shadows of the cliff which lay all along the deep eddying river below.

A stalactite cave is to be visited on the opposite side of the river, but without a Native guide it is not easy to find, and the Natives being all absent from the village I had not the opportunity of seeing it, but it is said to be worth a visit.

About ten miles below Orakeikorako, and about two miles above Niho-o-te-Kiore, or the Rat's Tooth (where the river is crossed by a bridge), near to the Constabulary post, is an extremely beautiful waterfall, called the Rainbow Fall. A long and rapid reach of the river, of a breadth of two or three chains, suddenly turns at right angles to its course, and dashes headlong over a ledge of purple rock, rolling past a wooded islet in the centre of the fall, in broad green waves and lumps of foamy white, over which hangs suspended the beautiful rain-

bow, which gives it its name. Below, the river widened out
runs deep and swiftly through a large pool, in which is
another islet covered with the greenest foliage, kept fresh by
the ever descending spray. A few hundred yards below, on
the eastern side of the river, and at its very margin, is a
moderate-size cistern of hot water, capable of containing
fifteen or twenty bathers, if closely packed. The facilities of
this spot for bathing are not very great ; but the combination
of the picturesque Rainbow Fall and the neighbouring
Powhatu Roa, a gigantic pyramidal rock of 500 feet high,
rising all alone from the bare level plain, and with a tradition
of Maori history attached to it, might afford inducement
sufficient for a moderate-sized establishment.

From Niho-o-te-Kiore the road to Rotorua Lake leaves
the Waikato River altogether, and the rest of that river's
course is, I believe, westward of the limits of the hot-spring
district, as defined by Hochstetter. The road is uninteresting
till within a couple of miles of Rotorua, when, after crossing
a low ridge, it suddenly brings the traveller into the midst of
a great group of most curious and repulsive-looking mud
volcanoes, boiling in a sluggish and most laborious manner
like very thick soup, and surrounded each by a viscous flooring
of the same material, diversified with little spitting craters,
from each of which sputters up a supply of the thick half-
fluid mass. It looks like the natural home of a family of huge,
ugly. bull-frogs who, were it not for the heat, would doubtless have been placed there by Nature to sprawl and croak and
enjoy their slimy life. Though wonderful evidences of the
fiery action going on below, they afford little attraction in
their present condition for sanatory experiments. I would be
sorry to say, however, that they will never be utilized for such
an object. A good many years ago a quack doctor travelled
over England advocating as a cure for all diseases the burying
of his patients up to the neck in the earth. A beautiful

young girl who accompanied him used to be immured as an example.   She was afterwards known to the world as the celebrated Lady Hamilton, whose name is historically connected with that of Lord Nelson.   Though the man was a quack, his remedy is said to have been efficacious, and possibly the mud *puias* of Rotorua may some day be found capable of similar application.

In front, at a distance of a mile, lies Rotorua Lake, with the Native village of Ohinemutu jutting into it on a long narrow headland, and away across three miles of water is the island Mokoia.   This is the scene of Mr. Domett's poem of "Ranolf and Amohia," in which, with a warmth of sentiment and fervour of expression of quite 212°, he has endeavoured to clothe savage life and character with charms and dignity which it would be difficult to recognize in the realities of any Maori pah on the shores of Rotorua at the present day, and which probably never had any existence except in the romantic day-dreams of the poet.   I am bound to express, however, my admiration of the truthfulness and splendour of his discriptions of the scenery, and the thorough New Zealand atmoshpere in which he has enveloped his, in many parts, beautiful tale.

Rotorua affords facilities for bathing " in the open," on the largest scale of any single place in the hot-spring districts. The whole bay in front of Ohinemutu (Ruapeka), some hundred yards across, has a temperature of from 50° to 110°, according to the set of the wind and the proximity to the hot springs by which it is fed.   These exist chiefly at the neck of the promontory on which the village stands, where they bubble, hiss, gush, and run into the cooler water of the lake.   Others emerge through the soft silicious bottom of the lake itself, and the bather is not unfrequently made aware of their presence by the sudden sting of a boiling jet when he sets down his foot.   This, however, is not attended with any bad consequences if he catches up his foot instantly, as he is pretty sure to do. This bay is the daily resort, morning and evening, of the whole population of the neighbouring village, and it is capable of accommodating regiments of soldiers at one time. It affords the finest conceivable opportunity of establishing a great sanatorium for Indian regiments.

There are isolated hot springs in other places near to the village, which could be easily adapted for bathing purposes. At a distance of a couple of miles is a group of most remarkable *puias*, the principal of which, Whakarewarewa, occasionally throws up a column of hot water to a height of 50 or 60 feet. Several others sputter, hiss, and heave in the same neighbourhood. These might, I think, be all utilized by a little hydraulic skill. At any rate, Ohinemutu and its surroundings can hardly fail to become one of the principal bathing-places in the country.

Leaving Ohinemutu by a new road which the Government of the colony is at present. (1874) constructing, and passing by Tikitapu Lake, with its waters of sapphire blue, and the more homely shores of Rotokakahi, Wairoa, at the head of Lake Tarawera, is reached. From this spot guides and canoes are taken for the trip to Rotomahana and the celebrated White and Pink Terraces. After a sail or paddle across the very picturesque Tarawera of six or eight miles, and a walk of a couple of miles, or a pull up a narrow creek for the same distance, the foot of the great Tarata is reached.

It is not my intention to dilate on the wonderful and beautiful which abound in connection with Rotomahana and its terraces. I wish rather to draw attention to the different groups of springs, with a view to their sanitary use. At the same time, the idea that these majestic scenes may one day be desecrated by all the constituents of a common watering-place has something in it bordering on profanity. I would not suggest that their healing waters should be withheld from the

weary invalid or feeble valetudinarian.   Doubtless their sanatory properties were given them for the good of suffering
humanity, and that they should become the Bethesda of New
Zealand would detract nothing from the sanctity and grandeur.   But that they should be surrounded with pretentious
hotels and scarcely less offensive tea-gardens, that they
should be strewed with orange-peel, with walnut shells, and the
capsules of bitter-beer bottles (as the Great Pyramid and even
the summit of Mount Sinai are), is a consummation from the
very idea of which the soul of every lover of nature must re-
coil.   The Government of the United States had hardly become
acquainted with the fact that they possessed a territory comprising similar volcanic wonders at the forks of the Yellow
River and Missouri, that an Act of Congress was passed
reserving a block of land of sixty miles square, within which the
geysers and hot springs are, as public parks, to be for ever
under the protection of the States; and it will doubtless take
care that they shall not become the prey of private speculators,
or of men to whom a few dollars may present more charms
than all the finest works of creation.

I will endeavour, as briefly as possible, to describe the
principal features of Rotomahana, premising, however, that
no description can convey a correct idea of what they are.   A
day spent among them is a new sensation, and must be felt
to be understood.

The Tarata, or White Terrace, rises by a succession of
chiselled steps, varying in height from 1 to 6 or 8 feet each, till
it attains an elevation of about 80 feet above the lake.   Here,
backed up by a semicircular wall of red rock, on the level
plateau of the uppermost terrace, is the great boiling *puia*,
the downward flow of whose waters, impregnated with impal-
pable white silicious sediment, has in course of centuries
deposited the "tattooed" rockwork of which the Tarata is
composed, and from which it has its name.   This great boiling

L

puia at the top is intermittent, and dependent, it is said, in that respect, on the direction of the wind, which, however, may be doubted. At times it sinks into its perpendicular funnel, leaving its rocky sides bare for hours. At other times it throws its water up to a height of 10 or 15 feet, till it gradually fills up its crater, and overflowing its beautiful-rounded lip glides down in endless broken ripples over the faces of the descending terraces till it reaches the lake below. In the course of its descent it fills a great number of cisterns between the different walls of the terraces. The water deposited in these is of the most exquisite turquoise blue, or something more beautiful than that, and there it lies semi-transparent and still, surrounded in every instance by a beautifully-defined and often sculptured rim of the nearly snow-white rock of which the terrace is composed. I say nearly snow-white, because it appears so in the bright sun and at a little distance, but when close at hand and looked down upon, it is seen to have a delicate, almost imperceptible, rose colour, which spreads over it like a blush on the human face, or still more resembles the tinted marble of some modern sculptors.

The temperature of the various cisterns in the terrace depends partly of that on the surrounding atmosphere, but chiefly on the length of time which may have elapsed since the overflow of the boiling *puia*. When it overflows, the cistern next to it and on the same level, which is only separated from it by five or six yards of snowy rock, is nearly as hot as itself, and far too hot for the bather, who must then resort to cisterns lower down, and of less size and depth. But when the upper *puia* has not overflowed for some hours, the cistern next to it attains a temperature just cool enough to be pleasantly borne, and perhaps, of all baths in the world, affords to a swimmer a most glorious " header." It is about 10 to 12 yards in diameter, a perfect circle, with a rounded lip overhanging inwards, and its exquisite pale-blue depth (unlike the colour of any other pool) cannot, I believe, be fathomed by any plunge, however energetic. But its greatest charm is that, instead of the sharp shock with goes through one like a knife on diving into a cold pool or the open sea, and which makes the bather feel like getting out again with immense celerity, here he is " lapped in the Elysium " of the delicious wave, at a temperature somewhere about 110°, and would be contented to stay there any number of hours that circumstances might permit.

The other terrace, Otukapuarangi, commonly known as the Pink Terrace, from its soft salmon-colour, well described by Trollope, lies at the opposite side of the lake. It is, except in the particular of colour, less remarkable than the Tarata, being of much smaller dimensions, and presenting fewer facilities for bathing purposes. It has, however, three cisterns immediately below the great boiling *puia*, which afford three varieties of temperature, all pretty warm, and which have space enough for a considerable number of bathers at once.

Immediately beyond the Great White Terrace, and all along the shore of the lake, and for a distance of some hundred yards back from it, up the broken hill side, there is a vast supply of active volcanic force in various forms of development. Conspicuous among these is the great Ngahapu or Ohopia, a rock-girt circular basin 30 or 40 feet wide, from which a violent geyser of boiling heat is constantly ejected to a height of 10 or 15 feet, enveloped in a perpetual cloud of steam. This great *puia* ever roaring, snorting, hissing, and heaving, and surrounded with gaping fissures, from which dense clouds of steam ceaselessly exhale, contains an unimited supply of boiling water, which might by artificial channels be made to supply many baths. There are, besides these, hundreds of other outbreaks of hot water and steam on the overhanging hill side. Sighing fountains, grunting fountains, fountains of mud, lucid fountains, fumaroles, and funnels, every imaginable indication of the *ignes suppositi cineri doloso*, which seem to lie within but a few inches of the fragile crust below the traveller's foot. The whole lake of Rotomahana is warm, as its name implies, and the creek which flows from it into Tarawera is full of hot springs every here and there.

I have endeavoured in this imperfect sketch which I have given (and for the details of which I am much indebted to Hochstetter, correcting my own less careful observation) to draw the attention of the Government to the great value of the sanitary provision which nature has made in the district described. It might be, and is probably destined to be, the sanatorium not only of the Australian Colonies, but of India and other portions of the globe. The country in which the hot springs are is not attractive for agricultural or pastoral or any similar purposes ; but when its sanatory resources are developed it may prove a source of great wealth to the colony. And not only so, but it may be the means of alleviating much human misery, and relieving thousands from their share of the ills that flesh is heir to. What is required is simply practical skill enough to make water run in pipes where it is wanted, and accommodation for those who may desire to avail themselves of it.

ACCOUNT OF OHINEMUTU AND LAKE DISTRICT.

Extracted from " New Zealand, its Physical Geography, Geology, and Natural History," by Dr. Ferdinand von Hochstetter.

THE Township of Ohinemutu is situated on the shores of Lake Rotorua, the second in size in the Lake District.

Rotorua means hole-lake, or a lake lying in a circular excavation. With the exception of the southern bight,

called Te Arikiroa, it has an almost circular form, with a
diameter of about six miles and a circumference of twenty
miles. Almost in the precise centre of the lake the island
Mokoia is situated, formed by a conical hill rising about 400
feet above the level of the lake, and with a pah on its top.
The circular form of the lake, the island in the middle, the
white steam-clouds ascending along the shores, all this might
easily induce the observer to take the Rotorua to have formerly
been a volcanic crater, while in reality this lake, like all the
other lakes of the Lake District, was produced by the sinking
of parts of the ground upon the volcanic table-land. The
depth of the lake is comparatively but small, perhaps at no
place more than five fathoms ; it has numerous shallow sand-
banks, and the shores also, with the exception of the north
side, are sandy and flat. It is 1,043 feet above the level of
the sea. On the south-west side the wood-clad Ngongotaha
Mountain towers up to a height of 2,282 feet. This is the
highest point of the range of hills encircling the lake. From
its summit an extensive view can be enjoyed, reaching to the
shores of the Bay of Plenty, and as far as the volcanic island
Whakari (White Island), which may be seen emitting immense clouds of white steam.

The principal Native settlement on the lake is Ohinemutu,
situated at its western extremity; it is a famous old Maori pah
—famous for its inhabitants, and famous for its warm baths.
The huts of the village are scattered over a considerable area
on both sides of the Ruapeka Bay, and on the slope of the
hill Pukeroa, which rises to a height of about 150 feet above
the lake. The whares and wharepunis, some of them ex-
hibiting very fine specimens of the Maori order of architecture,
are ornamented with grotesque wood-carvings, some of them
with human figures, intended to represent departed sires of
the present generation.

Ruapeka Bay forms the centre of the hot springs. There

they seethe and bubble and steam from a hundred places. The principal spring is the Great Waikite, at the south side of the bay. The basin of the fountain communicates with the lake, and it is to the immense quantities of hot water issued forth here that the whole bay owes its warm temperature, forming an excellent bathing-place. By approaching the fountain, more or less, any degree of temperature may be chosen. The water of the fountain is perfectly clear. For some short moments all is quiet in the large basin, only white steam-clouds ascending from it; then a powerful ebullition succeeds in raising the water to a height of from 4 to 6 feet, sometimes even to 10 and 12 feet. Little Waikite, a few yards above, forms a basin 4 to 5 feet wide, in which the water rises about every five minutes several feet high, sinking down again during the intervals to a depth of 6 to 7 feet. The temperature is about 201° Fahr. In going about between the countless pools of boiling spluttering mud the greatest care has to be taken. Whoever has once involuntarily bathed his feet in steaming water or boiling mud will certainly remember it all his life.

That even more serious accidents are of no rare occurrence is proved by several monuments in the shape of figures carved of wood, which are posted in those places where persons have met with an untimely death.

From the Ruapeka Bay the hot springs continue in a south-westerly direction on the foot of the Pukeroa, along the Utuhina Creek, as far as the small settlement of Tarewa. In this direction there are moreover two small warm ponds, Kuirau and Timara, fed by hot springs, both favourite bathing-places of the Natives. Also on the south and east sides of the Pukeroa steam is seen to ascend from various places. Tabular rocks of silicious deposit, 2 to 3 feet thick, of a mass resembling milk-opal, lie scattered about over the slope and the base of the hill, indicating that the activity of the

springs in former periods, especially on the east side of the
hill, was far more extensive than now, or that the springs
change their place from time to time.   The Natives have
special springs for bathing, for cooking, and also for washing.
On places where only hot vapour escapes from the ground
they have established vapour baths, and upon heated ground
they have warm houses for the winter season, of which it is
said that no vermin of any kind is able to exist in them.

The whole atmosphere in and about Ohinemutu is so
constantly impregnated with watery vapours and sulphurous
gases as to make them plainly perceptible to the sense of
smell.   This, however, seems only to improve the physical
condition of the inhabitants, for they are known to be an ex-
traordinarily robust set of Maoris.

Two and a half miles distance from Ohinemutu, in a
south-easterly direction, is the native settlement Whakarewarewa, where are springs exceeding those of Ohinemutu in
variety and extent.   Seven or eight of them are periodical
geysers, having, however, their own, as yet, unexplored
caprices, as they are not always obliging enough to satisfy
the curiosity of visiting travellers.   It is said to happen now
and then that they all play together.   The Natives assert
that such is generally the case during heavy easterly gales.
One of them, the Waikite, issues from the top of a flat silicious
cone, measuring 100 feet in diameter and 15 feet high, which,
rising between green manuka and fern-bushes, presents an
extremely picturesque sight.   The cone consists of white
silicious deposit ; it has numerous fissures and crevices,
which are all incrustated with neat sulphur crystals.   The hot
vapours, however, issuing from those fissures, smell neither of
sulphurous acid nor of sulphuretted hydrogen, but merely of
sublimated sulphur.   At intervals of about eight minutes the
Waikite throws out a column of water 2 or 3 feet thick to a
height of 6 to 8 feet.   It is in January and February, how-

ever, that it shows itself in its full glory, spouting to a height of 30 to 35 feet. A little south-east of the Waikite is the Pohutu ; its basin is 12 feet wide ; the masses of silicious deposit surrounding it are very extensive, and piled up to a height of more than 20 feet, fissured and broken by numerous cracks. The sulphur deposits are here still more distinct than on the Waikite. The range of hot springs extends from Whakarewarewa along the course of the Puarenga River, a distance of one and a half mile, to Te Arikiroa Bay, on Lake Rotorua. The number of smaller springs, of boiling mud-basins, of mud-cones, and solfataras, which are scattered over this extensive area, must be counted by hundreds.

The scenery of Lake Tarawera—distant about twelve miles from Ohinemutu—surpasses in wildness and grandeur that of any of the other lakes in the Lake District. The word signifies burnt cliffs. Its general form, exclusive of its deep side-coves, is that of a rhombus, with its main diagonal running from west to east. In this direction it is seven miles long, having a breadth of about five miles. The lake is probably very deep, for its shores are mostly rugged rocky bluffs, shaded by pohutukawa trees. The chief ornament of the adjoining landscape is the Tarawera Mountain, with its crown of rocks, divided into three parts by deep ravines. It is an imposing table-mountain, rising on the south-eastern side of the lake to a height of at least 2,000 feet above the level of the sea, and consisting of obsidian and other rhyolitic rocks ; and it is not to be wondered at that its dark ravines and vertical sides having given rise to many an odd story in vogue among the Maoris. Lake Tarawera receives the discharges of five small lakes : from the south-east the joint discharge of the Rotomahana and Rotomakariri—the warm and cold lakes ; from the north-west the waters of the Okataina and Okareka Lakes; and from the west the Wairoa River, which, flowing from the Rotokakahi, at a short distance from the missionary

station, forms a picturesque waterfall 80 feet high, and
empties into the lake through a narrow gorge of rocks. The
outlet of the Okareka Lake flows underground for half a
mile, and forms, when it comes to light again, the charming
waterfall of Waitangi.

The far-famed Rotomahana is one of the smallest lakes of
the Lake District, being not even quite a mile long from south
to north, and only a quarter of a mile wide. Its form is very
irregular on the south side, where the shore is formed by
swamps. In many places of those swamps warm water
streams forth ; hot-mud pools are also visible here and there,
and from the projecting points muddy shallows covered with
swamp-grass extend almost as far as the middle of the lake.
At its north end the lake grows narrow, and where the
Kaiwaka Creek flows out there are again on both sides nothing
but grass-swamps and shallows. Only in the middle the water is
deeper, and the shores east and west are high and rocky. It
justly bears the name of " warm lake." The quantity of boiling
water running from the ground, both on the shores and at the
bottom of the lake, is truly astonishing. Of course, the
whole lake is heated by it ; but the temperature is soon found
to be very different in various places. Where the rising of
gas-bubbles indicates a hot spring at the bottom of the lake
the thermometer will be often seen to rise to 90° or 100° Fahr.,
but in the middle of the lake and near its outlet 80° Fahr. may
be considered as the mean temperature. In bathing and
swimming through the lake the change of temperature is very
easily felt, but care must be taken not to come too close to
any of the hot springs. The water is muddy-turbid and of a
smutty-green colour. Neither fish nor mussel-shells live in it.
On the other hand, the lake is a favourite haunt of countless
water and swamp fowls. Various kinds of ducks, water-hens,
the magnificent pukeko, and the graceful oyster-catcher or
torea enliven the surface of the water. These birds have

their brooding-places on the warm shores, while they have to seek their food in the neighbouring cold lakes.   In certain seasons of the year the Natives institute regular hunts ; at other times, however, they refuse everybody, even Europeans, the pleasure of shooting, declaring the birds *tapu* (sacred). Numerous observations lead to the conclusion that constant changes are going on at the Rotomahana ; that some springs go dry, others rise ; and, especially, the earthquakes, which are felt here from time to time, seem to exercise such a changing influence.   The main interest is attached to the east shore, where are the principal springs, to which the lake owes its fame.

Te Tarata, at the noth-east end of the lake, with its ter-raced marble steps projecting into the lake, is the most marvellous of the Rotomahana marvels.   About 80 feet above the lake, on the fern-clad slope of a hill from which in various places hot vapours are escaping, lies the immense boiling cauldron in a crater-like excavation, with steep reddish sides 30 to 40 feet high, and open only on the side towards the lake.

The basin of the spring is about 80 feet long and 60 feet wide, and filled to the brim with perfectly clear transparent water, which in the snow-white incrustated basin appears of a beautiful blue, like the blue turquoise.   At the margin of the basin the temperature is 183° Fahr., but in the middle, where the water is in a constant state of ebullition to the height of several feet, it probably reaches the boiling-point.   Immense clouds of steam, reflecting the beautiful blue of the basin, curl up, generally obstructing the view of the whole surface of the water ; but the noise of boiling and seething is always distinctly audible.   The Natives assert that sometimes the whole mass of water is suddenly thrown out with immense force, and that then the empty basin is open to view to a depth of 30 feet, but that it fills again very quickly.   Such eruptions are said to occur only during violent easterly gales. The water possesses in a high degree petrifying or rather incrustating qualities. The deposit is silicious, not calcareous, and the silicious deposits and incrustations of the constantly-overflowing water. have formed on the slope of the hill a system of terraces, which, as white as if cut from marble, present an aspect which no description or illustration is able to represent. It has the appearance of a cataract plunging over natural shelves, which, as it falls, is suddenly turned into stone. The flat-spreading foot of the terraces extends far into the lake. There the terraces commence with low shelves containing shallow water-basins. The farther up, the higher grow the terraces, 2 feet, 3 feet, some also 4 and 6 feet high. They are formed by a number of semicircular stages, of which, however, not two are of the same height. Each of these stages has a small raised margin from which slender stalactites are hanging down upon the lower stage, and encircles on its platform one or more basins resplendent with the most beautiful blue water. These small water-basins represent as many natural bathing-basins, which the most refined luxury could not have prepared in a more splendid and commodious style.

The basins can be chosen shallow or deep, large or small, and of every variety of temperature, as the basins upon the higher stages, nearer to the main basin, contain warmer water than those upon the lower ones. After reaching the highest terrace there is an extensive platform with a number of basins 5 to 6 feet deep, their water showing a temperature of 90° to 110° Fahr. In the middle of this platform there arises, close to the brink of the main basin, a kind of rock island about 12 feet high, decked with manuka, mosses, lycopodium, and fern. It may be visited without danger, and from it the curious traveller has a fair and full view into the blue, boiling, and steaming cauldron. Such is the famous Te Tarata. The pure white of the silicious deposit in contrast with the blue of the water, with the green of the surrounding vegetation, and with the intensive red of the bare earth-walls of the water-crater, the whirling clouds of steam, altogether presents a scene unequalled in its kind.   The scientific collector, on the other hand, has ample opportunity of filling whole baskets with the most beautiful specimens of the tenderest stalactites, incrustated branches, leaves, &c., for whatever lies upon the terraces becomes incrustated in a very short time.

Altogether about twenty-five large *ngawhas* may be counted on the Rotomahana ; the number of smaller springs coming to light at innumerable places upon an area occupying about two square miles it would be difficult to estimate.   As these hot springs, according to the experience of the Natives, have proved very effective in the curing of chronic cutaneous diseases and rheumatic pains, there is no doubt that at no very distant period this remarkable lake will become the centre of attraction not only for tourists of all nations, but also as a place of resort for invalids from all parts of the world.

Lake Rotoiti is separated from Lake Rotorua only by a narrow isthmus scarcely half a mile broad.   The Ohua Creek, flowing from Rotorua into the Rotoiti, connects the two lakes. As regards the character of its scenery, Rotoiti is decidedly one of the most beautiful lakes.   It is of a very irregular shape, from west to east about six or seven miles long, and only from one to two miles wide.   Picturesque promontories and peninsulas jutting far out into the lake separate the various branches and inlets from each other.

VI.

DEFINITION OF ALL THE TECHNICAL TERMS WHICH APPEAR IN THE FOREGOING PAGES.

ABDOMINAL—Belonging to the abdomen, the lower part of the belly.

ACUTE—A disease of short duration, and with a certain degree of severity.

ALCOHOLISM—A collective term for the various morbid symptoms produced by an excessive indulgence in alcoholic drinks.

ALKALI—A substance capable of neutralizing acids.

ALKALINE—Having the qualities of an alkali.

ALTERATIVE—A medicine that gradually produces a change in a disease or constitution.

ALUMINA—An earth composed of aluminum and oxygen (pure clay).

ALUMINIUM—The metallic base of alumina.

ALUMINOUS—Containing alum.

AMENORRHŒA—Suppression of the periodical discharge of blood from the uterus (menses).

AMMONIA—A volatile alkali of a pungent smell.

ANÆMIA—Privation of blood.

ANALYSIS—The separation of anything into its elements or component parts.

ANTILITHIC—A substance preventing the formation of stones (calculi) in the bladder and kidneys.

ARTHRITIS—Inflammation of the joints, especially gout.

ARTICULAR—Relating to the joints.

ASTHMA—Great difficulty of breathing.

ATONIC—Wanting tone; debilitated.

ATROPHY—A wasting of the flesh ; defective nutrition.

BALNEOLOGY—A treatise on baths.

BI—As a prefix to words, has the same signification as twice, double.

BLENNORRHŒA—Inordinate secretion and discharge of mucus.

BROMINE—An elementary substance of a very volatile nature, found in sea-water.

BRONCHIAL—Belonging to the ramifications of the windpipe in the lungs.

BRONCHITIS—Inflammation óf the bronchia, the first two branches of the bronchus or windpipe.

CALCIUM—The metallic basis of lime.

CARBONATE—Containing carbonic acid.

CARBONIC—Pertaining to, or obtained from, carbon (pure charcoal).

CATARRH—A discharge of fluid from any of the mucous membranes.

CAUSTIC—Biting or burning in taste.

CHALYBEATE—Containing iron.

CHLORIDE—A combination of chlorine with a simple body.

CHLORINE—A greenish-yellowish gas obtained from common salt.

CHLOROSIS—The green sickness; a deficiency of red corpuscles in the blood.

CHRONIC—A disease of long duration.

CINNABAR—An ore of quicksilver; a native sulphuret of mercury.

CLIMATIC.—Relating to climate.

CLIMATOLOGY—A treatise on climates.

CONGESTION—Accumulation of blood in an organ.

CUTANEOUS—Concerning the skin.

DIABETES—A superabundant discharge of urine containing sugar.

DIARRHŒA—Looseness of the bowels, with unusual evacuation.

DIATHESIS—Predisposition to certain diseases.

DIPHTHERIA—A disease of the throat, characterized by the formation of false membranes.

DIURETIC—A medicine which increases the secretion of urine.

DYSENTERY—Inflammation of the mucous membrane of the large intestine, with frequent mucous or bloody evacuations.

DYSMENORRHŒA—Difficult or painful menstruation.

DYSPEPSIA—Difficulty of digestion.

DYSPNŒA—Short breath, difficulty of breathing.

ECZEMA—A skin disease, characterized by an eruption of small vesicles.

EMBRYONIC—Relating to an embryo or germ.

ENDEMIC—Diseases peculiar to certain countries or localities.

EPIDEMIC—A disease generally prevailing, but not dependent on local causes.

EPILEPSY—The falling sickness, consisting of convulsions, loss of consciousness, and foaming at the mouth.

FERRUGINOUS—Containing iron-rust.

FLUORINE—A yellowish-brownish gas, one of the acidifying and basifying principles.

HÆMOPTYSIS—A discharge of blood from the mucous membrane of the lungs.

HÆMORRHOIDS—Livid and painful excrescences, usually attended with a discharge of mucous or blood.

HEPATIC—Pertaining to the liver ; also another name for sulphuretted hydrogen gas.

HYDATID—A pouch or sac of a membranous nature, containing a clear, transparent fluid.

HYDROCHLORIC—A compound of chlorine and hydrogen.

HYDROGEN—A gas, one of the elements of water.

HYPOCHONDRIASIS—Low spirits ; vapours ; the blues.

HYSTERIA—An affection, occurring in paroxysms or fits, and consisting principally of alternate fits of laughing or crying.

INSOMNIA—Absence of sleep.

IODIDE—A combination of Iodine with a simple body.

IODINE—A substance found in certain sea-weeds or marine plants, which gives forth a violet coloured vapour.

LARYNGEAL—Belonging to the larynx, the upper part of the windpipe.

LARYNGITIS—Inflammation of the larynx, or windpipe. ·

LEUCORRHŒA—The Whites ; a discharge of a white, yellowish, or greenish mucous from the womb.

LITHIUM (Carbonate of)—A salt having the power of dissolving uric acid and the urates.

LUMBAGO—A rheumatic affection of the muscles about the loins.

MAGNESIA—-A white alkaline earth, used as a purgative.

MAXIMUM—The extreme or highest.

MENORRHAGIA—Immoderate flow of the menses, the monthly bloody evacuation from the uterus.

MINIMUM—The least or lowest.

MONO—As a prefix to words, has the same signification as single.

MONOGRAPH—A treatise on a single disease or medical subject.

MURIATED—Combined with muriatic acid ; brined.

MURIATIC—Hydrochloric ; a compound of hydrogen and chlorine.

NEURALGIA—Nervous pain or pang.

NEUROSES—Nervous affections.

OXIDE—A compound of oxygen with a metal or other substance.

OXYGEN—An elementary substance in a gaseous form, largely distributed in nature.

PALSY—Paralysis ; loss of the power of motion.

PARALYSIS—Loss or great diminution of the voluntary motions, or of sensation in one or more parts of the body.

PARASITES—Animals which live in or on the bodies of other animals ; also plants which attach themselves to other plants.

PARASITIC—Having the characteristics of a parasite.

PHOSPHATE—A salt formed of phosphoric acid and a base.

PHOSPHORIC — Pertaining to, or obtained from phosphorus.

PHTHISIS—Consumption.

PLEURISY—Inflammation of the pleuræ, two thin, perspirable membranes, which line each side of the chest, and are reflected thence upon each lung.

PNEUMONIA—Inflammation of the lungs.

POTASSIUM—The metallic basis of pure potash.

PROTOXIDE—When there are several different oxides of the same substance, the protoxide is that which is the first in the scale, or that which has the smallest quantity of oxygen.

PSORIASIS—A kind of scaly skin disease (dry scale).

PULMONARY—Pertaining to the lungs.

PUMICE—A porous volcanic product, consisting chiefly of silica and alumina.

RHACHITIS—Rickets, a disease of children, characterized by crooked spine and limbs.

REACTION—The process of applying a test for detecting the presence of certain other bodies.

RENAL—Relating to the kidneys.

RESPIRATORY—Appertaining to respiration, the process of breathing.

RHEUMATISM—A kind of shifting neuralgia, affecting the muscles and joints

RHEUMATOID—Resembling rheumatism

M

Saline—Containing salt.

Saliva—Spittle.

Sanatorium—An establishment for the treatment of the sick.

Sanitarium—A retreat selected for invalids owing to its salubrity.

Sciatic—Pertaining to the hip. ˙

Sciatica—Pain radiating from the sciatic notch in the course of the sciatic nerve.

Scorbutic—Relating to or affected with scurvy.

Scrofula—The king's evil, a disease characterized by chronic swelling of absorbent glands, particularly of the neck.

Scrofulous—Of the nature of scrofula.

Silica—A combination of silicium and oxygen.

Silicious—Partaking of the nature of flint. ˏ

Silicium—An elementary substance, the base of silica.

Sinter—A name applied to various minerals deposited from mineral waters.

Soda—The protoxide of the metal sodium.

Sodium—The metallic base of soda.

Spas—Springs of mineral water.

Splenic—Relating to the spleen.

Sulphate—A compound of sulphuric acid and a base.

Sulphuret—A combination of sulphur with an earth, metal, or alkali.

Sulphuric—Pertaining to sulphur.

Sulphurous—Like or containing sulphur.

Therapeutic—Appertaining to therapeutics, that branch of medicine which treats of the application of remedies and the curative treatment of diseases.

Thermal—Appertaining to heat.

Tonic—A medicine augmenting the strength.

Tubercular—Full of knobs or pimples.

URATE—Salts, formed by the combination of uric or lithic acid with different bases.

UREA—The nitrogenous constituent of urine.

URIC ACID—An acid existing in human urine, consisting of urate of soda or urate of ammonia.

UTERINE--Relating to the womb.

VASCULAR—Pertaining to blood-vessels.

APPENDIX.

THERMOMETRIC SCALES,

AND HOW TO CONVERT THE DIFFERENT KINDS.

1. FAHRENHEIT's Thermometer is divided into 180 degrees, the freezing point being marked 32°, and the boiling point 212°. (This scale is used in England, the United States, and Australasia.)

2. CELSIUS, or the Centigrade Thermometer, the freezing point of which being marked 0°, or zero, and the boiling point 100°. (Generally used in France and many other countries of Continental Europe.)

3. RÉAUMUR's Thermometer; in this scale the freezing point is marked 0°, and the boiling point 80°. (Used in most parts of Germany and Italy.)

NOTE.—In this, and also in the Centigrade, the degrees are continued of the same size below and above these points, those below being reckoned negative.

The Centigrade scale is reduced to that of Fahrenheit by multiplying by 9 and dividing by 5, and adding 32, on account of the difference of their zeros, thus : C. 100° × 9 = 900 ÷ 5 = 180° + 32° = 212° F. That of Réaumur is reduced to that of Fahrenheit by multiplying by 9 and dividing by 4, and adding 32, thus : R. 80° × 9 = 720 ÷ 4 = 180° + 32° = 212° F. That of Fahrenheit to either of these, by reversing the process, thus : F. 212° – 32° = 180° × 4 = 720 ÷ 9 = 80° R.; F. 212° – 32° = 180° × 5 = 900 ÷ 9 = 100 C. To reduce Réaumur's degrees to those of Centigrade, multiply by 5, and divide by 4, thus : 32° R. × 5 = 160 ÷ 4 = 40° C.; and, lastly, to reduce Centigrade degrees to those of Réaumur, multiply by 4 and divide by 5, thus : 40° C. × 4 = 160 ÷ 5 = 32° R.

TEMPERATURE OF BATHS.

Cold Bath—From 33° to 60° F.

Cool Bath—From 60° to 75° F.

Temperate Bath—From 75° to 85° F.

Tepid Bath—From 85° to 92° F.

Warm Bath—From 92° to 98° F.

Hot Bath—From 98° to 112° F.

Hot Air Bath—From 100° to 130° F.

Vapour Bath—From 122° to 144° F.

Sand Bath—A term applied to an iron dish, containing fine sand, placed on a fire.

Artificial Sea Water Bath—A solution of one part common salt in thirty parts of water.

Sulphur Bath—Take of sulphuret of potash, 4 oz. ; hyposulphite of soda, 1 oz. ; strong sulphuric acid, 1 drachm ; hot water, about 30 gallons.

WEIGHTS, MEASURES, ETC.

Weights and Measures of the British Pharmacopœia.

Weights.

1 Ounce (avoir) oz. = 437·5 grains.

1 Pound lb. = 16 ounces = 7000 ,,

Measures of capacity.

1 Fluid drachm, fl. drm. = 60 minims.

1 Fluid ounce, fl. oz. = 8 fluid drachms.

1 Pint, O = 20 fluid ounces.

1 Gallon, C = 8 pints.

Relation of measures to weights.

1 Minim is the measure of 0·9114583 grains of water.

1 Fluid drachm is the measure of 54·6875 grains of water.

1 Fluid ounce is the measure of 1 ounce, or 437·5 grains of water.

1 Pint is the measure of 1·25 pound, or 8750·0 grains of water.

1 Gallon is the measure of 10 pounds, or 70000·0 grains of water.

APOTHECARIES' WEIGHT.

20 Grains make one scruple—Ɔ.
3 Scruples   „   drachm—ʒ, = grs. 60.
8 Drachms   „   ounce—℥, = grs. 480.
12 Ounces   ,,   pound—℔., = grs. 5760.

APOTHECARIES' MEASURE.

60 Minims (♏) make one fluid drachm, = fl. ʒ.
8 Fluid drachms   „   ounce, = fl. ℥.
16 Fluid ounces   ,,   pint, = O.
8 Pints   „   gallon, = C.

RELATION OF THE WEIGHTS AND MEASURES OF THE B. P. TO THE METRIC SYSTEM, AND VICE VERSA.

Weights B. P. to Metric weights.

1 Pound = 453·5927 grammes.
1 Ounce =   28·3495   ,,
1 Grain =   0·0648   ,,

Metric weights to weights B. P.

1 Milligramme   = 0·015432 grains.
1 Centigramme =   0·15432   ,,
1 Decigramme =   1·5432   ,,
1 Gramme   =   15·432   ,,
1 Kilogramme   =   2 lb. 3 oz. 119·8 grs., or 15432·349 grains.

Measures of capacity B.P. to Metric measures.

1 Gallon = 4·543458 litres.

1 Pint = 0·567932 litres, or 567·932 cubic centimetres.

1 Fluid ounce = 0·028397 litres, or 28·397 cubic centimetres.

1 Fluid drachm = 0·003550 litres, or 3·550 cubic centimetres.

1 Minim = 0·000059 litres, or 0·059 cubic centimetres.

Metric measures to measures B. P.

1 Millimetre   =   0·03937 inches.
1 Centimetre =   0·39371   ,,
1 Decimetre   =   3·93708   ,,
1 Metre   = 39·37079   ,,   or 1 yard 3·37 inches.
1 Cubic centimetre   15·432 grains.
1 Litre = 1·76077 pint, or 1 pint 15 oz. 1 dr. 43 m.

(The cubic centimetre is a standard at 4° C. (39·2° F.), the grain at 62° F. (16·66° C.).

*Ready way to reduce the weights and measures of the B. P.
to those of the Metric system, and vice versa.*

(*a.*) Grains or minims, multiplied by $6\frac{1}{2}$, give centigrams,
thus : 20 grains × $6\frac{1}{2}$ = 130 centigrams, or 1 gram and 30
centigrams, expressed thus—1·30.

(*b.*) Drachms (fluid or dry) multiplied by 4, give grams,
thus : 4 drachms × 4 = 16 grams, expressed thus—16.

(*c.*) Ounces (fluid or dry) multiplied by 32, give grams,
thus : 4 ounces × 32 = 128 grams, expressed thus—128.

(*d.*) Centigrams multiplied by 2 and divided by 13, give
grains or minims, thus : 130 centigrams × 2 = 260 ÷ 13
= 20 grains.

(*e.*) Grams divided by 4, give drachms (fluid or dry), thus :
16 grams ÷ 4 = 4 drachms.

(*f.*) Grams divided by 32 give ounces (fluid or dry)
thus : 128 grams ÷ 32 = 4 ounces.

NOTE.—These rules do not give the exact values, but they are near enough for
all practical purposes.

www.ingramcontent.com/pod-product-compliance
Lightning Source LLC
Chambersburg PA
CBHW030600040726
47497CB00008B/2803